Praise for **The Lurking Place**:

T0160994

"There aren't many memorable novels about the 1960s and its counterculture, nor many about poets, nor many about interracial couples. But all those subjects are found in this searching novel, its contents wonderfully supported by Major's chastened style and painter's eye. Meditative and ethical, yes, but the narrative is also leavened with subtle comedy."
— Alfred Corn, author of *Miranda's Book*

"In this subtle exploration of avocation and racial identity, Major resists conventional narrative structure in favor of taut, dialogue-driven scenes that capture the randomness of violence, the arbitrariness of prejudice, and the poignancy of love." — Lucinda Roy, author of *The Freedom Race*

"What a fun ride/read! A real view into the late 1960s of downtown NYC to Mexico — the struggles of 'becoming a poet' (and being in love) — with all the details of time & place. Reads like a lost artifact: long missed, sorely needed." — Tama Janowitz, author of *Slaves of New York*

"*The Lurking Place* might well be the best of Major's very distinguished body of fiction. Generous, humane and written with a poet's touch, it is a work of rare beauty. He is an extraordinary artist."
— Steve Yarbrough, author of *The Unmade World: A Novel*

"*The Lurking Place* is a riveting and remarkable portrait of a young man negotiating the conflicts in poetic ambition, untested talent, maybe-love, and routine racism. This tale unfolds through New York and Mexico in a superb evocation of the late sixties, a time when anything could happen and usually did. A wonderful book." — Joan Silber, author of *Improvement*

"Vivid, canny, propulsive, and cool, *The Lurking Place*, Clarence Major's endlessly engaging new novel, probes the tensions of two interlocking moments – a young artist testing his creative powers and a young generation declaring its independence." — John Beckman, author of *The Winter Zoo*

The Lurking Place

a novel

Clarence Major

Manic D Press
San Francisco

Cover photograph by James Jowers, [People crossing street intersections] 1966. Courtesy of the George Eastman Museum. Used with permission.
Back cover author photo by Neil Michel.

This is a work of fiction. The characters and their names, the places or events, the incidents and actual people, are used fictiously, or they are the product of the author's imagination. Any resemblance to reality, including names of characters, is entirely coincidental.

Library of Congress Cataloging-in-Publication Data

Names: Major, Clarence, author.
Title: The lurking place : a novel / Clarence Major.
Description: First edition. | San Francisco : Manic D Press, [2021]
Identifiers: LCCN 2021022828 (print) | LCCN 2021022829 (ebook) | ISBN 9781945665288 (trade paperback) | ISBN 9781945665295 (ebook)
Classification: LCC PS3563.A39 L87 2021 (print) | LCC PS3563.A39 (ebook)
| DDC 813/.54--dc23

Failure is the foundation of success and success is the lurking-place of failure; but who can tell when the turning point will come?

—W. Somerset Maugham, *The Painted Veil*
after Lao Tzu, *Tao Te Ching*

I

THE WARREN LOWERY SCHOOL OF FINE ARTS was in Nola Alley, one of the last little cobblestoned streets left over from the 19th century in New York's Greenwich Village, south of Houston between Essex and Norfolk South. Not just in name only, Nola was really an alley turned into a narrow street, spiffed up with class lent by a prestigious artsy school of higher learning.

Lowery, as we called the school, was the only building back in there. Housed in a structure built in 1836, the outer walls were of sturdy faded salmon-red 19th century brick. The grey mortar holding the bricks together over time in places had turned green with moss and algae growing along the cracks.

Beyond the school building was a dead end created by the backside of a building with no windows. It was also an old three-story 19th century structure, once a factory where immigrant women, in the late 1890s and early 1900s, sweated over sewing machines for fifteen to twenty hours a day. From the 1920s to the 1950s, the factory was a third-rate apartment building.

Now, with interior walls knocked down, it was converted to studios for artists. Lowery art teachers were among the artists who had their studios there. To get to them they had to walk all the way around the block to the front entrance. A standing joke was that someday they would bulldoze a doorway through that back wall for easier access.

But it was relatively quiet back in the alley. The old faded high walls muffled much of the city sounds of traffic and other noise from beyond.

Lowery opened in 1902. It was launched as part of the modernist thrust at the turn of the century, and its progressive reputation grew steadily throughout the decades that followed. In its early days, it attracted students in their mid-to-late twenties and thirties.

The students nowadays tended to be younger and less formal than the average Lowery student in, say, the 1920s and 1930s, when male students wore suits and ties to class and the female students came to class dressed in their Sunday best. Photographs of early classes show them standing together looking stiff and grim.

The degrees, then and later, were Master of Arts and Master of Fine Arts in Fashion, Dance, Music, Theatre, Graphic Design, Architecture, Studio Art, Art History, Creative Writing, and Nonfiction Writing. The latter two were added to the curriculum soon after the Iowa Writers Workshop commenced in 1936.

In addition to these degrees, there were degrees offered in Literature in English, Philosophy and Religion, Foreign Languages, Linguistics, and Psychology. Like all college-level liberal arts schools, for the faculty, Lowery had a publish-or-perish policy.

Mr. Kenneth Jeremiah, chairman of the English Department, had invited me to the Warren Lowery School of Fine Arts to read my poetry. I arrived at noon on the second Friday in March 1968. A man was standing outside smiling as I walked along the narrow sidewalk to the school's entrance.

"Hello, Mr. Lowell? I'm Kenneth. Glad you were able to find us back here hidden away from the busy world." His chuckle was restrained.

We shook. He was a little man in brown tweeds, with a kindly twinkle in his eyes and a soft voice, very Harvard.

As we walked along the remodeled corridor, Mr. Jeremiah said, "I think you will be pleased with your audience. The entire student body and faculty will be in attendance. Well, let's put it this way: they have to be." He gave me a weak smile.

And it was true. Mr. Jeremiah's introduction was overly generous. He'd read my poems in various literary magazines and greatly admired them. I'd published only in periodicals. I was already twenty-five and I had yet to publish a book. Having no book to my name often caused me to seesaw between self-doubt and extreme ambition. It was hard to keep the anxiety under control.

Many poets had published early. Arthur Rimbaud finished *The Drunken Boat, A Season in Hell,* and *Illuminations,* three great books, all before the age of twenty-one. Lord Byron was still in his teens when he published *Fugitive Pieces* and *Hours of Idleness.* I knew it was a silly idea to compare myself and my progress to anybody else's, and I tried not to, but I couldn't help it.

The entire student body and faculty were indeed there. Staff people, of course, were not. They had to keep the school running. The place was abuzz with expectation. I was hoping I was going to keep those who were there on the edges of their seats. Listening to poetry required concentration, and I knew I was facing a crowd conditioned by the glamour and quickness of TV shows to have a short attention span. The challenge was to read the poetry so that it filled the room with excitement.

I read new unpublished poems. My manuscript's working title was *Rendezvous in the Rain.* It was the title of one of the finished poems. I was hoping no one would ask why that title for the book, and no one did. Titles were sometimes best left unexplained. I didn't want to dissect the relationship. I often puzzled over poetry book titles and their relation to their book's themes or subjects: Whitman's *Leaves of Grass,* Plath's *Ariel,* Eliot's *The Waste Land;* titles, at least for me, that retained a certain amount of mystery.

During the question and answer period, one of the young teachers stood up and said, "I'm Amy Lawrence, I'm an adjunct here. Where do you get your inspiration? What motifs do you use? Do you rely on your own experiences or is it all from your imagination?"

I said, "Inspiration comes from any and everywhere, motifs too, and yes, I rely on my own experiences and my imagination. I'm interested in writing about both the natural world and the world made by people."

Another young woman, this one I assumed to be a student, stood and said, "We've been studying Langston Hughes. He writes about race. Do you ever write about race?"

"Yes, I do, but remember, most of Langston Hughes' poems are not about race. They are about Black Americans living their lives and dealing with universal issues."

Hughes had died the previous year and his poetry was suddenly now getting a lot of fresh attention. I wasn't surprised to hear the student say they were studying the poetry.

There were several other questions, questions mainly about subject matter, but also a few about rhyme, rhythm, line-breakage, and the like. After the reading, an older man I assumed was a professor came up to shake my hand. He was heavy-set and balding, with very alert eyes. He said, "Loved your reading. I'm Ralph Kirkpatrick, English department. I'm teaching the Creative Writing workshops until we can hire a real poet. I'm a Shakespearean by training." We shook hands.

After Professor Kirkpatrick stepped away, Amy Lawrence moved in and extended her hand to be shaken, and she said, "I loved your reading."

I thanked her.

"I teach American and British literature here." She blushed.

I nodded. She was a plainly attractive young woman with clear skin, a large forehead, a small nose and thin lips, brown hair and brown eyes. She was wearing a grey sweater and a blue skirt. I guessed she was about twenty-three or twenty-four, maybe fresh out of graduate school.

She said, "I'd love to pick your brain sometime on what makes a good poem. Right now, I'm teaching Whitman."

"Sure, that would be fun. Want to have lunch sometime?"

"Absolutely," she said, and wrote down her phone number on a notepad, tore off the page, and handed it to me.

Alas, I didn't call her.

The next day, Kenneth Jeremiah called and said, "If you get your book placed before we fill the poetry position, we'd love to consider you for the poetry slot. If it's any comfort to you, we're looking around very slowly. We're in no hurry. If all goes well and there is no hiring freeze, we can start the process. Since our poet Emily-Marie Powell died last year, the position has been open. I don't mind keeping it open another year. Professor Kirkpatrick doesn't mind holding the fort till then. As a private institution, we don't really have to put out a call for applications in the same way public institutions must. The students and faculty adored your reading yesterday. You saw it; you got a standing ovation. We all think you'd be a wonderful addition to our faculty. Do keep in touch, and let us know when the book is under contract."

I assured him that I would. I felt the pressure. He'd said, "...when the book is under contract," and I was thinking, *if* the book is ever under contract. I already sensed how difficult it could be to get a book published.

Consultants Unlimited, Inc. started as a social science model project at Amadel Institute, a conservative Washington, D.C., think tank. Professor Basil Levi Goodman created CUI. Originally it was launched to help political candidates of either party win an election.

In New York, the Consultants Unlimited office was on the seventh floor of the old General Motors building, an intricate brown Gothic structure. It was a triangular building, and we always entered the West 57th Street and Eighth Avenue side. The other side of the building was 1775 Broadway.

Several of CUI's sister companies were studying international situations. There were uprisings in Poland, East and West Germany, France, Italy, Yugoslavia, Mexico, Spain, Czechoslovakia, and other countries. In Paris, the protest movement of students and workers of May 1968 would give rise to a call for "L'Imagination au Pouvoir!" ("Power to the Imagination!"). Bravo for Paris! Long life to the imagination!

Ours was a small research outfit whose findings would be turned over to the National Advisory Commission on Civil Disorders headed by Senator John Whittington. The full riot report would eventually appear in book form as *The Whittington Report*. The President's administration did not agree with the findings of the report. Recommendations were not implemented. Among many other things, the report said police mishandling of initial incidents caused many of the riots.

The upstairs people and the downstairs people at CUI hardly had any contact with each other, except when someone up or down ran out of something, such as pens or pencils or paper or even newspapers that needed to be searched and subjected to our analysis formulas or schemas.

I'd come upstairs to borrow a box of red pencils from the supply shelf. About twenty young men and women were sitting at desks in rows. They were all hard at work applying the scheme we used on newspaper articles.

She was reading a newspaper. I walked over to her and said, "What's your name?"

"Sophia."

If there was such a thing as love at first sight, this was it. I felt a strong surge of emotion as though some magnetic force was pulling me to her. My heart beat faster. My throat was dry. I loved her smile, loved the way the light from the high windows played on her face and body, highlighting her beauty—a beauty not confined to her face alone, but in her whole presence: the way she sat in the chair, the delicate touch of her hands on the newspapers, her slow, regular breathing.

Still smiling, she asked my name, and I told her.

Sophia kept smiling pleasantly, as though she was pleased to be noticed. We exchanged phone numbers.

A short time later I visited her on the Upper West Side, where she shared a small studio apartment with another young woman, Ethel. Sophia was playing the music of the Beatles. She was humming and singing along with the music. I sat at her little kitchen table and watched and listened.

Sophia was an attractive girl. She had a prominent nose and large friendly eyes. Her face was pear-shaped and framed by a generous splash of dyed blond hair. Smart, she was an aspiring anthropologist. She talked a lot about her plans to go back to school for a higher degree in anthropology, and to eventually do field research, and possibly someday teach. She was ambitious and I liked that about her.

Everything about her was beautiful, but she disliked her flat behind, and she had a tendency to slump forward in an effort to minimize the presence of her large breasts. She felt they were a burden. Except for a small amount of facial acne, which she covered with makeup, she had a smooth complexion. Because of nervous insecurity and contact lenses, she blinked a lot, especially while talking. Her innocent response to a simple male glance often caused men to approach her. She loved the attention, but didn't know how to handle the approach. The attention helped to quiet her insecurity about her appearance. The more attention she got, the more she needed it.

Sophia was from the Bronx and I was from Brooklyn.

I never met Sophia's mother, Sara, or her father, Saul, or her brother, Jacob, the youngest of the three, but I met Sophia's sister, Belinda. She was a year younger than Sophia, smaller and shorter, a pretty girl with an olive complexion, and with a serious face with large dark eyes and thin lips and a small turned-up nose. Her face was framed by a thick crown of dark brown hair. She was considerably shorter than Sophia. She had a decided Mediterranean look, while Sophia had a Swedish or Norwegian look.

Belinda always ignored me. I was offended but, because I didn't want to get into a fight with her or with Sophia, I kept my hurt feelings to myself. I knew each time she came to see Sophia that it was to try to convince Sophia to leave me. There was no way I could have stood before her, pointed to the door and shouted, "Get out! Don't come back!" She was Sophia's sister.

Their father had raised Sophia and her sister and brother. The mother was estranged from the family. She lived somewhere in New Jersey with her common-law husband. Sophia refused to talk about the trauma in her family that caused the separation.

Sophia's father worked at a variety of jobs such as car salesman, factory worker, and clerk in a supermarket. Until she ran away, her mother was a homemaker.

Each time I visited Sophia, we sat and talked about the current political situation in our country, or about movies or books we each had read, and we listened to music from her record player, Buffy Sainte-Marie or the Beatles. It was a couple of weeks before Sophia and I made love on her narrow bed. When we did, it was sweet and leisurely. Afterward, we lay there holding each other and listening to Joni Mitchell and Pete Seeger, two of Sophia's favorite singers.

One afternoon she said, "My landlord is going to raise the rent."

"Why don't you move downtown with me?" I said. The thought had not consciously entered my mind till the moment I said it. Perhaps it was already there unconsciously. I realized I wanted more time with her, wanted us to be together. It wasn't that I was lonely—although I was. I loved her. She was not the first white girl I had dated, but she was the first that I wanted to have a lasting relationship with. Sophia was an intellectual, an aspiring anthropologist, and a serious reader. Those were qualities I admired and respected. She would fit in the East Village scene nicely.

"Sure," she said, "if you want me to, but not till I help my roommate find somebody to replace me here. I'll have to place an ad in the newspaper."

Luck was with her. The following week, a young woman Sophia's age, twenty-two, responded to the classified ad.

My apartment was on the Lower East Side on Twelfth Street between Avenue A and Avenue B. The bathtub was in the kitchen. There was a small bedroom, a tiny closet, and an area that passed as a living space with a couch and a couple of chairs I'd picked up at a used furniture store. The rent was forty-five dollars a month.

From the Bowery and the East River to Canal Street and Houston, old tenement buildings like mine were packed densely together. They were built in the 19th century to house the influx of Russian and Polish Jews and other Eastern Europeans.

They came through Ellis Island between the 1850s and 1910s and they were, like we were now, seeking the American dream. They were packed like sardines into these tiny, airless apartments. Often ten to fifteen people were crammed in two rooms. Usually the bathtub was in the kitchen near the sink, because that was where the plumbing was.

Now here we were, the bohemians, the artists, and the poets—the new tenants—taking up residence in these dilapidated apartments. Why? Because we were not rich, and they were affordable. Being here together also gave us a community, one held together by the idea of creativity and intellectual pursuit.

In mid-June, I was invited up to Harlem to read my poems to a group that turned out to be composed mostly of young militant Black men and women who were, like me, aspiring poets. I knew that Malcolm X, not Martin Luther King, was their hero. Malcom X had been assassinated three years earlier. While I admired some of Malcolm X's political and social positions, I was more firmly a follower of the non-violence preached by Martin Luther King. Like the rest of the country, on that day and in that hour, I was still shocked and upset by the assassination of King two months earlier. Now, as I approached Harlem with these thoughts on my mind and these feelings weighing heavily in my heart, like the rest of the country, I was feeling a new layer of shock over the assassination of Bobby Kennedy just a few days earlier, on June 6th. I was angry. What was our country coming to? This was my state of mind as I approached Harlem.

The gathering was in an assembly room at the YMCA on West 125th Street. My host was the poet Perry Obadiah Willoughby, a New Orleans native now living in Harlem. He was the author of one self-published book of poems.

When I finished the reading, Perry and a group of them gathered around me at the podium. Perry, a tall pointy-headed guy with buck-teeth, said, "We didn't hear anything about the Black experience in your poems. Do you consider yourself a Black poet? What are you?"

I said, "I try to write poems that speak to universal issues, not simply always writing about my own cultural identity—I do that, too. I'm trying to come from a deeper place."

"What kind of deeper place?" Willoughby asked with a skeptical frown.

"I subscribe to what Langston Hughes said way back in 1926 in his manifesto, 'The Negro Artist and the Racial Mountain,' when he said essentially that we Black poets—or writers or artists—will write with freedom and without fear, and what we produce is a legitimate expression of Black life. He said, 'We stand on top of the mountain, free within ourselves.'"

Willoughby and the others looked at me suspiciously. Their philosophy was well known. They were Black Nationalist poets who believed that poetry should be a political weapon against racism. For them, that was the only useful function of poetry. They also had a limited definition of Blackness that I did not share. For me, the culture was rich and diverse, consisting of many different types of people with many different types of agendas.

Sophia and I had been together about six months when our research jobs ended. Now that we were free, one day I said, "How would you like to go to Mexico?"

It took her a moment to respond, then she said, "I was thinking the same thing."

Maybe it would be good for both of us to go to a slower, quieter place, to get away for a while from the city and from bad news every night delivered by TV newsman Walter Cronkite, affectionately known as "Uncle Walter." His was the heavy voice of authority. I always thought he sounded like the great actor Walter Pidgeon. In Mexico, I could get my book finished.

Sophia said, "Wonderful! Let's do it! You must have read my thoughts, or I somehow planted the thought in your mind."

We needed to sublet our apartment. We made arrangements with Agnes Ludovic, a young woman upstairs who played "Sgt. Pepper's Lonely Hearts Club Band" and "Lucy in the Sky with Diamonds," all day, every day, and much of the night. Passing her in the hallway, she always smelled of marijuana. That didn't sound so bad. She said she saw the movie *Yellow Submarine* twenty-six times. On the Lower East Side at that time, she seemed normal.

Agnes had a roommate, another young woman, Debbie, but Agnes had been looking for an apartment of her own. We didn't know Agnes and Debbie well, only in passing, but despite the marijuana, she seemed pleasant enough to trust. She assured us she could pay the forty-five dollars a month rent.

Later that day, to Sophia I said, "I've had poems in a magazine in Mexico City called *Nuevo Mundo*. The editor is a guy named Frank Garrick. You mind if we visit him?"

Sophia said, "No, not at all. I'm glad you know someone there."

I sent Frank a postcard telling him when we would arrive, and I got a postcard back inviting us to dinner the night of our arrival in Mexico City.

A few days before our departure, we made arrangements with the phone company to disconnect service on the day we were leaving.

That same day I went to see my parents on 14th Street in Park Slope, Brooklyn. They lived in one of the row houses, a brownstone with the usual iron railing alongside the single purple stone stairway up to the landing. It had an ancient front door with the usual classic window of dense antique glass through which you could see a distorted image of a person on the other side. This was where I grew up.

The minute Mom opened the door, there was the pleasant vanilla smell of cookies recently baked. Mom loved to bake cookies. It was one of the reasons Dad had diabetes. He also secretly ate Baby Ruth and Mars candy bars, and sometimes a whole pint of chocolate or strawberry ice cream.

Mom was sixty-five and Dad was sixty-nine. Mom—Elizabeth Williams-Lowell—had gained a lot of weight since her recent retirement from the public library. She mostly now stayed in the house. Her hair was grey. She walked with a wobble, and her teeth had all been replaced. She'd developed the annoying habit of moving them around in her mouth with her tongue. A person with alert and friendly eyes, Mom had small ears and fat cheeks.

Dad—Wendell Sinclair Lowell—before retirement, was manager at the Bank of the United States on Prospect Place in Park Slope, Brooklyn. He'd been tall and lanky like me, but now he was stooped a bit, bald on top. He had very little hair left. It was a reef of white circled around his head. He had big ears and a big nose. I worried that someday I would look like him.

They both were light brown-skinned, my complexion, and the older they got, the more they looked like sister and brother rather than husband and wife.

When I arrived, Dad was taking a nap. Mom made tea and she

brought out the vanilla cookies and placed them on the coffee table. I sat in the living room with her and sipped tea.

Mom said, "Now that the research job has ended you need to start looking for a real permanent job. When you took on the research job you knew it would be temporary. Your dad can get your old job back for you at the bank. The people there like you, and it would be a good place for you to work. You could start again as a teller and work your way up like your dad did to become manager." She paused. "But you can't take a job like that and then go running off to Mexico."

"I don't want to go back to the bank, Mom," I said. "If I can finish my book and get it accepted somewhere, I hope to get a job teaching, maybe at the Warren Lowery School, or at some place like that. They've asked me to apply when I get my book under contract, but I have to finish it first. That's what I want to do in Mexico."

"Oh, Jimmy, that all sounds so iffy. How can you depend on something like that?"

"I don't. I depend on myself. I know what I can do, Mom."

"Okay, if you say so."

Dad came out into the living room, rubbing his eyes. "Oh, Jim-boy, hi. Didn't know you were here."

Mom said, "Wendell, Jimmy is going to Mexico. That new girlfriend of his, Sophia, is going with him."

Dad said, "Good. Why not?"

"I'll miss you guys. I'll write, though, and let you know where we are."

Dad sat down in his favorite armchair. It was green with purple stripes. It was badly worn on the armrests and in back where Dad's back and head had made indentations. From excessive use, the seat was lumpy. I'd never sat in it. It was a pretty disgusting thing to look at.

He said, "Listen, son, are you still writing poetry?" He ran his hand across his bald head.

"Sure."

"Well, it's a good thing you saved a lot of money while you were working at the bank, but you know that money is not going to last forever. What I'm getting at, son, is that in addition to the poetry, you need to do something practical that will earn money. Now that the research job has ended, you need to concentrate on something that is going to benefit your future."

"I still get checks from the *Brooklyn Daily Observer* for the freelance editing work I do for them on feature columns."

"I know, son, but that's not a lot of money."

Mom added, "You can't depend on a thing like that, Jimmy."

"I don't, not entirely. As you know, I started that work while in grad school, and I've put every check in my savings account. Besides, Dad, I want to do work I can be proud of. The poetry is what I want to keep at the center of my life."

"Work you can be proud of? Pride? You talk about pride? You were born proud, Jim-boy. It's in your blood. I'm proud of working my way up at the bank to bank manager. Jim-boy, your ancestor, John Lee Lowell, was proud of the work he did. Boy, pride is in your blood. You don't have to strive for it. In bondage, John Lee Lowell worked as a blacksmith in Springfield."

I'd heard this same pride lecture countless times.

"John Lee was an expert blacksmith, the best in the county. He shoed horses and made anything out of iron that people needed. He worked his way out of servitude in 1753. Then he bought the blacksmith business he'd worked in since he was a boy, and he ran that business for forty years, serving his community right up till he died. Don't tell me about pride! Like I said, you were born with pride, pride is in your blood, but I don't see how being proud of writing poetry is even in the same category."

"That's your opinion, Dad. I know how you feel about it, but I think I can get a job teaching and write poetry while I teach. A lot of poets do that."

"That would be good, but, son, those jobs are hard to come by. You know that, especially for a Black man. When you were in college the poetry didn't matter so much, but now you're out in the world. You need to get serious, son. I'm worried about you and this Mexico thing… Why do you need to go to Mexico?"

"Because I can."

Mom said, "Wendell, let the boy find his own way. Jimmy is a sensible boy. He'll eventually make the right decisions for himself."

Dad shook his head and said, "I certainly hope so."

On my way back to the Lower East Side on the 2nd Avenue Local, I thought about Mom and Dad's worries. At least they weren't unhappy with my choice of Sophia as a girlfriend.

Sophia and I decided to have a going-away party. She had not kept in touch with friends made in college, nor had she kept in touch with friends made on the job at CUI.

So we invited my friends and their wives or girlfriends.

For the party we bought wine, beer, lots of pizza, peanuts, pretzels, and Sophia picked up from the local deli what she called "finger food," which were bite-sized, little breaded snacks stuffed with meat or cheese.

The people who came to the party:

Darius Wright was a slender guy with keen features and a secretive smile. He was from Jamaica, West Indies, and had been in New York for many years. He wrote poetry.

He was married to Josephine Cuyp, and they had lived for several years in Morocco and Europe. Josephine was from Idaho. She had brown hair and blue-grey eyes. She kept a diary, and she devoted herself to Darius, and she worked to support him and herself.

It was also well known that Darius had a daughter, Erminia. Several years into his marriage, he got an eighteen-year-old Puerto Rican woman named Flavia pregnant. In passing, I'd met both Flavia and Erminia. The child was now about four or five. This affair and the lovechild were something else Josephine was putting up with.

Darius and Josephine lived in a large rambling apartment in a tenement walk-up down on lower Avenue C.

Alvin Johnson was a perpetually high young man with curly hair and dimples. Alvin carried around all the time a notebook in which he wrote an endless sequence of poems. He was sidekick to Darius and Josephine.

Alvin slept on the couch or the floor in Darius and Josephine's apartment, and he'd done this for years wherever the couple lived, including during their stays in England, France, and Morocco.

Herbert Griffin was a lanky, sleepy-eyed fellow. He also edited our poetry journal called *Up Against the Wall: A Journal of Literature and the Arts*. He wrote poetry, and published it in our journal as well as in other East Coast and West Coast literary journals.

Herb was a loner. He was never seen with a girlfriend and he never married. Even where he lived was a mystery, a well-kept secret.

David Williams was the supreme jive-talker. He always wore dark glasses and a big engaging smile. He loved nothing more than having a cigarette in one hand and a glass of wine in the other. He also had a love for marijuana. David had been writing the Great American Novel for many years. He never talked about it, and no one ever saw any part of it.

His common-law wife, Carla Armand, was pretty and quiet. She had grey eyes and a beautiful mouth. Carla worked as a receptionist at Empire Real Estate in midtown. She was easygoing and always laughed at David's jokes and humor. She no doubt loved him.

David and Carla lived in a dingy little apartment on First Avenue near St. Mark's Place.

Glen Harrison was a painter from Atlanta, Georgia. Glen was tall and thin and cross-eyed. His hair was red and kinky, and he wore it cut short. He looked like a parrot. Glen had a patron, a wealthy woman out on Long Island, who bought his paintings on a regular basis. He made a modest living in this way.

His wife, Bianca Castile, was a tall, elegant young woman with dark hair and a very light complexion. She was graceful and soft-spoken. She was office manager at Bush & Wells law firm in Soho.

Glen and Bianca lived in a walk-up tenement on 11th Street between Avenues A and First.

Maurice Neal was originally from the Dominican Republic. Maurice was a barrel-chested guy with a booming voice. He had a flat nose and thick lips. We all knew he had a very violent temper, especially when he had a few drinks in him.

He was author of the science fiction novel, *Dominican Woman*, published in 1966 by Jones & Gillman, one of the major trade houses. The novel was set both in the Dominican Republic and in an alternate reality called Tremois. The protagonist is a creature from Tremois who comes to Earth, to the Dominican Republic, to kidnap a young fertile female and take her back to Tremois. A virus has rendered all of their females sterile. The story was not my cup of tea. After struggling through about twenty pages, I gave up.

His wife, Ruba Murdock, was devoted to him. She had a BA from Radcliffe and had inherited family money. She was good-looking, with a face framed by dark brown hair that fell to her shoulders.

She hardly ever said anything, but she seemed to always be listening sharply to what people were saying. She taught pottery in a local Lower East Side community center.

Maurice and Ruba lived in a high-rise near the East River promenade.

Lorenzo Mallory was a big, bumpy-faced guy, and he always wore dark glasses. Lorenzo had a degree from the English department at Yale. He wrote long poems that he loved reciting in public. He published them frequently in *Up Against the Wall* and several other literary magazines.

He was a favorite at the various poetry events sponsored by St. Mark's Church in-the-Bowery. Lorenzo was known to be working on a history of slavery. No one had ever seen any part of it.

Lorenzo would always show up with a woman. Each time he appeared, he was with a different woman. We all thought he lived a secret life because these women came from other worlds we had no contact with. Some he apparently picked up at his readings; others he must have met in random places, such as the supermarket or who-knows-where. He was very outgoing, and apparently had no problem approaching women he didn't know.

These were some of the people I knew at that time, Lower East Side poets whom I had met since leaving college. I called them friends, but they were friends I didn't see frequently.

Uncelebrated, they were often home writing, as was I. We didn't have much time to socialize. Hemingway once said that the writer had to be prepared to work "always without applause." He might have added "and without a social life."

These friends came that night to the going-away party. They were not always the best-behaved people.

Herb locked himself in the toilet for a long time. People knocked on the door, but he took his time coming out. When he came out, the toilet reeked of marijuana smoke.

"How long you guys going to be in Mexico?" Maurice said.

"For as long as we can afford to stay," I said.

I noticed that Maurice Neal was smoking a joint. He was passing it around. It worried me because I knew Maurice tended to get hostile when he smoked weed. At the very least, he would start an argument with one of us.

Sure enough, ten minutes later, Maurice was into a heated argument with Lorenzo Mallory. By now, Lorenzo was drunk.

Glen tried to calm them down. "Hey, guys, cool it."

Maurice said, "Shut your damn mouth, Glen!"

Sophia gave me a warning look.

Before I could turn around, Maurice had jumped on Lorenzo and knocked him to the floor.

As Lorenzo tried to get up, Maurice grabbed him by the collar and pulled him out into the hallway. We heard scuffling, then *bump, bump, bump, bump* and *bump*.

I rushed into the hallway. Lorenzo was lying on the floor. His dark glasses lay unbroken a few feet away.

I said, "Jeez! Maurice, man, this is not cool. You guys are going to get us kicked out of this building."

He hissed, "Lorenzo started it."

I knew that was not true. His friends quietly and affectionately called Maurice crazy. He grew up in Jersey City, New Jersey, where, as a teenager, he was arrested several times for street fighting and petty theft.

Lorenzo stood up and picked up his glasses and put them on. He brushed off his pants and adjusted his shirt, tucking it back into his pants.

I said, "There's no need for this kind of craziness."

They shook hands and followed me back into the apartment.

The party lasted till midnight.

I turned off the music, a mix of jazz, pop, rock & roll, and blues. After everybody was gone, Sophia and I looked at the mess: beer cans, wine bottles, pizza boxes, dirty glasses, and a mess of dirty paper plates.

"Let's leave it till morning," she said.

"Sorry about my roughneck friends."

"It's not your fault. Those things happen when people drink."

"And smoke."

"Yes, and smoke."

About three days before Sophia and I were to leave, she said, "Do you mind going to the zoo? As a teenager, when I was stressed, I used to go there to calm down. I always feel at peace there among the animals."

"Are you nervous about flying?"

She said, "Very."

"Last time I was at the Bronx Zoo I was fifteen."

We took the bus up to the zoo on Southern Boulevard. It took an hour and nine minutes, and it was interesting seeing that part of the city from the window: the buildings, the people, the cars, and the taxis; the metropolis in motion but not so much motion that the parts became indistinguishable.

We walked in under the big letters: Bronx Zoo. Immediately I noticed that Sophia was smiling. Holding my hand, she was almost skipping along like a six-year-old. She seemed happier than I'd seen her in several days. Inside immediately we passed between the sculptures of the two giant water buffalos.

We stopped at the ice cream stand and bought ice cream on cones: she, vanilla, and I, strawberry. While walking around and eating ice cream, I was thinking that after Sophia moved downtown with me, I often noticed how restless and agitated she got if I spent a lot of time at the typewriter. I said, "When we get to Mexico, after visiting Frank, I think we should go to Puerto Vallarta. I've heard that it's a quiet, sleepy village. I can try to finish my book there. Are you going to be okay while I work on my book?"

"Absolutely! Don't worry about me! I'm interested in studying the culture." She paused. "Puerto Vallarta! Great idea! My friend Ruth went there on vacation once. She loved it!"

The zoo grounds were as I remembered them. They were pleasant, with the water fountain of sea horses and other mythical figures. We stopped to watch the seals swimming around in their pond. A couple of them were sunning on the rocks. Sophia said, "They seem so carefree. Not a worry in the world! Just look at them!"

Then, for a while, we watched the peacocks strut about displaying their colorful plumage. They were co-existing with the other big birds and even frisky monkeys.

Sophia was beside herself with happiness. It improved my own mood. Her face and her whole body beamed. We leaned on the circular railing and watched the sea lions lazily sleeping on the rocks.

We watched a mother lion licking her young cubs. They were tawny and most of them had black spots. One cub, with no black spots, wandered away and didn't get licked.

Smiling, Sophia said, "He's the one that's going to grow up with a problem."

We spent the day watching the monkeys in the open, playing or grooming each other, or seeing red kangaroos, polar bears, tigers looking very majestic, or seeing gorillas looking at us with human-like eyes.

Sophia said, "The mission of the zoo is not just to put animals on display for people to look at. The zoo has a higher purpose: to protect and sustain the lives of these animals. Some of them are becoming extinct in their natural habitat."

"Says the anthropologist."

"Well, human behavior and animal behavior are not that far apart. There is no getting around it, we are animals, too."

Unexpectedly, the whole experience gave me comfort as well.

Just before we were to leave for Mexico, Belinda came again to visit. I was sitting at my desk in the living room, working at the typewriter. She sat on the edge of the couch as if she was scared to relax too much. She might catch some kind of disease in our apartment. She sat very primly with knees together and her hands together on her lap. She looked up pleadingly at Sophia, who was standing before her.

"Sophie, Poppa says you must not go to Mexico with somebody you hardly know. You know he is against this relationship."

"Tell Poppa I am a grown woman. I make my own decisions."

"He said you would say that. He says he has nothing against colored people, but the world is against this kind of relationship. He says you are just asking for trouble. You will not be happy, Sophie, not with a, a colored man, a Negro. Please come home. You would make Poppa so happy."

Belinda was talking about me as if I were not in the room. Her attitude toward me was annoying, and I could see that Sophia was embarrassed by her sister's lack of manners. As before, I kept my anger to myself rather than confront Belinda. Where would confronting her get me? Would it improve my relationship with her? I doubted it. Wrong or right, I felt that confronting her, demanding she be polite, would not achieve a positive end.

"Belinda, tell Poppa I am going to be fine, not to worry."

"It's not me, Sophie," Belinda said. "It's Poppa. I'm only delivering his message. I have nothing against you, James."

I turned around. She was looking at me.

I decided to stay out of it. I said nothing.

II

ARLY JULY. WE WERE AT THE AIRPORT. We had our travel permits. While we were waiting for our flight, I heard my name called over the public address system: "Mr. James Eric Lowell, please come to the ticket counter." The counter was only a few feet from where we were sitting.

I walked over to the counter. The uniformed ticket agent, a thin Mexican woman with very red lips, said she wanted to check my identification again. I showed her my driver's license. Satisfied, she said, "Thank you," and that was that.

Soon we boarded Mexicana Flight 906 and waited for takeoff. Sophia and I were in Row 12, and I was aware of the hot nauseating plastic smell, the stuffiness and airlessness of the cabin. The plane was about two-thirds full.

It was five minutes past departure time.

I was in the aisle seat and Sophia was by the window, nobody in the middle. The plane jerked, then wobbled a few times, then slowly started taxiing out to the runway.

The two thin Mexican stewardesses sat down, still smiling. Both had perms. Now I counted four empty seats ahead of us, the backs of heads. Our seatbelts were tight as they could be.

The pilot spoke on the intercom, first in Spanish, then in English: "Despegaremos pronto. Sentarse y disfrutar del vuelo. We'll be taking off shortly. Sit back, folks, and enjoy the flight. Think Mexico City!"

I looked out the window. The sky was a dull grey.

Yet we waited and waited, then the pilot finally said, "We're next, folks. Make sure your seatbelts are fastened." As we continued to wait, the plane was roaring.

The plane suddenly shot forth out along the runway, picking up great speed. We felt the grinding of the wheels lifting, being tucked up into the belly of the plane. We felt the liftoff, felt ourselves leaving the earth, climbing into space. My ears began to clog.

Sophia said, "I've never been outside the country before."

She was wearing a white cotton shirt and tight jeans. Her long legs were a bit cramped as they touched the back of the seat in front of her. She was about five-nine and I was five-eleven. My knees were pressed firmly against the seat in front of me. There was nowhere else to put them.

I said, "This is my first time, too."

The ascent was a bumpy, dull grind, shaking our insides. As the plane continued to climb, it was like we were inside some heavy animal struggling up a hillside. The plane's push against gravity was laborious. I felt Sophia's left hand fearfully digging into my arm.

I reached up and turned on the air spigot, releasing the airflow down upon me, trying to dispel the heavy warm plastic smell of the cabin, but relief was slight. Sophia reached up and turned on hers, too.

When the plane finally reached a cruising altitude of about thirty-nine thousand feet, my stomach began to settle a bit. Sophia also relaxed more. She gave me a nervous smile, scooted over, then leaned her head against my shoulder.

During the five hours and forty minutes of bumpiness, we tried to read. She had a cultural anthropology book about tribal warfare among Central Africans in the 18th century.

I was reading a translation of Paul Verlaine's early Symbolist poem, but my stomach was so upset from the unsettling flight that I couldn't concentrate. Without comprehension, I kept reading the same lines over and over till I gave up and put the Selected Poems back in my baggage under the seat in front of me.

I leaned over Sophia and looked out the window. Despite queasiness, as we approached Mexico City International Airport, I felt a growing sense of excitement.

Sophia and I were holding hands. I looked at her eyes. They were filled with controlled fear. She said, "They say most crashes happen during landings."

"Don't worry, we're not going to crash."

As we were landing I saw the airport's modest building stretched out white under the sun. We filed down the portable silver steps from the airplane to the hot tarmac, walked single file across to the airport entrance. We went through customs quickly. Then, inside at a currency exchange kiosk, we exchanged dollars for pesos.

Outside on the sidewalk, we waved for a taxi. There were only three, and a couple of old buses. Diesel fumes from the buses were thick in the air.

A taxi driver got out and came toward us. He was a short stocky man with a bald spot on top. We started toward him, and he met us and took the luggage.

He put our luggage in the long trunk of his old lime-green Ford . He said his name was Juan. All the while he was asking us questions about our flight. He started talking about the last time he was in an airplane. Sophia and I got into the back seat. The interior was hot and stuffy. A plastic replica of a human skull lay inelegantly on Juan's dashboard.

He said, "Where you folks from?"

"New York," I said.

"Ah, New York! My brother Matias went to New York once for a little while. They deported him. I don't think he was doing nothing bad. Ah, poor fellow, he's not doing so well these days."

Sophia said, "I hope he gets better."

"He lives in Chapala now. He's a handyman for the retired Americans living around the lake. He works farms, too, but he gambles and loses the little money he makes as a handyman and doing farm work. Me? I take care of my family and try to put a few pesos aside. You never know when you going to need emergency money. Right?"

"Right," said Sophia.

As we moved through the streets, I saw old, beaten-up American cars everywhere, both parked at curbs and in motion.

Juan said, "Señora, you have a sister?"

"Yes. Why?"

"Well, I too have a sister, Valentina. She's two years younger than me. Poor Valentina, she's crazy. I don't know what's wrong with people. She had a bad drinking problem. My sister, she prayed to Saint Sebastian to cure her from drinking. Because she was drunk, in a tavern once she got into an argument with another woman over a man, this no-good man named Cristobal. He had a wife and fifteen children. The woman Teresa somebody-or-other, she shot my sister. She pulled out this little pistol from her purse and shot Valentina, but the bullet only grazed her thigh. She says all the time she would be dead if Saint Sebastian had not been watching over her. He saved her life."

Sophia said, "I'm glad your sister survived."

We were on our way to a cheap hotel, Comandante on Izazaga near San Pablo in downtown Mexico City, which our travel agent had secured for us.

People were demonstrating on the other side of the street.

I said, "There were recent uprisings in Paris. Anything like that here?"

Juan said, "Not yet, but problems are coming."

We arrived. I paid Juan, and a young hotel porter came out and took our bags into the little modest lobby with deep purple walls.

It was what we could afford. The hotel was in an unimpressive building with three floors. It was of stucco painted a bright red bordering on an orangey pink. The lobby was small and crammed with old dusty furniture. There were metal plants in pots in two corners, and the floor was composed of a profusion of tiny marble blue and green rectangles. Silver metal ashcans stood alongside many of the chairs.

The clerk, an ancient heavyset man at the small check-in counter, greeted us warmly.

In the room, which smelled of mildew, Sophia and I took turns taking a shower. The shower walls were of grey stone. The water was slow and tepid. We had a little time to relax. The bed was comfortable. I stretched out there on my back to rest for a few minutes.

After we got dressed, we went out and found Gringo Heaven, an outdoor café with square metal tables and chairs. It had a blowup image of Aunt Jemima high on a placard above the entrance. We spotted an empty table and sat down on the little iron chairs. Sophia and I ordered coffee.

American tourists were there eating dinner. They were mostly over-weight and elderly couples. The women were wearing bright gabardine and the men were dressed in shorts and colorful sport shirts. The café served American-style hamburgers and pancakes. The rate of exchange was one peso equaled eight cents. 12.50 pesos equaled $1. It was a good exchange for Americans.

From where we sat, I saw American tourists on the street with cam-eras, milling about and taking pictures, mostly of themselves and each other.

A little boy with an angelic face came from the sidewalk up to our table with an armful of newspapers. It was an English-language paper out of El Paso, Texas.

Sophia said, "How much?"

"Six pesos," he said.

She handed him, in peso paper money, the equivalency of a five-dollar bill and said, "Do you have change?"

Rather than answering her and then handing her a newspaper, he snatched the money and ran away.

Sophia, with a smile, said, "A lesson learned. In the future keep smaller bills."

It was just after four in the afternoon. We'd gained one hour. In New York, it was five o'clock. Sophia and I were expected at Frank Garrick's house at six-thirty for dinner.

Frank was a well-known New York poet who was publishing a high-ly respected bilingual literary journal, *Nuevo Mundo*, out of his home in Mexico City. Frank's "new world" journal was distributed in Mexico, South America, and the States. Always printed on fine paper, it carried reproductions of contemporary art as well as poetry, fiction, and essays on art and literature.

During the five years since the journal started, he'd published many fine poets, fiction writers, and essayists of the United States, Mexico, Brazil, Peru, Colombia, Argentina, Bolivia, Venezuela, and the Caribbean.

I'd circulated a bit in the New York poetry world, but I'd never met Frank. My contact with him was through the mail after he moved to Mexico. That was the extent of the connection.

Frank knew we'd be in Mexico City a couple of days before moving on to Puerto Vallarta, where we hoped to find an apartment.

At six, Sophia and I, dressed casually, went down and flagged a taxi. It was a short ride to the San Miguel Chapultepec area. The taxi stopped in front of a house wide and low with a big unremarkable front yard.

The grass was dead, and there was a decrepit car tire lying on the grass and a rope-swing hanging from an old tree on the left side of the yard.

I paid and we got out. The air was hot and humid.

A man I assumed was Frank Garrick came out onto the front porch. He had the kind of face you saw every day everywhere. A face hard to describe, hard because there was nothing unusual about it; his were regular features.

He was neither handsome nor was he unpleasant to look at. He didn't frown and he didn't smile. His brown hair wasn't long nor was it short. He was average height, and he was wearing a light blue dress shirt with the sleeves rolled up, jeans, and house slippers.

As we walked up onto the porch, the boards of the steps and the planks of the porch squeaked. Lying on the arm of one of the porch chairs was a copy of Mao Tse-Tung's little red book. It was dog-eared.

I shook hands with Frank Garrick. I introduced Sophia.

He said, "Great to see you guys, come on in! I'm cooking! I gave my cook the day off!"

The front door was opened. Immediately, through the screened door, the cooking smells from the kitchen area at the far end of the huge room were pungent, spicy, and sweet.

"Good to finally meet you, Frank," I said.

He turned around with a big ironic smile and said, "Yeah, but damn, man, I didn't expect you to be so handsome with a movie-star chiseled face, and so tall, too! I think I'm a bit jealous!"

I laughed, and he laughed. Sophia didn't laugh.

We followed Frank inside. We were in a room even bigger than it had seemed looking in from the porch. It served as living room, dining room, and kitchen. Clearly it was a much lived-in space, with books and magazines everywhere.

On the far wall was a framed poster of the Argentine Marxist revolutionary Ernesto Che Guevara, who had died in La Higuera, Bolivia, a year before in October, and all over the world he was quickly becoming an even bigger cult figure than before.

As Frank led us in, he was talking over his shoulder to us. "I haven't had any news from the States lately. What's happening with the Beats, with Ginsberg and Kerouac, with the Yippies, with Abbie Hoffman and Jerry Rubin, with Timothy Leary, with Huey Newton and Bobby Seale, and Germaine Greer and Betty Friedan? How about Norman Mailer and his antics? What is Truman Capote up to these days? I read a Gore Vidal interview in an English language newspaper we get here in the city. He sure doesn't mince words. They all seemed to be getting the establishment very worried."

"Many of them are still raising hell trying to lower heaven," I said. Abbie and Jerry I knew because I had met them while donating things to the Diggers' Free Store on East Tenth Street. I'd also joined them in anti-war demonstrations. Abbie called me "The Poet," a title I was not yet worthy of. The day before leaving for Mexico, I saw them on St. Mark's Place. Abbie said, "Hey, James, you coming to the demonstration? You could maybe write a poem about it." I said, "Wish I could, Abbie, but I got to go home and pack. I'm going to Mexico." He said they were on their way to demonstrate on Wall Street against big business corruption. I gave him two thumbs up.

Over the couch was a large framed cover print of the first issue of Frank's journal, *Nuevo Mundo*.

In the room were two women and two girls about eight and nine years old. The two women, on the couch, were deep in conversation. The two girls at a table to the side of the couch were playing some sort of card game.

From the kitchen, Frank introduced everybody.

The two girls, Selena, eight, and Bonita, nine, were introduced as Frank's daughters. Pretty little girls, they were clearly sisters: they looked alike, except Selena had freckles and Bonita didn't. She had a dimple in her chin and Selena didn't. Sitting at the card table, they were now quietly staring at Sophia and me.

Carol Leland, a young woman with short light brown hair and a toothy smile, was from New York. She was drinking beer. Her fingers and fingernails were also short and on thick hands, and her thumb bent back farther than usual. The nails were not painted.

Frank introduced her as his girlfriend. She was wearing a pullover with the face of Mao Tse-Tung front and center. Underneath his face, two words: Social Democracy.

I shook hands with the two women and the little girls.

Arleta Mandel, with freckles and hair hanging loosely down her back, was Carol's best friend, also from New York. She had excessive blue shadow over her large eyes.

Carol got up and fixed drinks for everybody. Arleta was already drinking white wine. I accepted a glass of white wine. Frank had beer. Sophia never drank alcohol. Carol continued with her beer. The girls were drinking soda.

Frank shouted, "By the way, my ex-wife is also coming to dinner."

Looking at Sophia and me, Bonita said, "Our mother is a lawyer. She was in court today."

Selena said, "She's always late because she's busy. She was in *El Universal* today. Want to see?"

Before I could answer, she ran from the room and returned with a sheet from a newspaper and handed it to me. It was in Spanish, of course. I quickly read that abogada Suzette Lopez-Garcia had just "defendido con exito." She'd recently defended a man falsely accused of murder.

I said, "You must be very proud of your mother?"

"Yes," they said in unison. I was sure they could have responded in Spanish. They were growing up completely bilingual.

Frank shouted, "Say, James, what is our country coming to? So many assassinations! Four years ago, President Kennedy. Two years later, Malcolm X, and this year, Dr. Martin Luther King preaching togetherness. Just last month, our attorney general, the president's brother."

I said, "Yes, it's horrible and stressful for the whole country."

Frank called out again. "Sophia! Are you Jewish?"

She hesitated, smiled, and turned red, then called back, "Yes. Why?"

"Your name, Sophia! My mother was Jewish," he said. "Her name was Naomi Roth, bless her soul. She's in heaven now. Also, I don't see many blond Jews. You guys are the first interracial couple that's ever set foot in this house. You know, recently some American Black Nationalists came through Mexico on their way to South America. I wanted to invite them to the house for drinks and conversation, but they wouldn't talk with me. I guess because I'm white." He chuckled. "May I ask, where were you born, James? Isn't Lowell kind of an unusual name for…?" He didn't finish the sentence.

Sophia's face turned redder. She said, "James is from a very old New England family. There were white people named Lowell and there were Black people also named Lowell."

I said, "As far as I know, they were not related by blood. I'm not related to Amy or Robert Lowell—if that's what you were wondering. My family is originally from Springfield, Mass." I paused. "But I was born in Brooklyn."

"James Eric Lowell," said Frank.

I said, "My mother's brother was named Eric. That's where the Eric comes from. He was an officer in the army, died in a car accident when he was just thirty-two." I paused. "Do you have a middle name?"

"No, just Frank. I didn't qualify for a middle name." He laughed, clearly thinking he'd said something very clever.

Sophia said, "James' great-great-grandfather was the second or third Black man to graduate from Harvard."

"Harvard, huh?" said Frank.

Carol said, "Sophia, you're very pretty." It was obvious she was trying to change the subject, and for that I was grateful.

"Thank you," Sophia said, blushing.

"I love that dress," said Carol.

It was light blue, a sleeveless seersucker that sat well on Sophia's wide hips. She blushed again, smiling, and thanked Carol again.

Frank called, "James! Do you prefer to be identified as Afro-American or Black? I know Negro and colored are out. Both were out before I left the States."

I hesitated. "I prefer James, actually." His questions annoyed me. I said to myself, "Here we go again." I am sure he meant well with his naïve and artless question, and for that reason I felt tolerant.

Frank was silent for a moment—perhaps realizing his faux pas—then called out, "When I published your poems, I didn't know you were Afro-American. A buddy of mine in New York read your poems in the journal and happened to mention it. He said. 'James Eric Lowell is Afro-American.' "

Maybe, for Frank, discovering he'd published a Black poet was like discovering when you got home and took a closer look, that you'd picked a male puppy from the litter when you thought you were selecting a female, or vice versa. People made assumptions based on their assumptions.

It led me to another thought. Maybe for many Americans the difference between white and Black was like the difference between classical music and rock 'n' roll. Clearly one was thought by many to be superior to the other.

Another moment of silence, then he said, "This is the first time my daughters have seen an Afro-American in person. Here in Mexico we see them on TV all the time but…" He suddenly stopped talking. "Am I embarrassing you?"

"No," I lied. He clearly didn't feel like he was embarrassing himself. He rattled on innocently and incessantly. Sophia looked angry. The two women looked embarrassed for Frank. Poor innocent guy!

Sophia and I had not had a good meal since New York.

When Frank shouted, "Dinner is served!," we all got up and gathered around the long wooden table just below the two steps up to the kitchen. It was already set. Frank brought out the steaming hot platters and bowls, and placed them along the middle.

There was a platter of delicious-looking chicken enchiladas verdes, a pot of hardy carne en su jugo made with pinto beans, chunks of pork and beef in tomatillo sauce, a bowl of refried red beans, and one platter of spicy rice, well-seasoned. The aroma of the food was intoxicating.

Frank said, "James, where'd you go to school?"

"Brooklyn College."

"English?"

"Yes, I have an MFA in English. I taught creative writing while I was in grad school. It's what I hope to do as a career."

"Oh? Where?"

"Hopefully, some college or university, maybe at Warren Lowery. Fingers crossed."

"That's a highly rated and highly respected private school. If you get on there, you're set for life. They offer advanced degrees now."

"Yes, it's a great school. Right now, I'm focused on trying to finish my first book of poems, then we'll see what happens."

Outside, apparently next door, a dog was barking. The barks sounded like those of a big dog. A woman's voice called out and a child responded. The dog stopped barking.

"Suzette is always late," said Frank. "We won't wait. Please help yourself." As Carol filled her small soup bowl with the carne en su jugo, the front door opened.

I looked. A good-looking Mexican woman, with her hair dyed a decisive henna-red, came in smiling. She wore long false eyelashes. "Sorry I'm late," she said.

She came directly over to the table and sat down in the chair reserved for her at the end of the table. Frank was at the other end. "Suzette, this is Sophia and James, both poets from New York. What's your family name, Sophia?"

"Schwartz." She paused. "And I'm not a poet."

"Oh? What do you do?"

Carol said, "Frank! I hate that question. Don't answer, Sophia!"

"I don't mind," Sophia said. "I graduated last year from City University in Manhattan with a degree in anthropology."

"Neat!" Frank smiled. "What do you get out of anthropology?"

"A lot. Anthropology makes you think about why people do what they do."

"Example?"

"Well, for example, as a result of studying tribal peoples, I've come to think that clitoridectomy and circumcision, both religious practices, are meant to reduce private pleasure for better social control."

"Wow! If that's true, I've been had!" said Frank, laughing.

Everybody laughed.

Now we were all eating and talking at a vigorous speed. At one point, Frank said, "I'm thirty-two. When I was a teenager, I thought I'd be famous by now, a world-famous poet with my picture on the cover of *Time* magazine and poems published in *The New Yorker* every week. How old are you, James? Did you think you'd be famous by now?"

"I'm twenty-five."

"Did you think you'd be famous by now?" he said again.

"Nope! Never had such thoughts. I knew I wanted to write good poems, and if I managed to get them published, all the better."

While this conversation was going on, Suzette was asking the girls about their violin lessons, which, apparently, they had had that morning. Carol and Arleta were talking about something that happened in New York at a party.

We finished dinner and went back to the living room area, and Frank brought over a pot of hot coffee and placed it, with cups, on the coffee table. "Help yourselves, folks!"

Now Frank was sitting on the floor facing Sophia and me. We were in armchairs. "So, how long you guys going to be in Mexico?"

Sophia said, "We don't know."

I said, "As long as we can afford to stay. I guess till our money runs out. I'd like to finish my book here."

Frank laughed and sipped his beer. "Yes! Money is always a big issue, isn't it?" He chuckled. "So, James, what'd you do for a living? I know you've published in a lot of little magazines. I know you want to teach, but what do you do now to make ends meet, to put bread on the table?"

"I just finished working as a research analyst."

"Wow! What was that like?"

"Intense," I said, "Sophia and I both worked for the same research company."

"Sounds interesting. You mentioned finishing your book. How is it coming along?"

I laughed. "As you know, you can't hurry poems. The next hurdle will be getting it published."

"Yes, it's not easy," said Frank. "I've tried to get a book of my poems published without luck. I've had a full collection ready for two years now, but no luck with publishers. Maybe I'm sending it to the wrong places."

I nodded. I was thinking, at least you have a finished manuscript. I had yet to accomplish that much. I didn't know if I would ever get a book published. Frank and I were in the same condition.

It was after nine and not yet completely dark. Frank called a taxi for us. We waited, then when we heard the car pull up outside, Sophia and I thanked Frank and his family and friends for their hospitality and said our goodbyes.

Unloading a stack of back issues of his magazine on me, Frank walked out to the car with us. On the way out, he asked if we knew where we were going to stay.

"No," I said. "We thought we'd just wing it. To start, we'll try to find an inexpensive hotel. From there, look for an apartment."

"Hotel Rosita isn't bad," said Frank.

"Hotel Rosita," I said. "Thanks."

After we got in the taxi, he said, "James, let me know how things go in Puerto Vallarta. Send me some new poems! I'm working on the next issue now."

Back at the hotel, exhausted, we got ready for bed. We had to be at the airport by seven for our eight o'clock flight to Puerto Vallarta. We would be on a small twin propeller Otter plane. Since before leaving New York, Sophia had been nervous about flying in a large jetliner but especially in something as small as an Otter. Now lying in bed, she said, "You hear about small aircraft crashing all the time."

"Don't worry. It's not going to crash," I said, feeling there was nothing to worry about. "Now let's go to sleep."

There were only four other passengers: two businessmen from Texas and a couple from Flint, Michigan on their way to try to find their runaway seventeen-year-old daughter in Puerto Vallarta. The couple was sitting across from us. They introduced themselves. They were Brenda and Robert Muller. He was about forty-five and she was about forty.

He said, "We got word our daughter, Bessie Marie, was living in a house with a bunch of dope-smoking hippies. She'd become pretty wild before she ran away."

Nervously clutching her purse on her lap, Brenda Muller said, "She wouldn't listen to us anymore."

Robert Muller said, "You hear about those dirty hippies demonstrating at the New York Stock Exchange? They should lock them all up and throw away the key."

I looked away, saying nothing. I could have said, "Why?," but that would have only started more discussion. His comment about hippies didn't merit a response. I was in no mood for a confrontation. I wasn't going to go through life confronting every jerk that made a dumb remark.

Soon the pilot landed the plane at the small airport closest to Puerto Vallarta without incident. I saw the relief in Sophia's face. We said goodbye to the couple and wished them luck in finding their daughter.

Outside the airport we got into one of the two taxis at the curb. Like our driver in Mexico City, he was also named Juan. I told him in English we wanted to go to Hotel Rosita. Juan's smile was both friendly and a bit mocking.

In English, with a heavy accent, he said, "You'll like. Across from Bahía de Banderas. Very nice! Pretty, pretty, you'll see. You can walk el Malecón and, not far, Nuestra Señora de Guadalupe. You like church?"

Sophia said, "Yes, we like churches."

On the way, he asked where we were from. When he heard New York, he said, "My brother, he's in New York. Big city, big city!" He laughed heartily.

We arrived.

Juan stopped the taxi alongside the three-story red and white hotel. Several old cars were parked alongside the curb. The street was cobblestone.

When we got out, I looked down the street to the bay and saw the Malecón Juan had mentioned. It was lined with palm trees. The walkway was lined with a sequence of oval-shaped stones. Above, the sky was grey, and in the distance, beyond the bay, the mountains were pale blue.

I paid Juan and thanked him. He grinned and counted the money. He waved and got back in his car and turned around, I guessed, to go back to the airport.

We had two pieces of luggage. We picked up our two pieces of luggage and, going inside, we got checked in. The lobby was quaint. A worn carpet on the floor of faded pink flowers was badly frayed at the edges. A tropical plant in a large pot on the floor by the desk looked in need of water. Behind the clerk there was a row of wood slots for room keys. The clerk was a handsome young man with smooth skin, long sideburns, small ears, and a pleasant smile. We had no reservation, but they had plenty of empty rooms. This was the off-season.

In clear English, he said, "Welcome to Hotel Rosita!"

"Thank you!" Sophia and I said.

I paid in pesos and he handed me a big iron key.

The room was small, with two tiny twin beds, and there was no air conditioning. The toilet was hardly big enough to turn around in. It was hot and stuffy and humid in the room.

I said, "Let's walk down to the Malecón."

Holding hands, we walked down the dirt road to the sand. There were little wooden open-air kiosks and stalls along the way. Kiosk clerks were sitting in the shade of their stands, waiting for customers. One woman, sitting on a wooden crate, called to us to stop and look at the beautiful straw hats hanging on hooks all around her little kiosk.

Down at the beach, we went up the stone steps to the amphitheater called Aquiles Serdán. It was an open, circular area. In its center was a giant cactus growing out of a stone cup planted in a fountain.

We looked out beyond the bay at the sea. It was a cloudy afternoon. In the distance we saw two or three small fishing boats. Out past the boats, behind the clouds, the sun was setting on the sea. It was about to disappear below the horizon. We kissed.

Sophia said, "I like the raw fishy smell of this place." She was smiling as she spoke. She seemed happy.

Back at the hotel, we ate dinner in the hotel restaurant. Then we went back to the room, but it was very hot in there. By now it was dark. To escape the heat, we went up to the roof, which, in the daytime, they said was used for sunbathing. The sky was black-blue and full of yellow and white stars and planets. I imagined I could see Saturn following Jupiter.

We were alone up there. We stretched out together on one of the lounge chairs. We hugged and kissed. Sensing we were safely alone, under the stars we quietly made love. I was in love. It was enchanting.

Then we lay side by side, hugging each other.

Sophia said, "When I was a little girl, I didn't like my name. I used to make up new names for myself: Isadora, Antoinette, Jovita, Tanya, Clarissa, Erna, Fifi. Actually, Fifi is a nickname for Sophia. I also used to try spelling Sophia a lot of different ways to see if the sound would change, and to see if I could learn to like the name better."

"Such as?"

"I tried Sofi, Sophey, Sophie, Sophy, Sofia. It was not until I was in college that I learned to like my name. It's an old, old beautiful name. It means holy wisdom. It's the name of a basilica in Constantinople. Do you like your name?"

"You mean James? I don't dislike it. It's harmless. Everybody's named James. I guess that makes me everybody."

"Well, when we first got together, I looked it up," she said. "It's a Latin variation; it's from the name Jacob. James is the one who supplants; he follows the leader. He is one of the twelve apostles who followed

Jesus of Nazareth."

Then we lay there in silence for a long while.

Finally, Sophia said, "We've been in Mexico five minutes and already the poverty I've seen just in passing is heartbreaking."

I didn't know what to say in response. I understood her emotions, but her timing seemed odd.

After breakfast the next morning, we stopped at the front desk. A man was already there, talking with the desk clerk. When we walked up, the clerk stopped talking with the man and said, "Yes, Señor Lowell? May I help you?"

"Excuse us for interrupting," I said.

"Not at all, no interrupting. We talk of nothing important."

And both men laughed.

I said, "I wonder if you could help us. We are looking for an apartment. Is there a real estate company around here?"

The man standing beside us said, "Perdón. My name is Nicolas Gonzalez." He smiled. "You want apartment?"

"Yes."

"You no need real estate, not far from here apartment for rent. I draw you map."

The desk clerk tore a sheet of paper from a tablet on the desktop and handed it to Señor Gonzalez. On the paper with a pencil, he quickly drew lines and wrote names along the lines on the paper, making a crude map.

I offered him several American dollars for his efforts but, with a smile and a wink at Sophia, he refused the money.

Sophia said, "Do they speak English?"

Señor Gonzalez said, "The manager, he is good at English. Nombre, Señor Tomas Perez. Es la casa de la lado, white casa bottom of Hidalgo, es donde gira, it's where la carretera turns. It runs along river. Okay? Piso de arriba. Upstairs, ring doorbell."

"Thank you, señor. We'll find it," I said.

We walked out of the hotel and Sophia screamed. There on the sidewalk, looking up at us, was a giant iguana with a brown head and a green body.

Señor Gonzalez came running out to the sidewalk. When he saw what had caused the scream, he laughed heartily. He told Sophia that the iguana was harmless. He reentered the hotel.

I took Sophia by the arm and we stepped around the beastly-looking creature and continued.

We found the white casa without any trouble. It took less than ten minutes to walk there. As Señor Gonzalez said, it was a white two-story building on the right-hand corner of Hidalgo. It consisted of two apartments on the ground floor and two on the upper floor.

There were two identical two-story buildings. The other one was on the opposite side of the street facing this one. We figured it was this one because a sign alongside the door to the upstairs stairway said: Se Renta Apartamento.

Sophia and I climbed the steps to the second floor. Both doors had doorbells. I pressed the one on the right with a small card alongside the door that read Gerente.

A man I assumed to be Señor Tomas Perez opened the door. He was very tall, unusually tall compared to most locals. His hair was thin and slicked down to his head. He had a thin moustache. He wore a white dress shirt and brown slacks and brown sandals. He smiled at us. "Hola, señor."

"We're here about the vacant apartment."

"Americans?"

"Yes," I said.

His smile grew broader. "Certainly," he said. "Let me show it to you. I'll get the key."

We waited at the opened door till he returned, then he opened the vacant apartment's door and let us enter first.

We stepped into a vast space, with a kitchen area and bar with high red stools to our immediate right. Beyond was the bright, sun-kissed living room. Through the glass doors, we saw a stone balcony, and the Malecón with the bay and the sea beyond.

There were five windows along the far wall, and they looked out on the river that ran from the bay. The walls were white, and there were green and light blue armchairs and a blond sectional couch arranged strategically around the room.

Señor Perez said, "I lived in Los Angles for many years, so the minute I saw you two I knew you were Americans. You like Mexico?"

"Yes," I said. "We just got here yesterday. How much is the apartment?"

"One hundred dollars a month. I can rent this cheaply because we are in the off-season right now. You like it? You want to rent it?"

I looked at Sophia and she smiled and nodded.

I said, "Yes, we'd like to take it." I was thinking we needed to go to a bank and buy more pesos.

"Good! Then you don't need to pay in pesos. American dollars will be fine."

I took out my wallet and pulled out five twenties, and handed them to Señor Perez. "Do we need to sign anything, a lease?"

"No, we don't need to sign anything. You pay every month. Everything will be fine. How long you plan to stay?"

"We don't know yet. Hopefully a long time."

"I understand," he said.

"There are two other couples living downstairs, Cedric Ainsley Brathwaite, and his wife, Regina Santiago. She's from Puerto Rico. He's from somewhere in Canada. They are in the apartment on the left. On the right is an American couple, Estelle and Grant Oppenheimer. They're an older couple. Been here only a couple of weeks. Cedric and Regina came just last week. They say they plan to stay a month or maybe longer. You will meet them, I'm sure."

A rooster crowed.

I said, "A rooster crowing this time of day?"

Laughing, Señor Perez said, "Yes, he's across the street. He's one of those blue Andalusians. He's a strange-looking fellow: the usual red-plumage, but he has white earlobes and red wattles. Noisy as hell! They must have come over with the Spanish." Señor Perez laughed. "That rooster crows anytime, day or night. There have been times when I wanted to go over there and ring his neck."

Sophia said, "I just got the scare of my life: a large iguana right in front of the hotel." She held her hands out in a helpless gesture. "Daytime crowing roosters and monstrous iguanas!"

Señor Perez laughed heartily. "Oh, yes, they're all over the place. Don't fear, the iguanas look like monsters, but they are harmless. They are not going to attack you."

"Thank God!" she said. "He looked like some sort of prehistoric beast. He was about the size of a little dog."

Sophia walked away across the living room and disappeared into the bedroom. I could see she was looking around, getting the hang of the place.

"How far is the bank from here?" I said.

Señor Perez said, "Banco de Commercio de Guadalajara is a ten- or fifteen-minute walk up the hill into town. You'll see the shops. The bank is on the right-hand side. Here in Puerto Vallarta, there is no telephone service to the States. If you need to send a telegram anywhere, you have to go to the bank to send it."

"No telephone service to the States, huh?"

"We have only one stoplight. It's up by the square where the church is. You'll see it. It's really just a kind of joke."

"No cars?"

"Not enough cars yet to require stoplights."

"Just my kind of place," I said.

Sophia came back and stood at my side.

Señor Perez laughed and said, "I live across the hall and the office is there, too. If you need anything, just let me know. There is a maid and her daughter who come here twice a week."

He told us what we should pay. It was very reasonable.

He said, "Her name is Camilla Gomez. Her daughter's name is Miranda. Camilla will wash your clothes and change the bed and wash the sheets. If you like, she will also cook for you. You have to tell her what you want. The little girl will help a lot. She will sweep the floor and take out the trash and things like that. Generally, she helps her mother."

Sophia said, "Sounds good."

Señor Perez said, "You can also arrange to go horseback riding. Diego will bring the horses to the door. All you have to do is climb up on them. They are very gentle horses. Just let me know a day in advance and I'll arrange it for you. I hope you both will feel welcome in my country and be happy here."

"I'm sure we will be," I said. "Thank you, Señor Perez."

"As I said, I lived and worked in the United States, and it wasn't always easy. I didn't always feel welcome in your country. I was made to feel that being Mexican was not a good thing." He smiled broadly. "I was glad when President Johnson passed the 1964 Civil Rights Act for fair housing. Now, just six months ago, I hear that he's signed another Civil Rights Act outlawing discrimination in public places. Must be nice for you to get away from all the fury going on in the States right now, huh?"

Sophia said, "Yes, sure is."

"You should know that everything closes at one o'clock and does not open till 4 p.m. It is out of respect for the traditional siesta."

I said, "Thank you."

"You are welcome," he said, turning to leave. He then looked back and said, "Enjoy the apartment."

Then he was gone.

We were lucky! The apartment was large and comfortable, and it was inexpensive. It had the largest living room and bedroom I'd ever seen. The bathroom was bigger than most bedrooms I'd seen. The rooms were bright with high ceilings and the walls were white. Large tropical plants flanked the doorway to the balcony. There were succulent plants on the balcony along the front and side railings.

The sectional couch was pretty-looking, imitation 19th century Spanish, and the two chaises were imitation Madame du Barry. The two armchairs were also fakes: one was upholstered in light blue imitation silk. The chair was fake Madame Élisabeth and the other imitation bergère chair was not-too-clever fake Jean-Baptiste-Claude Sené.

I had some knowledge about historical furniture because, as a subtext, it was included in a European History course I was required to take at BC.

The kitchen was small, but we didn't need a large kitchen. We were not planning to do a lot of cooking. I didn't know much about cooking. Sophia, in the months we'd been together, hadn't done much.

The next morning, we found the tienda de comestibles, the grocery store, and bought a few things we needed right away: milk, bacon, eggs, bread, butter, coffee, salt, pepper, sugar, and cream. Together we made breakfast. I scrambled the eggs and she toasted the bread in the toaster. Sophia was obviously happy now that we were doing something together.

As we finished, we heard footsteps in the stairwell. Then there was a knock at the door, which we'd left ajar. From where I was sitting, I could see a woman, probably in her late thirties or early forties, and a little girl about twelve years old standing in the doorway. "Come on in," I said.

The woman was thin, with a dark reddish complexion, and had what looked like a permanently worried look, yet she had a handsome face. The little girl was a small version of the woman minus the worried look and she was lighter in complexion.

They stepped timidly into the apartment. I suspected they did not speak English. I read Spanish better than I spoke it. Sophia understood it fairly well. She was also brave enough to attempt to speak it more often than I had the nerve to do. Again, the rooster across the street was crowing.

The woman said, "Hola, soy la doncella de este apartamento." She then said her name was Camilla, Camilla Gomez, and that this was her twelve-year-old daughter, Miranda, Miranda Gomez, who would help clean the apartment.

We greeted them and gave them our names.

Sophia then said, "Estamos felices de tenerte."

Camilla said in Spanish that she was a talker, "Me encanta hablar." She would get started with her work and Miranda would wash the dishes and dust, but Sophia told Miranda she didn't have to wash the dishes.

Miranda ignored her and started gathering our dirty plates, cups, and glasses from the counter. She scraped the remaining scraps on them into the wastebasket, then took the plates to the sink, which was just behind her. She filled the dishpan with warm sudsy water, and she started washing the dishes.

Camilla had already taken a vacuum cleaner from a nearby closet and was vacuuming the rugs spread around the living room's tile floor.

As she worked, Camilla was talking to Sophia in Spanish, "You know, I am very religious. I trust in the Holy Virgin to guide me in my daily life. I just wish my relatives were more like me. I have a cousin, Valentina, she became a prostitute, and her pimp ended up killing her and for no good reason, over a few pesos. That girl strayed too far from the watchful protection of the Holy Virgin. Another cousin, Maria, likes women rather than men. She is in love with a girl named Josefina who wears pants and cut her hair short. Maria prayed and prayed to the Virgin for guidance, but it didn't do any good. Our family has disowned her. My uncle Adrian tried to cross over into Texas illegally and the border patrol caught him and now he is in jail there in Texas, but Adrian was always doing crazy things like that. He says he will pray to the Virgin when he gets old but the way he is living he may not live to get old. A dog bit Adrian's ten-year-old daughter Martha on her way to school. Our Sweet Virgin saved her from getting rabies. A cousin of mine, Felipe, tried to cross the Rio Bravo and almost drowned. I have some crazy relatives!" Camilla laughed.

She turned off the vacuum cleaner and pushed it across the floor and into the bedroom. We could hear her in there singing as she cleaned.

Keeping out of the way, Sophia picked up my copy of an English translation of Zola's *Nana* and settled down on the couch with her back to the light.

I got my notebook and went out on the balcony and sat in one of the big wooden chairs. I was waiting for the first line of a poem, but it stubbornly refused to come out of where it was hiding. While sitting there I watched, below on the street, a donkey pack go by. A taxi had to stop and wait for it to pass.

When Camilla finished with the vacuuming, she took a broom from the broom closet and started sweeping the floor in areas not covered by rugs. She also came out onto the balcony and, sweeping around me, swept its tile floor.

Then she went back inside.

While Camilla worked, she kept talking with Sophia. She said she had four other children, all boys, boys that were no good for housecleaning. She laughed.

When she was finished cleaning, I came back in and sat at the typewriter.

In Spanish, Camilla said, "Señora Sophia, wait till you have children, you will see. My boys are so busy. They can't sit still. That is the way boys are. They have accidents too, bloody noses, dirty pants. They bring iguanas and frogs into the house. Just yesterday my oldest boy, Rodrigo, eleven, was pushing my youngest boy, Lorenzo, seven, in the rope swing, and the rope broke, and poor Lorenzo fell and got a bloody nose, but he was not seriously hurt. I thank my dear sweet Holy Virgin that Lorenzo did not break an arm or a leg. Rodrigo, he wants to be a priest. I tell him it's not easy to be a priest. It's not as easy as it looks. With boys there is so much to worry about. Last week Francisco got bitten by a neighbor's dog. Dante, trying to light the stove, accidentally started a fire in the kitchen and I'd told him not to play with matches. I pray to Our Lady of Tepeyac to keep them safe. Lorenzo two weeks ago had a bad fall. I am sure Our Lady of Tepeyac saved him from a bad head injury. I talk too much. It is a bad habit. Forgive me, Señora Sophia."

"Me encanta oirte hablar. I love to hear you talk," said Sophia.

Camilla said that Sophia was wise to have married a man darker than she, it made for "ninos mas coloridos," more colorful children. Camilla said her husband looked like a white person and that their children were many different colors.

Camilla and Miranda finished two hours later. Then Camilla said, "Vendremos pasado mañana."

She went on to say, rather than just twice a week, she and Miranda would come every other day for the same amount of money as twice a week. They would take the bed sheets and our dirty clothes away and wash them.

Sophia said, "Bueno!"

I watched Sophia count out pesos on the counter to pay Camilla the agreed amount plus some, and she gave Miranda her own handful of pesos.

When Camilla and Miranda were gone, Sophia and I sat together on the couch, not knowing what to do next. Before we left New York, we'd read a lot of tourist pamphlets about Puerto Vallarta.

One of the things we wanted to do, we had said, was visit the nearby remote fishing village, Yelapa, where singer and songwriter Bob Dylan once lived. Sophia's friend, Ruth, had told her that it was now the home of Australian and Canadian hippies.

Sophia was interested in meeting the hippies. I was willing to go because she wanted to, but there were other things that seemed much more interesting to me such as hiking up the hillside where the small villages were or exploring the shops in town or visiting and studying the pre-Columbian ruins.

Right now we had more urgent things to do. First, we needed to go to the bank and get more pesos, then go to the post office and get established so we could receive mail. We needed to go to the market and buy fresh fruit and vegetables. While I knew we were not going to do much cooking, we needed things in the kitchen that could be cooked, just in case.

All the errands done and the shopping finished, late in the afternoon, naked, we were in bed making love. The bedroom had a window onto the stairway landing. To let cool air in, it was open with only a curtain over it. Suddenly we heard footsteps in the stairwell.

Since we were not expecting anyone, we had pulled the curtain across the window without closing the window. It was too hot in the bedroom with the window closed. We lay still, listening. The footsteps stopped on the landing.

Then a small hand pulled the curtain back. I looked up and saw Miranda's little face looking in on us.

I groaned just as Miranda closed the curtain. Sophia was on her back, looking up at the ceiling. I said, "It's Miranda. She saw everything."

"Don't worry," Sophia said. "There's nothing that child has not seen before now. She's already a hundred years old."

I sat up and started dressing.

Sophia said, "I'd better get dressed and see what she wants."

Then Sophia went to the door and let her in. I was still in the bedroom, but I could hear them talking in the kitchen. The girl said she'd come back to see if we needed anything done. Did we need her to wash dishes again or go to the store?

Dressed now, I walked out of the bedroom and across the living room, and Miranda looked at me and smiled. She said, "Buenas tardes, Señor Lowell." She didn't seem a bit embarrassed about having seen us naked.

I said, "Buenas tardes, Miranda."

Sophia said, "Let me think. Ah! Let's go see if the plants on the balcony need watering."

Together they went out onto the balcony. Miranda came back in and got a watering bucket with a spout from under the kitchen sink. She filled it at the tap.

Leaning sideways from the weight, she carried the bucket outside where Sophia was leaning on the railing and looking out toward the bay where the sun was going down.

The little girl struggled with the bucket till it was almost empty as she watered the succulent plants, cacti, in pots strung along the walls and side railings.

When Miranda finished, Sophia gave her a few pesos.

After Miranda left, Sophia, with a sad smile, said, "The plants didn't need watering, but she needed the money, so I pretended with her that the plants needed water."

After Miranda left, I went across the hall and asked Señor Perez to arrange for the horses in the morning at nine o'clock.

We were up early. The doors to the balcony were opened. We kept the balcony doors open all day. We were finishing breakfast when someone knocked twice at the door. We looked at each other. It might be Miranda or Señor Perez. I got up and went and opened the door.

There was an elderly woman, perhaps sixty-eight or sixty-nine, maybe older, standing there. I took her to be an American. She looked curiously at me. She seemed a bit surprised, then hesitant.

Her body leaned to one side, the right side. Hers was like the body of someone who had carried a heavy load for many years on the right side of their body and the body had caved in to the right. She no doubt had curvature of the spine.

"Hello," she said, "I'm Estelle Oppenheimer." Her earrings were small, and obviously not heavy. Heavy earrings over the years had stretched her earlobes so that they hung unnaturally halfway down her neckline.

I half-expected her to extend a hand, but she didn't. I never knew if this was proper with women or not, so I always waited for the woman. Some women shook, others didn't.

"Me and my husband rent the apartment downstairs on the right side. Señor Perez said you folks arrived a few days ago. I just wanted to come up and say hello. Doing my friendly neighbor thing, you know." She tried to grin, but it came off as a grimace.

"Oh, sure," I said. "I'm James Lowell. Would you like to come in? Perhaps join us for breakfast?"

"Oh, no thank you. We've already had breakfast."

Then I heard footsteps on the stairway and presently an elderly man, a bit stooped in the shoulders and back, stood behind Estelle. He had bushy eyebrows and neck skin that hung loosely.

Estelle said, "This is Grant, my husband. We're from Iowa."

Grant and I shook hands. I told him my name.

"Are you sure you don't want to come in?"

"Oh, no. We're going out soon to the market."

"Well," I said, "It's a pleasure to meet you both."

She looked critically at Grant, then turned back to me. "We've only been married ten years. Grant's a retired engineer and I worked in an insurance office for forty years. We both have grown children from previous marriages. We figured we'd travel now that our kids are grown and settled in their lives. We both have grandkids. We figure we don't have much time left. We said, 'What the heck, let's do it!,' and we took off for Mexico and here we are." She chuckled. "You and your wife are here together?"

I wasn't about to explain so I said, "Yes." I turned and called Sophia to the door.

She came, and I introduced her to Estelle and Grant.

"Well, we'll let you young folks get back to what you were doing." As she spoke, she was craning her neck to see into the apartment. "You have lots of light. It's a nice apartment, isn't it?"

"Very nice," I said.

"Ours is a bit dark but we like it okay. We don't get as much light as you're getting up here, and we can't see the bay from down there. I like to watch the people on the Malecón. We go walking there. It's a nice place to walk after a large meal, but I can't eat much these days. I have so many medical issues…" and her voice trailed off.

Grant looked a bit embarrassed. Just as Estelle turned to leave, she turned back and said, "I thought that if you folks would like to join us for a snack get-together kind of thing… I'm a pretty good cook but I can't eat sweets, though, I'm diabetic."

"Sure, we'd love to come to your get-together," said Sophia.

Then Estelle said, "We're both retired: Grant was an engineer. He built bridges, lots of bridges all over the Midwest." She paused and smiled as if waiting for applause.

"Bridges, huh?" I said.

Estelle said, "The other couple, across the hall from us, Cedric and his wife, Regina, has already been over. We like young folks. We just get together for a little conversation and snacks. That's all."

Again Sophia said, "We'd love to join you."

"Great! I'll let you know the next time we have a get-together."

And they were gone.

What could we possibly talk about with Estelle and Grant that would be of common interest? But I was willing to give it a try. Why not?

That same morning, at ten minutes to ten we heard downstairs the *clippity-clop, clippity-clop* of horses, then a voice calling out, "¡Señor y señora, sus caballos están aquí!"

We were ready. We trotted down the steps, and there was old man Diego and two brown horses at the front door. Diego gave us a toothless smile as he held both reins in one hand. He asked if we knew how to ride. Sophia said no, I said yes.

He helped Sophia up onto the horse, but he kept the reins. This was Sophia's first time on a horse. She was one hundred percent city girl from the Bronx.

I'd had a little experience riding in upstate New York, in the Finger Lakes area. To get out of the hot summer city, my mom, dad, and I used to go up there in Dad's 1958 yellow and white Ford Ranch Wagon.

We'd stay at Radcliffe's Bed and Breakfast for a week each summer during the years when I was growing up. Betty and John Radcliffe were very liberal-minded people. It was one of the places Black families knew they could go in the summer without running into a lot of negativity.

I learned to ride at Ludlow's Horse Ranch near Cayuga Lake.

I was now in the saddle and holding the reins, ready to go. Diego let me go first, then he walked with Sophia's horse, holding onto the reins, leading her along. Diego said the name of Sophia's horse was Sula and mine was called Ursula.

I looked to my right and there was that crazy blue-black rooster standing on that fence across the street. For once, he wasn't crowing, just watching us.

We went slowly out along Rodriguez, with the river to our right, and went clippity-clop onto and across the old footbridge. As we crossed, I looked down. Women, dressed only in slips and bras, were down there on both embankments reaching down into the stream, washing clothes and pounding them on the rocks embedded along the edges of the water.

We went past the little grocery store, Gutiérrez Rizo, where we'd shopped. Then, making a circle, going along una pequeña calle, we headed back toward the bay, and we reconnected with Hidalgo beyond our place. We worked our way down Hidalgo and stopped where we started. It took all together about fifty-five minutes. We'd paid for an hour.

Two drunken white Texans in ten-gallon hats and cowboy boots came along the street and stopped by Diego. With red eyes and leering grins, they stood there swaying and looking up at us. One said, "Ma'am,

I sure like the way you sit on that horse."

Sophia blushed from ear to ear. Both of her ears turned red.

I got down, and Diego started helping Sophia down. We thanked Diego, paid him, and tipped him generously.

We walked past the two drunken Texans and entered our hallway. Looking stunned and baffled, they stood there watching us pass.

The next day, as usual, I was at the typewriter by 9 a.m., working.

Sophia walked over to me and placed her hand on my shoulder. "I'm going for a walk," she whispered.

"Okay."

The next morning while I was getting settled at the typewriter, ready to return to the poem I'd been struggling with, Sophia, already standing at the door, said, "I'm going for a walk."

"Okay. Enjoy!"

That weekend she did not go for a walk, but I worked at poems. Instead of walking, Sophia sat on the balcony and read a novel.

Monday morning around nine, we walked over to the boat rental place. I was wearing my red and green dashiki and jeans. Sophia was also wearing jeans.

The rental place was a shack by an inlet on the coast of the bay. You could rent boats there, or you could book a ride on the water taxi that went to and from Yelapa a few times a day.

An old white man with an Oklahoma accent came out and stood in the entrance. As he scrutinized us, he had his thumbs tucked under his suspenders. I had not expected an American.

I said, "We'd like to book a ride to Yelapa."

The round-trip rate was posted on the wall of the shack.

He took off his baseball cap and scratched his bald head. "Come back in an hour," he said. "The next boat leaves at ten-fifteen. If you're late, you'll miss it. My skipper's not waiting for nobody."

"We'll be here," I said, while counting out the pesos in his out-stretched crusty hand.

To wait out the hour we went back to town and walked around. We stopped and looked in shop windows. There were signed photographs of Ava Gardner and Richard Burton in many of the shop windows. They'd not long before been here making the movie *Night of the Iguana*.

Coming along the street, a young woman, obviously American, stopped and spoke to us. "Hi you guys, where you from?"

Sophia said, "New York."

"So am I," she said, grinning. She was a pretty girl, in jeans, with red-blond hair, obviously dyed. "I've been here now for six weeks and, boy, let me tell you, it's been rough. The locals think we're just a bunch of hippies here to smoke dope. They don't like us. They call us gringos and worse. It's such a pity too because I adore the culture here and I don't smoke weed. I'm here with two other girls. We rent a house on Adolfo Lopez Mateos. It's so sad. How long you guys here for?"

Sophia looked at me.

I said, "We don't know yet. Probably till our money runs out."

The girl laughed and said, "By the way, my name is Rebecca."

We told her our names.

"Nice to meet you both." She looked at her watch. "I got to get going. See you guys. Have fun!"

"See you around," I said.

We got back to the boat rental place at five minutes to ten. The old man was sitting outside on a crate by the wall. He was staring off into space, but he looked up as we approached.

The boat for Yelapa was not there yet, but I heard its motor off in the distance. The morning smells of the water were fishy, and the air was still damp and foggy. On a clear day, you could see Yelapa from Puerto Vallarta but not today. Yet, in the distant morning mist, finally, I could see the boat coming this way. Only the skipper was in it.

It was about an hour-long trip. We were the only ones on the boat. The boat was small, and the water surface was smooth. Fog in the distance was lifting. On arrival, I climbed out and walked onto the sandy beach. The old skipper helped Sophia off the boat. In the process she lost one of her sandals. He picked it up and handed it to her, then turned off the motor. He'd wait here about a half-hour to see if there were any passengers before he'd head back to Puerto Vallarta.

Down the beach, a boy with a donkey was walking this way. He had a bundle of sombreros thrown across the back of the donkey. He was calling out, "¡Compra tu sombrero, compra tu sombrero!"

Sophia and I walked up to a food stall palapa on the beach. There was an elderly local woman in attendance. We stood there looking at the menu posted to the side of the counter. Typical offerings: tacos, ceviche, and Dos Equis beer. I wasn't hungry and it was too early for a beer.

Just then we heard a woman's voice, "Yoo-hoooo! Yoo-hoooo!"

We looked down the beach and saw a white woman wading her way across the stream running parallel with and behind the palapa. She was coming up the beach. It was clear she was waving to us, so we stood there waiting for her arrival.

When she was finally standing in front of us, barefoot and out of breath and grinning widely, with her right hand resting against her chest above her breasts, she said, "I saw that gorgeous shirt in *Ramparts* magazine! That is so beautiful! I saw you in the boat coming and I just had to see that shirt up close. It is so beautiful!"

She had an Australian accent. "Thank you," I said.

"My name is Louise Weaver. I live here on Yelapa."

We introduced ourselves.

"Why don't you guys come and meet my family? We're the only family living here by the beach. People come and go, but we stay."

Sophia said, "Sure, we'd love to."

We walked with her back to the stream crossing—the shallowest point in the stream. It was only about twelve feet wide. I took off my shoes and rolled my pants halfway up my legs. Sophia took off her shoes, too. The three of us waded through the stream.

At one point there were logs, no longer used. One end of a log they'd used for crossing was resting in the water. The embankment, where it had wedged on the far side, had washed away.

The water in the stream was not deep. It came up just above my ankles. While we were crossing, Louise Weaver said, "This place is heaven, truly heaven!"

As we gained the embankment, I saw six people coming toward us: two men and four women. Behind them was a dilapidated shack, leaning to one side. A plastic tablecloth was nailed above the doorway, serving as a door.

"Hello, there!" said the older man in a loud voice. "Welcome to paradise!"

When we were standing before them, Louise Weaver introduced us. The older of the two men, probably in his mid-thirties, also had an Australian accent. He was tall with long hair, long arms, and big hands. He had a hatchet face.

He extended his hand to me. "I'm John Sharp."

I shook with him. He was wearing a heavy set of colorful love beads. His t-shirt said Free Love. He was dressed in cutoff jeans, and he was barefoot. I suspected he was the group leader.

The younger man, Roy Underwood, we later learned was from Canada. So were Lisa Garner and Betsy Mae Williams. Roy was handsome with brown unruly hair, freckles, and was dressed in dirty slacks and sandals. He was looking at us suspiciously.

Lisa and Betsy Mae were smiling cautiously.

The two other women were from the States: Jean Stone and Janice Schneider. Jean Stone was from Sacramento, California. Her blond hair looked chopped off hastily. She had a wide welcoming grin. Janice Schneider, a woman as tall as John Sharp, was from Philadelphia. She'd been a fifth-grade schoolteacher.

They were all in their mid-to-late twenties or early thirties.

They were all soon very friendly and accommodating.

After asking where we were from and how long we planned to stay in Mexico, John Sharp said, "Let me show you around. This is an amazing island. Everybody is very happy here."

As he spoke, a dog-sized iguana was scurrying along in the sand coming slowly this way. He stopped, gazed at us, then turned around and started toward a nearby cluster of rocks and undergrowth. He climbed into the rocks and disappeared behind one of them.

We walked away with Sharp and the others toward the shack where there were two small children playing in the dirt. We later learned that the girl, Lenora, was ten, and Baxter, five.

John Sharp said, "Call me John. James, you and Sophia would be very happy here. If you would like to join our family, we'd love to have you. We don't want everybody who comes to this place. We're very careful about who we invite to join us." He paused, then said, "I'm a good judge of people, and the minute I saw you two, I knew you would fit in nicely."

I looked at Sophia. I saw the excitement in her eyes. The tips of her ears turned red. The idea appealed to her. I, on the other hand, couldn't think of anything less appealing.

"Can we, James? I'd love to join!"

I said, "We'll think about it," but I was just saying that to stall and to prevent an argument. I had no intention of joining a commune.

"Let me show you our magnificent waterfall. We get fresh spring water."

John led us to an embankment behind the shack where there was a small stream of very clear water pouring down the crevice of a rock formation. I assumed it eventually reached the stream we'd crossed.

"We just hold our bucket under here and get the purest spring water you've ever tasted." He took a tin cup hanging from a nail driven into a small tree. He filled it with water and handed it to Sophia.

She sipped it. "That's the best water I've ever tasted," she said. Then she handed the cup to me.

I drank the rest of the water. It was good water, but pure water was not enough to get me to change my mind.

"You have a couple of hours before the boat comes back," said John. "Think about my offer. We'd love to have you both here. You can contribute so much, and we have so much to offer."

"We're thinking," I said.

Sophia gave me a disappointed look.

When it was time for the boat to return, we said goodbye to Sharp and the others, and crossed the stream again, and waited in the shade by the palapa. We heard its motor before we saw the boat.

Early evening, the ocean had turned blue-black, and the sky above it was a vivid pink from the light of the sun going down at the horizon.

Back in Puerto Vallarta, as we were walking from the boat rental place, Sophia said, "I think we should accept Sharp's offer."

"No way." I spoke firmly.

"How come?"

"Because."

"What does 'because' mean?"

"Just because."

"That's no reason. You're being unreasonable."

"There is no way we're going to give up this nice apartment with a comfortable bed for just a hundred dollars a month to go sleep on the ground in a shack crowded with nine other people."

Sophia, fuming, said nothing. She was angry, and she was going to stay angry for a while, but I thought she would get over it and we would be okay again. We'd had disagreements before. Sometimes she won, sometimes I won. This time I was going to win. I had no doubt.

On the way in, we picked up the mail. There was a check from the *Brooklyn Daily Observer*. I kissed it and put it away for later.

We were here to experience things together and to do things couples do together. Hopefully, to see our love grow deeper. I was also here to write, to write the best poems I could possibly write. We were here too to absorb a culture different from our own, to learn as much about it as we could, and to appreciate it.

I knew, from an anthropological point of view, Sophia would observe the culture. I had hoped she would also read a lot. She always had. I'm sure if I had asked her, "What are you going to do in Mexico while I am making poems?," she would have said, "Don't worry about me. I'm not going to be bored."

I had a project, but I was her project, and I wasn't always available. This gave me some anxiety, and it gave her a lot of frustration. I was beginning to worry about us.

In college, Sophia had a friend, Ruth, who had come to Puerto Vallarta and fallen in love with the country. Ruth had also had a hot affair with a handsome local man that warmed her every fiber. Sophia talked about Ruth's Mexico experience with a lot of fascination and awe.

Sophia certainly had sufficient inner resources necessary to keep her engaged or happy, especially while I was busy writing. Then why was she so restless when I was at the typewriter? I'd already seen some evidence of this in New York; if I were at my desk writing, she would ocassionally show signs of displeasure and agitation.

She would often then say she was going for a walk, or she would sit on the couch and brood, pick up a magazine, flip through it, then angrily throw it on the floor. We had a TV but neither one of us cared much for what was available on it. We could take only so much of *Laugh-In, Bewitched, Beverly Hillbillies, Lawrence Welk, Red Skelton,* or *Gomer Pyle.* Despite the fact that she was a prolific reader, there were times when Sophia picked up a book and started reading, then soon tired of it and put it down. Restlessness would overtake her.

At such times I got the impression that it was the fact that I was doing something that did not include her that annoyed her most. That I was not focused on her, and I didn't know what to do about the situation, didn't know how to change it, and now, here in Puerto Vallarta, I was concerned that Sophia might be feeling restless, bored, and unhappy.

The day after we returned from Yelapa, while I was at the typewriter, Sophia went for a walk. After a couple of hours, I got tired and stood up and walked out onto the balcony.

I was tired of sitting so I stood at the railing, leaning on it. I gazed out at the bay. The fog was lifting earlier than usual. In the afternoon, as usual, it would rain.

Then, on some impulse, I looked down at the street, then up the street, and there was Sophia, a block away, standing at the intersection, talking with a handsome young local man I'd never seen before. He was gesturing wildly with his hands.

She was listening quietly. She shook her head affirmatively. He lifted her hands to his cheeks, kissed each of them, then turned and walked up the street.

Now she started coming down this way, obviously to come home.

I went back inside and sat at the typewriter and waited for her. I was feeling jealous and angry and frustrated. I was also feeling guilty for not spending time with her.

When she came in, I said, "Have a good walk?"

"Yes. I bought this necklace." She pulled a beaded string necklace from a paper bag in her shoulder bag, and held it up to the light. It was costume jewelry, multicolored in pinks, purples, and greens. "Do you like it?"

"I do," I said. "Let me see what it looks like on you." While she was unclasping it, I said, "Where did you walk?"

"Just up the hill, looking in shops, window-shopping. It's interesting, so many of these little craft shops."

That following Friday, Estelle would have her get-together. We were to be there at six o'clock. The other couple, Cedric Ainsley Brathwaite and Regina Santiago, would also be there.

Now Friday evening was here. We went down to the Oppenheimers' apartment. There was a circle of two armchairs and a couch with a coffee table in the middle.

Cedric and Regina were already there. Sophia and I went through the introduction and greeting ritual with Cedric and Regina, then sat down on the couch alongside Grant. He was sitting at one end of the couch. Cedric was in an armchair and so was Regina.

I noticed right away that Cedric was a dark-skinned and handsome lanky young man with curly hair and a dimple in his chin. His expression was noble and serious. His arms were very hairy.

Regina was beautiful. She was slender and shapely. She had a small nose and a full mouth. She had naturally red hair and green eyes. She was sitting there with a secret Mona Lisa smile.

Estelle was busy bringing food out from the kitchen, which was situated exactly like ours, just inside the entryway. She said, "I had a hard time finding stuff to make American food."

She'd placed something she called "ants on a log" on the coffee table. It was cream cheese on celery sticks with olives lined up in the cream cheese. It was a narrow boat with figures. Then she brought out a dish she called "Frito pie." It consisted of salsa and beans and rice stacked on corn chips.

Regina said, "That Frito pie looks more Mexican than American."

Estelle said, "It probably is, but it's very popular in the Midwest. When I have my lady friends over for bingo, it's what I serve them. They love it."

Then she brought out a little platter of cupcakes with cream filling and placed it on the coffee table.

Cedric said, "Estelle, I think you did all right."

Soon we were all deep in conversation with several different conversations going on at the same time.

There were no other chairs, so Estelle pulled a footstool to the circle and sat on it. She said, "I made the cupcakes for you young folks. I can't eat even a crumb. I'm diabetic, but don't get me started telling you about all my illnesses. I'm sixty-eight. If I'm lucky, I figure I got about another ten years or so." She laughed. "That is despite my high blood pressure." She laughed again. "But that's enough about me. What kind of work do you do, James?"

"Research. We both were doing research on the riots and on newspaper coverage of the riots."

Grant said, "Riots, huh? I think people have gone crazy, out there in the streets killing each other."

Cedric said, "There's nothing wrong with peaceful protesting."

Grant said, "Yeah, I guess you're right, but that's not what some of them are doing."

Sophia said, "James is a poet."

"A poet?" said Estelle. "How do you make a living as a poet?"

"You don't, but I hope to land a teaching job."

"Oh? Where?" Estelle said.

"If I'm lucky, at a university or college."

Sophia said, "He stands a good chance of getting one at Warren Lowery."

"Sweet," said Cedric. "That's a good school."

Regina said, "That's one of the colleges where students were protesting."

"They were protesting on a lot of campuses," said Sophia.

Estelle said, "You young folks are all from big cities. Cedric here is from Toronto; you, Regina, you're from New York. James and Sophia are also from New York. Grant and me, we're from a tiny small town in Iowa called Keokuk. Nobody's ever heard of Keokuk. I doubt the population is more than ten thousand. I don't care much for big cities myself. They make me feel crazy."

I said, "Nothing wrong with a small town."

Estelle said, "James, I see you're holding your glass with your left hand. Are you left-handed?"

"I am."

"My grandpa used to say if you are left-handed, your brain was installed backwards." She cackled.

"That's me, backwards in every way."

"Sophia, if you don't mind my asking," Estelle said, "how did you and James meet?"

"We worked together."

"When did you and James marry? I see you don't wear wedding bands."

Grant said, "Estelle! Estelle! Estelle, you're asking too many personal questions."

Estelle looked innocently at me, then at Sophia. She said, "Oh, I'm so sorry! I'm just trying to make conversation. I didn't mean any harm. I guess I'm a chatterbox. I just can't help it. Mama used to tell me my mouth ran a mile a minute. She also said my eyes were bigger than my stomach because I ate so much." She chuckled. "Don't pay me no mind."

Grant said, "Cedric is an actor."

"Oh?" said Sophia. "What kind of acting do you do, Cedric?"

"Stage, mainly. I'm trying to break into film, but it's not easy."

Estelle said, "Cedric is from Canada. Born there, right, Cedric?"

"That's right." He spoke with an interesting accent.

"His parents moved to Canada from Jamaica," said Estelle. "Regina, you're from Harlem, right?"

"Not originally. I was born in Puerto Rico and grew up in el barrio,

East Harlem, otherwise known as Spanish Harlem."

"Regina is a professional dancer. You studied dance at Juilliard, right, Regina?" said Estelle.

"Yes, that's right. How about you and Grant? Let's talk about you guys for a change."

Estelle laughed. "Oh, we're boring old folks. You already know everything about us. We're retired. Grant was an engineer. He built bridges. I worked in an insurance office, typing, filing, answering the phone."

Grant added, "We're retired and happy to be retired."

The erratic uneasy conversation eventually slowed and came to a stop. Regina and Cedric stood.

To Sophia and me, Regina said, "It was nice meeting you both."

To Cedric and Regina, I said, "I have a feeling we'll be seeing each other again."

Cedric said, "We feel the same way."

Then to Grant and Estelle he said, "Thank you both for your hospitality."

Sophia and I stood up. "Goodbye, Grant. Goodbye, Estelle," I said. Sophia was at my side ready to go.

The four us left the Oppenheimers' apartment together. Out in the hallway we said goodbye to them again, this time with hugs.

Saturday night Sophia and I walked up to Our Lady of Guadalupe and sat on one of the park benches in front of the church and watched the courting boys and girls. They were dressed in pretty, colorful clothes. Sophia said, "In anthropology and folklore, I studied this kind of courting. It's so fascinating and sometimes so strange. You always recognize a corresponding element in our own society. I studied the charismatic ritual practices of the North Mekeo in Papua New Guinea, but I found cannibal courtship in the Amazon region more interesting; it was really highly regulated."

"How?"

"Through ritual and law."

"Huh. How does that relate to courtship in America?"

"You mean the Indians? The tribes in the northern region of the

Mississippi Valley have been observed: their ceremonies and dances, their customs and games, their marriage and courtship; there's been research done on the Pacific coastal area's Flathead tribes, but I haven't really done much work in those areas."

"Huh."

"As an undergraduate, a lot of my study was of the sub-Himalayan region of India; but most of my time was spent on African tribes, such as the Bantu group. I did work on the Basotho, the Bemba, the Swahili, the Maasai, the Zulus, and the Wakamba."

"Impressive."

"At some point I want to go to graduate school and get back into anthropology. I'm interested in studying the fieldwork done on courtship practices among Germanic tribes: their bundling, their love songs, and their riddles. They had a custom where the groom had to pay for the bride."

"A reverse of the dowry?"

"Yes, a bit like that."

"You ever study the Mexicans?"

"Not the Mexicans, but the Indian tribes, such as the Huichols and the Tarascos of the Sierra Madre. There has been fieldwork done in that region, but mostly on deities and diseases; there may have been courtship studies, too, but I haven't come across them."

While Sophia was telling me about the fieldwork studies she was familiar with, I was watching the boys and girls on the various benches around the church plaza. They were nervous and tentative. The girls were shy, but the boys were shyer. The girls covered their mouths when they giggled; the boys fidgeted and snickered.

"It's interesting," Sophia said, "to watch these kids; you can't see rivalry unless you look closely and watch where the girls' eyes are focused. You can tell which girls they envy, and the boys too are giving signals. See that boy there on the red bench with that girl? He really wishes to be over here to our left with this girl in yellow."

"How do you know that?"

"Watch their eyes."

I watched the eyes, but I couldn't see what Sophia saw.

"In my second year, I wrote a paper on the role of alcohol in courtship rivalry among teenagers in the Zuni tribe, but there was more research already available on risk behavior among the natives of Alaska."

"Risk behavior?"

"Yes. In courtship studies we are beginning to see how marijuana is often replacing alcohol as a key component in risk behavior."

"These kids don't seem to be drinking or smoking weed."

"No, they seem to be innocent kids, but you can't tell by how they look. Much of the risk behavior takes place among those who later may score somewhere in the dark."

I said, "I don't think of any of them are actually having sex."

"Well, very few of them will. The drinking, of course, is the white man's influence, but these kids are not remote tribal people. Many of them will go home to radios and TVs, electric stoves and electric refrigerators, and indoor plumbing."

Again, Sunday night, Sophia wanted to go and observe the timid courting of the teenagers. While we were watching the courting, she said, "Folklore and anthropology got a bad reputation because of their historical focus on tribal people. Someday I would like to apply modern techniques to people in Manhattan or Boston, for example, to so-called 'advanced society.'"

"Isn't that what they call sociology?"

"I guess you could say that, but sociology isn't anthropology. Sociologists are interested in the relationships of people in society and anthropologists are interested in the cultural aspects of peoples."

"Huh. Did you notice there were more couples last night?"

"Yes, well, it's Sunday, isn't it? That fact may have something to do with it. You notice they are better dressed tonight and are not as engaged. They're still wearing their Sunday best, the clothes they wore earlier today when they went to mass. That couple there is holding hands, not hugging. Last night they were hugging."

Monday morning, I settled down with coffee beside the typewriter to get back to working on the poem that had dogged me for days.

Sophia, dressed in a colorful skirt and white blouse, said, "I'm going for a walk." And with that, she was gone.

When she returned three hours later, she took a shower, pulled on a shirt and a pair of jeans. We tended to stay dressed in the apartment during the day because we never knew when little Miranda would pop in.

She was now showing up almost every afternoon to see if we needed anything. Her mother, Camilla, tended to come every two or three days, mostly to change the bed sheets and take away clothes that needed to be washed. We didn't need her to cook.

That night when we were undressing and getting ready for bed, I saw deep purple bruise-marks on the backs of Sophia's thighs. The pattern was in the shape of hands, and there was a circular bruise on the right side of her neck.

I said, "How'd you get those bruises?"

"What bruises?" She seemed surprised, even a bit panicky.

"On the backs of your thighs."

"Oh, those! I probably got those sitting on a bench somewhere. I sat down on a park bench over by the bay."

"And there's a hickey on your neck."

She rushed to the mirror and looked. Then nervously she said, "You must have done that."

Well, I knew I had not sucked her neck like that. That was not my thing.

Her eyes blinked repeatedly, and she couldn't make eye contact.

I said no more and got into bed. I was tired and ready to sleep, but I felt bitterly disappointed in what had happened to our relationship. I was also angry with her. And myself.

It was Wednesday around six-thirty in the evening. The usual late afternoon rain had stopped. This was not only the tourist off-season, but not quite the end of the rainy season as well. The sky was turning black, the tip of the bright white sun was still visible at the top of the mountain range, a dusty gold-green color.

A truck rumbled by below. In the back, a bare-chested boy was lying on a stack of burlap sacks full of something, probably corn.

"Why can't we do something together sometime?" Sophia said. "All you do is sit at the typewriter."

"Okay," I said. "When the bullfight starts, let's go. Would you like that?" I'd just read a pamphlet on bullfighting some previous tenant had left in the apartment.

"Sure," she said. "When is it?"

"It's too late to get tickets for today. Next Wednesday the bullfight starts at five in the afternoon. It lasts about an hour and forty-five minutes."

"How'd you find out about it?"

"A pamphlet. Posters are also posted all over town," I said.

"Oh. I guess I never noticed."

The next morning, as usual, while I was at the typewriter working, Sophia left to go for a walk.

Ten minutes after she left, a knock came at the door. I thought it might be little Miranda looking for Sophia. There was no specific time of day when the child would come knocking.

I got up and walked slowly to the door. It was Regina, smiling with her head slightly lowered. I was surprised.

"May I come in?"

"Come on in."

She walked past me, looking back over her shoulder. "I saw Sophia leaving just a little while ago. Where does she go every day?"

"For a walk. I don't know."

"Oh, I see. Well, I thought I'd come up and keep you company. Cedric had to go back to Cabo San Lucas to meet with a Hollywood director. We were there before we came here. If things work out with this director, Cedric might land his first movie role, but Cabo is, I don't know. I got bored lying on the beach every day, but I do like the natural archway and the sea cliffs."

"I've never been there. Let's go on the patio."

She followed me out and we sat down, side by side, in the wooden chairs. "I was down there looking through dance magazines and I just got bored."

"Tell me about Regina and dancing."

She laughed, her green eyes reflecting the daylight. "Regina is twenty-three. You already heard where she was born and grew up. In case you forgot, she was born in Puerto Rico and grew up in Spanish Harlem. After high school, she went to the Juilliard School at Lincoln Center for the Performing Arts."

"That's a great school. What was it like going to school there?"

"It was heavenly! I felt so lucky to be accepted there. I couldn't have gone without financial help and scholarships. It's a very expensive school."

"I would imagine. What kind of dancing are you most interested in?"

"I'm interested in the language of the human body, the art of the human body in motion. The kind of dancing I do is an art, not a sport. I know there has been a debate about whether ballet, for example, is a sport or an art."

"I always assumed ballet was an art."

"Good for you, James. It is an art. At Juilliard I first studied classical ballet, then romantic ballet, then neo-classical ballet. I wanted a good grounding before going to any other kind of dance, such as contemporary ballet. I went through the Bournonville method, the French method, the Cecchetti method, and the Vaganova method, all before moving on to contemporary ballet, which is what I do now."

"I'm impressed."

"Oh, I set the bar high for myself. Even as a little girl, long before I went to Juilliard, I saw myself, in my daydreams of course, dressed in Renaissance costumes or Baroque costumes dancing across a stage in, say, Paris or Rome." She closed her eyes as if seeing herself again.

"Have you been to Paris or Rome?"

"Not yet!" She laughed, her red lips sliding back from her perfectly shaped teeth. She wagged a finger in the air. "But I will go! When I was growing up in the barrio we used to brag, 'I'm down and brown,' a declaration of pride, and we used to sit on the front steps and daydream about what we would do in life when we grew up. I always said I want to dance in Paris." She laughed. "And I can assure you, I will go, and I will someday dance in Paris and in Rome."

"I know you will."

"I will be a ballerina doing my relevé en pointe to music by Tchaikovsky, maybe in *The Nutcracker*! I can assure you of that!"

"What's 'relevé en pointe'?"

"It's when the ballerina is balancing herself on one foot with her butt sticking up. It's called 'attitude derriere'. In other words, 'smart ass'. Just kidding." She laughed.

"I love it!"

She said, "Have you ever seen Degas' ballet paintings at the Met?"

"Degas?"

"Yes, the French painter, Degas."

"Oh, yeah. I remember seeing those ballet paintings. Oh, yes, Degas. I know who you mean." But I wasn't sure if I remembered seeing those paintings at the Metropolitan Museum of Art. Maybe what I remembered was seeing reproductions of them in magazines and newspapers.

"I love those paintings. He must have been an exceptional man to capture ballet so well."

I looked at my watch.

Regina stood up. "Oh, are you concerned about the time? Are you busy? Am I interrupting…?" She gently laid a hand on my chest.

"No, you're not interrupting, I was just working at the typewriter. I needed a break." I stood up, too.

"Let's go inside," I said.

She followed me inside.

We stopped by the couch.

Coyly smiling, she said, "I was down there all by myself and lonely. I came up to see if I could play with you?" She was now standing only a couple of inches from me.

I knew what she meant. I said, "Right now?"

"Yes, now." She moved closer. I felt her hand cup the back of my head, and her lips softly touched mine. She pressed her lips harder against mine, while gently pressing the back of my head.

Then she pulled back and smiled.

"You know, I can hear your typewriter all the way downstairs. I sometimes fantasized about coming up here and sitting on your lap while you type."

"What an imagination you have."

We sat down, side by side.

On the couch we kissed for a long time. The fragrance of her perfume was fruity and spicy. I was breathing heavily. So was she.

Lying back, she pulled up her dress and parted her legs. She was wearing no panties. I stood up and stood before her with my knees balanced on the edge of the couch, holding her by the backs of her thighs with her legs far apart.

Without undressing, we made love slowly.

When we finished, I saw that my hands had accidentally made purple bruises in the shape of hands on the backs of the delicate pink flesh of her thighs, same as the marks Sophia had on the backs of her thighs. I had not meant to do that. I worried that the bruises might be seen by Cedric.

Then Regina went back downstairs.

Cedric returned the next day, Friday. I ran into him at the entrance. He was just returning from his trip and I was coming back from the grocery store where I'd bought our usual staples: fresh fruit and vegetables, milk, bread, bacon, and eggs.

He said, "James, my good man, I just got back from Cabo. I caught a cold, but I'm okay. I just need to rest. Say, why don't you come down later this afternoon and have a beer with me?"

"Sure. Around two or three?"

"Make it three."

"See you then."

Sophia had stayed in that morning baking cookies. When I got upstairs the apartment had the pleasant smell of warm cookies. There were about thirty cookies in the tray.

"Yum, yum," I said while putting away the things from the store. Finished, I picked up a cookie and ate it. It was delicious. Then I ate another one.

"Be sure to save some for Miranda. I baked them for her."

Around two-thirty, Sophia said she was going for a walk.

"You want me to go with you?"

"No, I like the alone time, to just be to myself, if you don't mind."

"Okay."

At three o'clock I knocked at Cedric and Regina's door. Regina opened the door with her finger to her mouth, indicating she wanted me to be quiet. She whispered, "He's asleep. He caught a cold in Cabo. Come on in."

Quietly she led me to an armchair across the room. She then gently pushed me down into the chair and unzipped me.

Seeing what she was about to do, I whispered, "No! Not here!"

"Yes!" she whispered.

"Let's go upstairs."

"No, right here," she insisted. She turned around, lifted her bright yellow skirt, and backed onto my lap. I groaned.

"Shhhhhhh!" she said.

She reached back and made the adjustments. Once I was in, I couldn't protest any more. My defenses were gone. We were in rhythm for a long time. Then I felt the tightening and releasing, tightening and releasing, then a massive release.

Just then there was a loud knock at the door.

She leaped up and I zipped up. I felt a rush of fear and guilt. My life was getting too complicated. How did I let myself get this caught up in such a mess?

At the same time Cedric came from the bedroom rubbing his eyes. "Oh, James, my good man, you're here. Sorry I fell asleep. How about those beers?"

Regina opened the door. It was Estelle. She said, "Hi, Regina. I was just wondering if I could borrow a cup of sugar?"

Calmly, Regina said, "Sure." The kitchen was just to the left of the door. I watched Regina fill a cup with sugar and hand it to Estelle.

Estelle said, "I'm baking a pie. Grant loves my pies." She thanked Regina and she was gone.

Smiling, Cedric eased down in the armchair opposite the one I was in and called out to Regina, "Babe, while you're in the kitchen please bring us two beers."

While we waited, Cedric said, "James, what kind of poetry do you write?"

That was a question I hated. I hated it because I never could answer it to anybody's satisfaction. I said, "I've been called an expressionist and even a romantic poet." It was not a good answer, but I hoped it gave Cedric something to hang on to. I added, "I try to keep my themes universal."

But Cedric surprised me. He said, "Funny thing. I'm Canadian, but I don't know much about Canadian poets beyond the obvious people like Robert Service and Elizabeth Bishop, and truth be told, I haven't read much of their work."

I said, "I know Bishop and Layton and Acorn."

Cedric continued, "You've read more Canadian poetry than I have. Very few Americans know Canadian poetry, but the poetry I know best is the poetry I learned in school, mostly by British poets such as Milton, Shakespeare, Shelley. Of modern poetry, I guess I like the Scottish Renaissance and the Georgian poets, poets like Rupert Brooke, Robert Graves, D. H. Lawrence, John Drinkwater, and Siegfried Sassoon."

"What about Jamaican poets?"

"I also like the Jamaican poets, especially Claude McKay, Roger Mais, Dennis Scott, James Berry, and Andrew Salkey. Do you know their works?"

"Not well. McKay I know well, but not the others."

"They are quite good. You should check them out. I think you would be delighted."

Regina brought over three beers and she joined us by sitting on the couch, with her legs tucked under her body. She sat there and sipped her beer. When Cedric wasn't looking her way, she winked at me.

Cedric said, "You said you did work on the riots. Tell me about that."

"The riots and riot news coverage. The federal government commissioned the study. Many universities and private companies worked together and came to the same conclusions."

"What were they?"

"One of the main ones was that most of the riots were caused by police mishandling the initial incidents."

"Fortunately, in Canada, we don't have many instances of that kind of violence. Did the government accept the recommendations?"

"No, the government wasn't happy with our conclusions, so they accepted none of the recommendations."

"Phew! I feel lucky to be Canadian." He laughed.

Regina said, "In Harlem, a few summers ago, a police officer shot an unarmed boy. He was running away, and the police shot him in the back, and people took to the streets protesting police violence, but an internal police investigation found the police justified in shooting the boy, and that was the end of it."

Cedric said, "We need to do something that's fun."

I said, "By the way, Sophia and I are going to the bullfight this coming Wednesday. Why don't you guys come with us?"

"Bullfight, huh? What a neat idea," said Cedric, grinning, showing his dimples.

Regina said, "I hope it's not too bloody!"

Cedric said, "Actually, bullfighting doesn't have to be bloody. I once read a book about bullfighting. I learned a lot, too, and in Spain I saw a bullfight when I was fifteen."

Regina said, "Was that the time when your parents took you to Europe?"

"Yes, exactly. As a modern sport it's almost three hundred years old, but much older since the Romans actually started it. It was a kind of added attraction to ceremonial occasions."

"Like what?"

"Well, if a member of royalty was being promoted or being crowned, or if a person of high office or high birth was marrying. Those were the kinds of occasions when they brought out the bulls. The first bullfights were on horseback, not like they do it in Spain or here in Mexico, with the bullfighter standing on the ground, and the bull charging at him."

"Still," Regina said, "I don't like the idea of tricking an animal and killing him with a sword hidden behind a cape."

Cedric laughed. "Tell that to the people of Ecuador, Venezuela, Peru, Colombia, Spain, Portugal, and here in Mexico. I don't think they'll listen to you."

"Bullfighting was ruled illegal in Puerto Rico long before I was born. Thank god! But I'll go," Regina said. "I won't understand or like what I'm seeing, but I'll go."

Cedric said, "All you have to do is remember a few simple things: the banderillero is a bullfighter who assists the main bullfighter. I don't know if they have that here in Mexico. The bullfight is called corrida. If he's a famous bullfighter, he's called a matador but only if he's famous; otherwise he's just a torero."

"Thanks a lot, dear. I knew that," said Regina. "In fact, I think my knowledge of Spanish is better than yours since I grew up bilingual, speaking both English and Spanish at the same time."

Cedric said, "When the bullfighter makes a pass with his muleta, it's called a veronica. Don't call the muleta a cape. It's not a cape."

Cedric was showing off his knowledge of bullfighting. I thought his going on and on about the terms was pretentious.

"Everybody calls it a cape," she said.

"Don't be everybody, Gina." He sounded snobbish.

"I've heard enough, Cedric. How'd you remember these things?"

"I have a good memory. I got interested when I was a kid and saw my first bullfight in Spain."

Not only was I trying to fully understand what drove Regina to do the things she was doing, I was also trying to understand why I was participating in her game. She clearly got a thrill out of the deceptive nature of infidelity. Was I simply driven by the powers of Eros?

I liked and respected Cedric. That made it even more baffling and difficult for me to, unintentionally and even accidentally, turn him into a cuckold, but if Sophia was doing what I suspected, I too was a cuckold.

What kind of excuse was I making for myself? I loved Sophia. Sure, it was easy to blame my actions on Eros. The Greek god Eros made me do it! As a poet, I'd studied Eros in all of his guises of desire and sexual attraction. I'd studied his primordial schemes, his relationship with his mother, Aphrodite.

Eros often favored illicit love. Then the name got changed to Cupid. The poet William Blake asked why the Greeks made the god of love, Cupid, a boy when such a god should clearly have been a girl. I didn't blame my actions on Eros or Cupid.

Wednesday afternoon, around four-thirty, the four of us walked together to Plaza de Toros la Paloma. The sky was overcast. The smells of dung and urine and animals were in the sluggish air. It had just rained for about twenty minutes. Now the air was also heavy with moisture.

"I can't believe July is ending in another day," said Cedric. "The time is really flying."

As we approached, I saw the plaza. It was a modest whitewashed stucco circular structure inside a square structure; and there was a giant metal black bull likeness perched high on the corner wall.

Painted on the bull was the word OPEN and below, also in English, on the wall: Wednesday 5 PM. Obviously, those words in English were not meant for locals. The entrance was just a few feet beyond. Above the plaza, stretched up to the bull image, were three lines strung with colorful flags.

As we approached I had misgivings about going to watch an innocent animal slaughtered. No matter how artful the act, in the end, it was about killing an animal for sport. It was an ugly business, but despite my conscience and emotions I was going anyway. We were all going. It was what people did in such countries as Mexico. In a sense, we humans were herd animals.

We paid at the gate, and inside it wasn't crowded. We climbed the steps to the cheap seats and sat on the benches in the sun. Sophia and Regina were together between Cedric and me. On the other side of the arena, a few people were in the more expensive seats in the shade.

A gunshot announced the beginning of the bullfight. Birds, nesting under the seats, flew up, scattering like black dots across the greyish white sky.

Two picadors on horseback with their lancers were already in the ring circulating, waiting for the bull to be released so they could start working on him.

Then the bull was released. You could tell he had been tortured just before being released into the ring, and he rushed excitedly into the ring. He was big for a bull and dark brown with massive horns. He stopped and looked around, as if confused; then started running around the ring. Finally, seeing no way out, he stopped again and looked at the picadors and horses.

The cudrilla came out.

Three banderilleros came out with their flags.

Two more picadors came out with their lancers.

Then the bullfighter came out. He was no torero. I didn't remember his name; but he was not famous, not a matador. Yet he was dressed in the traditional bullfighter's hat, jacket and pants and shoes. His muleta was red. He looked the part without having the credentials.

In this first stage, the tercio de varas, the bullfighter kept away from the bull, watching how he responded to the banderilleros and then how he responded to the picadors.

Sophia said, "I don't know about you guys but I'm for the bull."

Regina said, "I'm with you, Sophia. The bull is my hero."

We all laughed.

Soon the picadors kept moving closer to the bull, but they were very careful to give him room. This was still the tercio de vara.

When the bull charged at one of them, pounding his horns into the heavily padded horse, the picador jabbed at him repeatedly with his pica.

During stage two, where the banderilleros were trying to plant the barbed sticks in the bull's hump, Sophia said, "Oh, I can't stand looking."

Regina had her eyes closed. Though I was disgusted, I kept my eyes opened.

Now Sophia placed her hands over her eyes as another picador rammed a lance into the bull's hump and it stuck there, dangling as the bull jumped around trying to dislodge it. The smell of blood, animals, and dung were high on the air.

Cedric said, "When I saw my first bullfight in Spain, it just seemed like a game, but now this truly is a sport about death."

Regina looked at Sophia and smiled. She said, "Se pone peor."

Sophia said, "If it gets worse, I may have to leave."

The bullfighter came from behind the barricade. He called out to the bull, "Toro! Toro!" but the bull showed no interest.

Then the bullfighter started flapping his red muleta, trying to attract the bull's attention, but the bull remained more interested in the horses and the picadors.

Out of breath, he stood in the middle of the ring, showing no interest in the bullfighter. Exhausted, worn down, confused, bloody, the bull stood there panting, out of breath. The bullfighter was clearly a coward.

The bull was brave, even as he was dying. I didn't want to see the bullfighter gored, but I hoped that the bull would somehow be the victor.

Again, the bullfighter flapped his muleta and shouted to the bull, "Toro! Toro!"

The bull, still breathing heavily, now started toward the bullfighter, and as the bull got close, the bullfighter was not able to keep his feet still. Twitchy, he was clearly losing his nerve. Instead of giving the bull a smooth pass, the bullfighter flapped his muleta at the bull, all the while standing a safe distance from the bull as he passed.

Cedric said, "The great matadors don't move their feet as the bull charges. They let the bull pass close by, not far away the way this guy is. He's out there nervously flapping his muleta. This bullfighter is a coward."

The few spectators booed the bullfighter and it was all downhill after that. At one point the bull knocked the bullfighter down, but he wasn't seriously hurt, and the rest of the performance was a farce.

In the end, the picadors had to butcher the bull, and when the bull lay dead in the ring, the bullfighter raised his arms in victory as the crowd booed him. It was painful to watch such a travesty.

The four of us stopped at the refreshments stand on the way out and bought raspados, shaved ice in a paper cone covered with fruit syrup.

I said, "The whole thing was disgusting!"

Sophia said, "Worse than disgusting!"

Regina said, "I really needed this snowball. What a horror show we just saw!"

"I second that motion," said Sophia.

I felt sickened by what we'd just seen in the bullring. Cedric, among us, was the only one who didn't seem disgusted by the spectacle we'd just witnessed. Even if it had been an artful performance about the inevitable reality of death, the whole thing in the end was about killing a trapped animal for sport.

Many people in Puerto Vallarta went to the post office to pick up their mail. We usually didn't get mail, but because of an arrangement with the post office, our mail was delivered to the apartment. The carrier would drop it downstairs in the hallway. What we did receive were things forwarded by our New York post office.

There was a postcard from Amy Lawrence; it was addressed to my Lower East Side place. She said, "Still haven't forgotten our idea of getting together for lunch. Best wishes, Amy."

Among the other items was a phone bill for our telephone in New York. We had discontinued the phone service, paid the bill, and we were fully paid up. Sophia said, "Agnes must have turned the phone back on in your name."

That was obviously the case. I went and sat at the typewriter and wrote a letter to the phone company telling them the situation. How annoying!

Mostly what I got in the mail were rejection letters from literary magazines along with my poems returned in the self-addressed, stamped envelopes I'd supplied. I had published widely in such magazines, and occasionally poems were accepted and appeared in print.

The next day, Thursday, two letters came: one from Mom and one from Frank Garrick.

Sophia had returned from her daily walk. We were standing in the living room near the balcony doors where the light was better. "You want to hear the letter from my mother?"

"Sure," Sophia said. "Read your mother's letter to me. I like your mother."

"Okay. 'Dear Jimmy, you've been gone from home now for a number of years, so your dad and I have decided to convert your room into an exercise room so we can try to get in better physical shape. Since he retired from the bank, your dad has gained too much weight and his doctor tells him he needs to exercise more. He doesn't want to go to a gym. We're planning to buy a couple of those exercise machines.

" 'We hope you and your girlfriend, Sophia, are having a good time in Mexico. She seems like a nice girl. Love, Mom.' "

"Sounds like that chapter of your life has closed," said Sophia.

"How do you mean?"

"You can't go home again."

"I don't want to go home again."

"So sweet of your mother to say I'm a nice girl." Sophia was blushing. "I don't think she knows how you treat me."

"How do I treat you?"

"All you do is sit at the typewriter. Your mind is always on your work."

I knew what she meant and she was right, but getting my book done was so important that I'd placed the task at the forefront of my concerns.

"I love you," she said.

"I love you, too, Sophia. You should know that by now, but I've got to get this book finished."

"I know, I know, but I can't help feeling neglected."

Dropping the letters on a nearby chair, I put my arms around her and said, "You want to hear the one from Frank?"

"Sure. Sure, change the subject."

" 'Hello James and Sophia, I trust you both are well and are enjoying Puerto Vallarta. As for myself, I've gotten into a bit of trouble. I was helping some students at the university here by demonstrating with them against harsh and unjust university policies, and I got arrested. I'm out on bail now and I have to go to court next week. My fear is that I may be deported. If I have to return to the States, I'm pretty sure I can return to my old teaching gig at Willem Granville in Connecticut, but Suzette has gotten me a crackerjack lawyer and maybe things will work out here, but this is Mexico: you never can tell what might happen. Fingers crossed. Best wishes, Frank. P.S.: Don't forget to send new poems.

The next issue of *Nuevo Mundo* is closing soon.' "

Sophia said, "Wow! I hope he'll be all right. He seems like a nice man."

A few days later, Sunday, mid-afternoon, Sophia came in and said, "I don't feel well. I'm going to lie down on the couch. I feel hot all over. I feel dizzy."

I got up from the typewriter and went to her. She stretched out on the couch. I felt her forehead. It was hot. "Stick out your tongue."

She stuck out her tongue. It was white and dry. "Maybe you're dehydrated?"

"I have stomach cramps and I feel nauseous."

I got her a glass of water, sat on the edge of the couch, lifted her head and gently poured the water into her open mouth. She swallowed. I thought she might have eaten something that upset her stomach. I didn't want to think worse.

I ran to the bathroom and wet a towel, and rushed back to her and placed it on her forehead.

"I want to sleep," she said.

"Okay, sleep. You'll feel better. Maybe it's just a cold."

By nightfall, I was worried. Her complexion had changed. I feared she was dying. She clearly had a fever. Her whole body was hot.

"Sophia?"

Her eyes were closed.

"Sophia, can you hear me?"

She whispered, "Yes."

Five minutes later I asked the same question again.

She didn't respond. I felt her pulse. She still had a strong pulse. I had no blood pressure meter to take her blood pressure with. Holding her by the shoulders, I gently shook her, but she was out cold.

I leaped up and grabbed my wallet and shot out and down the steps. I ran all the way up Hidalgo to the drugstore in the little shopping district there. I'd been there before for aspirin. I knew the druggist spoke English. Out of breath I said, "My wife is unconscious. Can you get in touch with a doctor for me?"

"Yes," the druggist said. "This is very common affliction for foreigners here. They make the mistake of eating raw fruit without washing it good. Best not to eat anything raw if you're not native."

As he talked he had picked up the telephone and was waiting for somebody on the other end to answer. I heard him say, "¡Está muy enferma!"

"Gracias, Señor Mendoza."

"You have to go up in the hills to the doctor's house. Take a taxi. There should be one or two parked out in front. If not, you can get one by waving one down. Give this address to the taxi driver." He wrote down the doctor's address and handed it to me. "The doctor needs you to direct him to your house. Your wife will be all right, don't worry. She's not going to die."

"Thank you, señor!" I said, and shot out of there and almost immediately was able to flag down a taxi. I gave him the sheet of paper and he took off for the hills.

It took thirty minutes to get there. Dr. Martinez came out into the yard when he heard the taxi drive up and stop. He was putting on a jacket. Up here in the hills, the night air was chilly.

Dr. Martinez said, "Me acompañas en mi carro."

I understood him to say I should go with him in his car. I paid the taxi driver and he drove away.

I got into the passenger seat of the doctor's car. In English he said, "I will get my bag. One minute."

He ran back into the house and returned quickly with a black soft leather country doctor's medical bag.

When we got upstairs, Sophia was still unconscious. I brought a straight-backed chair over so the doctor could sit beside Sophia and examine her.

"I have to give her a shot," he said. He opened his bag. "Best to place it in her hip. I will cover her. You have a sheet?"

I got a sheet from the bedroom closet and he spread it over her. He then reached under the sheet with his needle and placed the shot in her hip.

I thought about this act of modesty. I remembered reading an article in the *New York Times* a few years earlier about medical practice and morality in 16th century Spain. Back then, the church laid down the moral rules for medical practice. Dr. Martinez was apparently following the ruling of the church.

He then balanced his prescription book on his knee and wrote a prescription and handed it to me. "Take this to the pharmacist. She'll need to take these tablets for a few days. Make sure she takes them."

"What is it, Dr. Martinez?"

"Stomach infection. They call it traveler's sickness."

"Montezuma's Revenge?"

"That's what the tourists call it," he said.

Sophia began to stir; her eyes fluttered and opened. The shot was taking effect. She blinked a few times and looked up at me. "Hi," she said, "I guess I passed out, huh?"

"Yes. Sophia, this is Dr. Martinez. He's treating you for a stomach infection."

She nodded approval and gave the doctor a faint smile.

After Dr. Martinez left, I walked up to the farmacia and Señor Mendoza filled the prescription. I thanked him for his help.

Back at the apartment, I then helped Sophia get ready for bed. Once she was tucked in, I got a glass of water and placed it on the bedside table and I had her hold her hand out. Then I shook from the bottle into her hand the first of the little white pills she was to take. Color seemed to be coming back to her face. Her fever was diminishing. She threw the pills into her mouth and took a sip of water.

"Better drink all of it," I said.

"Then I'll have to get up and pee all night."

Hearing her say this, I knew she was getting better. "Still, you should drink it."

And she drank all of the water.

We were four days into August. That night Sophia's sleep was restless, but the next day she felt better. I didn't go at all to the typewriter. I cooked breakfast.

After breakfast, I sat with her on the couch while Camilla and Miranda were working in the apartment.

Miranda washed the breakfast dishes, dried them, and put them away in the cabinets. Camilla ran the vacuum cleaner across the rugs and Miranda dusted. Camilla then brought the bed sheets out of the bedroom rolled up into a bundle. She said to Sophia, "Me pongo sábanas limpias."

Sophia said, "Muchas gracias."

Finished, I paid them, and they left with the bed sheets tucked under Camilla's arm.

The next day a letter came from the telephone company in New York saying they had turned off the phone. There was no apology, but we would not have to pay the bill.

Five days later, a Thursday, Sophia left the apartment to walk while I was at the typewriter.

I continued to work for about an hour before I started feeling cabin fever. I'd been inside too long. The balcony doors were open and fresh air was coming in, but I needed to stretch my legs and get fresh air at the same time.

I closed the apartment door and ran downstairs. I walked quickly over to the Malecón. To exercise my legs, I started walking up toward the amphitheater.

As usual, couples were strolling the Malecón, holding hands. I passed two or three elderly women in black and an old man pushing a wheelbarrow full of fish to some small market up the way.

Then, up ahead, I saw Sophia and that same handsome young man walking toward the amphitheater. They were holding hands. I felt a rush of anger and jealousy. I weighed the situation. Was I ready to break entirely with Sophia? No, I was not. She was having a fling. It annoyed and angered me, but I also feared that confronting her and her companion in the street at that moment could have no positive outcome.

Would I have felt differently had she been my wife? I didn't know, but the question crossed my mind. I was selfishly involved in my work. I felt a bit guilty, I guess, for neglecting her. I needed to spend more time with her, to do some of the things she wanted to do. I felt I had driven her away.

I wasn't surprised to see her with him again. I didn't want her to think I was out with the intention of spying on her. I wasn't. Doing such a thing had never crossed my mind. I knew that this would be the first thing she would think.

Maybe because I had become involved with Regina, I felt I had no right to complain about what Sophia was doing. Though I still loved her, seeing her with her lover deepened the growing distance I felt between us. My anger and jealousy gradually gave way to sadness.

Was there an assumed state of emotional and sexual exclusivity? We'd never talked about fidelity or loyalty, but certainly when she moved downtown into my apartment on the Lower East Side, she and I must have silently agreed by our actions to be exclusive—or had we? I didn't know.

If that was true, then exclusivity must have recently ended here in Mexico, and again without words spoken. We said we were in love, but we had never defined the terms of our relationship.

I'd read in a psychology class that women in a relationship considered emotional involvement with a person outside the relationship to be cheating, while men tended to define sexual involvement outside the relationship as cheating.

I thought seriously for the first time about trust, infidelity, cheating, and betrayal. These were hard concepts to swallow. By my clandestine episodes with Regina, I was betraying my acquaintance with Cedric. Never mind what Sophia might have been doing, I had in some essential way failed myself. I wondered how many things in life does one end up forgiving one's self for?

It was after dark when Sophia got back to the apartment. This was the first time she'd come in after dark. I was sitting on the couch reading a novel called *Wide Sargasso Sea*. I was determined not to question her. I said, "Hi," and kept reading.

She came over and stood in front of me. "Aren't you going to ask where I've been?"

"No."

"Went to see a movie," she said, looking away, fidgeting.

"That's nice." Sophia was not a good liar. Early on in our relationship I learned how to tell when she was lying. It wasn't difficult. She couldn't look me in the eyes, she stuttered and was visibly nervous.

While writing poems, I'd already stumbled into questions about the relationship between truth and lies. I saw poetry as an art form above and beyond the complicated nature of lies. Poetry sought to remain in the realm of a higher truth. So did fiction.

We human beings, in our earthbound day-to-day interactions, were subject early on to using lies to hide deficiencies, and lies were used also for self-protection or self-promotion or even self-deception. Sophia, I thought, was an amateur at lying.

But she was not pathological—not yet. Her voice got higher, it cracked when she lied. She batted her eyes a lot and she got fidgety and she tended to speak in shorter sentences, omitting references to herself.

"Aren't you going to ask the name of the movie?"

"No."

"You're mean."

"Mean? How?"

"You're just not nice at all. You wanted to come to Mexico to write your little obscure poems. I thought we were coming here to have fun together. All you do is stay in this apartment and sit at the typewriter. I'm sick of it!" she shouted, her face turning red.

"You said you were going to do research. What'd you come here for, to have an affair?"

"What? What? What is that supposed to mean?"

"You know damn well what it means." I hadn't planned to get angry, but she pulled it out of me. I made a conscious effort to control my temper. I shut up.

She was silent for a moment, then she said, "Today I ran into John Sharp and Lisa Garner from Yelapa. They were over here to buy supplies. They asked me if we'd given any more thought to coming to live with them."

"And?"

"Well, I've been thinking about it. If you don't want to, I think I might."

"You might what?"

"Don't be a wisenheimer! Move over there with them, of course. At least give it a try. You're not willing to try anything new. Why should I restrain myself because all you want to do is stay in this apartment the whole time we're here?"

"Suit yourself."

"You don't care?"

"Of course I care. I don't want you to go, but I can't stop you, Sophia. Do what you want."

Exasperated, she left the apartment, slamming the door.

The next morning at breakfast, Sophia said, "I need some money."

"Okay." I got up and went to the bedroom and took two hundred dollars from my wallet. I was sick at heart. One moment I was angry, in the next I was grief-stricken.

Back in the kitchen, I handed the money to her. She rolled it up and stuck the wad in the pocket of her jeans. Her interest in studying people was surely part of her motivation for wanting to go to Yelapa.

By nature, I was not controlling. I was not going to try and stop her. I didn't see Sophia as my possession. She was the woman I loved, my partner, my friend, my intellectual companion.

"Thank you," she said. "I'm going to pack my things."

With a breaking heart, I stood on the balcony and watched her walking toward the boat rental place with her suitcase bumping against her leg. I felt both sadness and compassion: sadness for myself, and compassion for her. I told myself that this foolish thing was something she had to do.

Now Sophia was headed for Yelapa—a new adventure.

There was a knock at the door. It was Estelle, looking wide-eyed and nervous. "I came to tell you and Sophia we're having another get-together tomorrow evening, say, about five o'clock."

"Sophia moved to Yelapa."

"She what?"

"Yes."

"But she's your wife, isn't she?"

"No, we're not married."

"I thought you were. I'm sorry to hear that, but you can come tomorrow night, right?"

"Sure, I'll come."

Morning. I typed three of the new poems and put them in an envelope with a note to Frank Garrick: Hope these three poems work for you and *Nuevo Mundo*. Let me know if you are okay. Best, James.

On the way back from the post office, I cut over to the Malecón and sat down on a bench and gazed out at the bay and at the soft blue and the deeper indigo mountain range in the distance. The shades of blues and blue-greens were constantly shifting and merging.

I listened to the tides coming in and washing back out. In the middle distance I watched the lime and emerald and shamrock greens of the tides as they moved in and out, producing sea foam. I almost went into a trance watching the colors shift.

The color turquoise lay along the coastline.

Farther out, the deeper blue blues shifted higher toward the sky: azure, cobalt, ultramarine, phthalo, Prussian and royal blues were all washing in and out of one another all the way to the horizon where there was a long belt of white light.

I smelled the fishiness of the bay and felt the dampness in the air. Later it would rain, with its *pit-a-pat, pit-a-pat* on the railing of our balcony. Lately, it rained every afternoon, but for only about a half-hour. I would often stop working and go out to the balcony and watch the rain falling through sunlight into the bay. Without knowing it at the moment, I was washing my sadness away in the ocean colors.

I got up and started walking aimlessly. On impulse I stopped at Café Chino for a cup of coffee. It was just off the Jardin Allende, in the shadow of the old church. The service here was quick and the coffee was good.

I took a sip sooner than I should have and burned my tongue.

A young American woman was the only other customer. With a ballpoint pen she was writing a letter. A stamp and an envelope lay on the tabletop near her arm. Her hair was light brown, her eyes grey, and she had a clear complexion and a square chin. Makeup almost covered a bit of acne.

How did I know she was an American? I just knew. Americans abroad can tell other Americans abroad. She was dressed in a red and white checked cotton shirt and tight blue jeans. She was wearing huarache sandals with the bottoms made out of tire treads. She looked very young. I said, "Hello."

"Hello," she said, with a smile. "You here on vacation?"

"No, I guess I'm living here right now."

"Oh, wow! That's so cool! You like living here?"

"I've been here only a month."

"Still, that's a long time. By the way, my name is Bessie Marie."

"I'm James. Good to meet you, Bessie Marie." For some reason that name sounded familiar. "What's your last name?"

"Muller, Bessie Marie Muller."

Sophia and I had met her parents on the flight down here. They were coming to Mexico to take her back home because she was only seventeen. Apparently, they had not yet found her. I said, "How long have you been here?"

"Six or seven weeks, I forget. My parents came down here trying to take me back home, but I turned eighteen the day they arrived, and that threw a monkey wrench into their plans. I'm living with my boyfriend. We like it here."

The coffee had cooled, and I finished drinking it and stood up to leave. I said, "Well, good luck, Bessie Marie. Enjoy Mexico!"

"Thanks!"

On the way back, I saw Regina coming around the corner of our house with a bag of groceries in her arms. She was carrying the bag against her belly, like some women carry babies.

"This morning, through the window, I saw Sophia leaving with a suitcase," she said.

I looked down at my shoes. "Yeah, she's moved to Yelapa."

"You guys separated?"

"I guess so. At least for now."

"Did you have an argument?"

"Yes, we did. She wants a bigger, brighter Mexican experience than she's been having."

"Oh, yeah, well, we women get restless. We can't help it. We need things to do. I get bored pretty quickly myself." She laughed. "That's why I've always had more than one lover at a time. I'm also bisexual. I like women, probably better than men."

"Somehow I'm not surprised. Does Cedric know?"

"Are you kidding? Cedric is such a conservative person. I mean, I love him, and I want to spend the rest of my life with him, but I would go crazy restricting myself to just Cedric."

"By the way, did Cedric get that part?"

"He has to fly to L.A. in two days for a screen test. Maybe he'll get it. It's not definite yet. He's been reading the part over and over and over. He's really trying hard. I hope he gets it. If he does, we'll move to L.A. for a little while, I guess. That might be fun." She shifted the bag. "I better get inside. This bag is getting heavy."

"Will I see you soon?"

"Yes, when I can. By the way, Estelle is having another get-together tomorrow evening. Are you coming?"

"Yes, I'll come. She stopped by this morning to invite us."

"Did you tell her about Sophia?"

"I sure did."

"Bet she's dying to know the juicy details." Regina giggled.

"Yeah, I'm sure."

I stepped aside to let Regina go in first.

Saturday, after being depressed all day, I went downstairs at a quarter after five. Grant opened the door. "Come on in, James, good to see you, boy."

I walked past him into their living room. Cedric and Regina were already there and so was another couple I didn't know.

Estelle had tacos, some kind of dip and crackers, and soft drinks, beer, and wine on the coffee table.

"James," Estelle said, "this is Darshita and Louis. They're from Los Angeles. Darshita is a pediatrician and Louis is a trial lawyer. They're staying in that new hotel over on the bay. James, your last name is Lowell, isn't it?"

"That's right."

Speaking to Darshita and Louis, Estelle said, "James is a poet."

I think I must have rolled my eyes. I hoped no one noticed. I didn't like being introduced as a poet, especially since I didn't feel that I had yet achieved the right to call myself such. A poet was someone who'd published at least one book of poems. Being called "a poet" somehow always either amused or bewildered people.

Speaking to me, Estelle said, "I met the Orlandos at the market. We hit it off right away. Didn't we, Darshita?"

"We certainly did," said Darshita. She had large white eyes, a narrow nose, and thin lips. Her skin was a beautiful blue-black and she had long straight silky black hair. Judging from her name, I assumed she was from India or she was a U.S. citizen of Indian descent.

Louis was brown-skinned with straight black hair, and he wore glasses, the kind with those little pads that rest against the nose. His basic expression was one of studiousness.

Balancing on her lap a paper plate containing crackers with dip, Darshita gave me a quizzical look. "How does a poet make a living?"

The same old question; it made me feel like a freak. "They don't, not as a poet. A lot of poets teach."

"Do you teach?" Her big eyes stretched, waiting for an answer. I was almost sure her expression was hostile.

"I'm a freelance editor for a Brooklyn newspaper. Till recently I also was a research analyst. I'm hoping to get a job teaching."

"Oh," Darshita said, "so that's how it works. Well, good luck with your prospective teaching job." She smiled, showing brownish nicotine-stained teeth.

"And Cedric here is an actor," said Estelle.

"An actor!" said Darshita. "How exciting!"

Cedric blushed.

Darshita said, "Cedric, are you on the telly or in film? Have I seen you at the cinema?"

"Not yet, but I've done lots of stage work, first in Toronto, my hometown; Toronto has a very active avant-garde theater scene. I've had parts in plays at the Hart House theater, Theatre Passe-Muraille, and the Royal Alexandra Theatre. You may know those theaters. In Canada they are big."

Regina said, "He's done *Macbeth, The Balcony, A Streetcar Named Desire, A Raisin in the Sun, The Glass Menagerie.* You name it!"

Cedric said, "But those plays were in New York, off-off-Broadway, Lower East Side. It was there that I made real progress. La MaMa taught me everything I know."

"Oh, I see," she said, clearly disappointed.

Grant said, "Who is La MaMa? You mean your mother?"

Cedric, smiling, said, "No, La MaMa is a theater in Lower Manhattan."

Grant said, "Oh. The things I don't know..." He laughed at himself. "Cedric, you're Canadian but you're also Jamaican, right?"

"Yes."

"How'd that happen?"

"I was born in Jamaica, but my parents moved to Canada when I was five years old. I'm essentially Canadian. Of course, while I was growing up, we often went to Jamaica to visit relatives."

Grant said, "Estelle and I have been to Canada, but never Jamaica. What's it like?"

"Jamaica?" He rolled his eyes toward the ceiling. "Where should I start? You want the textbook version or the personal version?"

"Whichever you think is best."

"Well, it's a beautiful island of flora and fauna, one of the biggest islands in the Caribbean, an island of ex-slaves and native people, the Arawak and Taino. We were ruled first by the Spanish in the 1500s, then by the British from the 1600s till just six years ago, 1962, to be exact. That was the year of our independence. My whole family went back for the grand celebration. There were fireworks, the whole works! It was a great liberation festival."

"Sounds wonderful," said Grant, eating a cracker and sipping a beer.

"But," said Cedric, "during the occupation, some of our people picked up many of the traits of the British upper-class, not all of them good. Despite that, we are a beautiful people."

Cedric picked up a cracker and pushed it in his mouth and chewed it slowly.

"Harry Belafonte is Jamaican, right?" said Estelle. "I've seen him on television."

Cedric said, "Yes, his parents are from Jamaica and he grew up there. We are famous for our music, sports, literature, and our food. The British also brought in Chinese and Indian laborers to work the land because, after 1834, they couldn't get the ex-slaves to do the work. The ex-slaves were done with taking orders."

With downcast eyes, Regina was sitting quietly and smirking at the conversation.

Darshita said, "My India was occupied by the British too for a long time. British rule ended in 1947: it was goodbye to the Empress of India, Queen Victoria, and the East India Company and all of that! But it was not all bad. The British also did a lot of good for India."

I was about ready to change the conversation.

Darshita said, "And you, Regina, what do you do?"

"I'm a chorus dancer," Regina said, looking Darshita squarely in the eyes, and without a trace of irony or friendliness.

Louis was gazing off in the distance. His eyes were half closed.

Cedric said, "She's more than a chorus dancer, she's had leading dance roles in *Golden Boy*, *Bye Bye Birdie*, *Porgy and Bess*, and *West Side Story*."

Darshita said, "Did you study dance? Who is your ideal dancer?"

"I studied at Juilliard. When I was a little girl I loved the Bomba and danced a lot in the traditional Bombas in Puerto Rico. Then I fell in love with Isadora Duncan when on TV I saw her in an old film dancing like an angel. Then in a 1905 film on TV I discovered Anna Pavlova dancing 'The Dying Swan,' and fell in love with her, too. These two women were my models. I'm a Juilliard-trained dancer. My background is firmly in classical ballet."

Darshita said, "Very high ideals, I must say, certainly not just a chorus dancer." She looked very smug and offended.

Regina said, "I hope to try out for the new musical called *Hair* that recently opened on Broadway."

"My goodness, everybody is so gifted," said Darshita, again with exaggerated smugness.

Louis raised his eyebrows and looked at his wife.

I was wondering what the hell I was doing here. I was trying to think of some excuse to leave. I didn't know how much more of this chatter I could take. I was also dreading the possibility that somebody might ask me, "Where is Sophia?"

I was sure I sat there for at least an hour, ate a few crackers and sipped some punch before I politely departed.

That following Monday morning Camille and Miranda came as usual to clean. Camille had been running the vacuum cleaner for about twenty minutes when she turned it off and said, "¿Dónde está Sophia?"

I was at the typewriter, letting Camille work around me. "Sophia fue a visitar a amigos," I said, turning around, looking at her.

She uttered, "Ahhhh."

Miranda was dusting. When she got to my desk she said, "¿Señor James, lavaste los platos?"

"Si," I said, realizing that I had inadvertently done her job, a job she looked forward to being paid for doing. I would make it up to her.

An hour later, when they finished, I paid Camille and Miranda what they normally got each time they came. Miranda smiled, happy that her fears turned out to be unfounded.

I was in the third and fourth revision stages. I had drafts of all of the poems I intended for the collection. Now I was polishing and polishing. In the process I was learning a lot about the craft of making poetry.

I remembered that poet Theodore Roethke said a poet is someone who is never satisfied with saying one thing at a time, and he said that

that makes the language take desperate jumps. I was beginning to trust something in myself that knew more than I knew.

All the while, I was trying to keep my grief under control while working on the new drafts. Whether or not true, I felt responsible for much of the grief I was now feeling. Had I treated Sophia better, had I spent more time with her, maybe she would still be here. I missed her and I still loved her.

I'd allowed time between the first draft, and the second, and the third. I double-checked opening lines and closing lines. Typically, those were the places where most of the problems lay. I went over the structure of each poem with a careful eye.

I removed unnecessary words, words including *very, like, that, really, much, only, certainly, probably, even, simply,* and *truly.*

I watched for repetitive words and phrases. If they were intentional and served a rhythmic purpose, I intensified them. If not, I fixed the problem. I checked transitions between lines and sentences. I made sure the opening line was strong and that the closing line had real closure.

Only about twenty of the poems were finished. I liked those twenty poems a lot. I read them out loud over and over to make sure they sounded the right way. Poems were tricky. If the language didn't flow, something was wrong.

A poem might sound fine one day, but sound like crap the next day. I had to make sure a poem sounded just as good no matter how many times I read it out loud.

Now I needed to keep plugging away till I got enough of them finished for a book of at least seventy or eighty pages, maybe even ninety pages. That meant a manuscript of about a hundred and fifty pages. No doubt about it: I saw my future dependent on getting that book finished. It was a risky gamble, but in the best sense of the word, I was a gambler.

Yet finding a publisher might be difficult. Trade publishers, known for quality books and great distribution, were unlikely to publish a first book of poems by an unknown person.

If I were a well-known poet with a flashy public image, that would help, but getting there was a catch-22: you couldn't get there without being published, and it was hard to get published without already being published and well-known.

I believed that most editors in trade houses were passionate about the art of writing, but at the same time they needed to always think about the profit margin, and poetry was a weak proposition for a trade house.

Small presses and university presses, on the other hand, were more open to publishing poetry volumes. Many of their editors were passionately committed to the aesthetics. Unlike the trade houses, they did not necessarily have to make a profit. Many of them were happy to survive and break even so they could continue to publish fine books. The drawback, especially for small independent presses, sometimes was poor distribution.

When the time came, I suspected I would try my luck with either the small presses or the university presses.

All afternoon I paced around the apartment. It had started with a line problem. I'd been puzzling over a line, unable to decide on exactly how to word the line:

> ... all that sunlight cultivates

or

> ... everything sunlight cultivates

or

> ... the things that sunlight cultivates

When it started raining, I went out on the balcony and sat down and watched the rain falling through sunlight into the bay. In the distance the light blue mountains seemed to blend with the sky. Sunlight lay across the ocean like a thin brilliant garment.

Thursday, in the afternoon, there was a timid knock at the door. I opened it. Regina stood there grinning. "May I come in?"

"You certainly may."

She walked past me into the apartment. She was wearing a white cotton sleeveless shirt with purple buttons and purple shorts and purple sandals. Her curly hair was different, but I couldn't tell how. Obviously she had done something to it.

"Your hair is different."

She patted it on the sides and in the back. "Yes, I went to the hairdresser. You like it?"

"It looks good." It was an updo. "Have you heard anything from Sophia?" She walked over to the kitchen counter and climbed up on one of the stools.

"No, not a word." I stood on the other side, leaning with my arms on the counter, facing her.

"I guess you miss her, huh?"

"Sure."

"I imagine you get pretty lonesome up here by yourself." She got down from the stool and came around the bar.

I faced her.

She placed her arms around my waist and pressed her body against mine. All the while she was looking up into my face and still smiling that sunny smile of hers. She wiggled her hips a little bit. "Are you horny?"

"Now I am."

"Well, that's just too bad," she said, frowning, "because you are not going to get any today."

"Why not?"

"Because I'm on my period."

"Oh, I see."

"But I suppose I can take care of you another way."

"Where is Cedric?"

"Downstairs, reading a script."

"Does he know you're up here?"

"Yes. I told him I was coming up to borrow something to read, you know, like a novel or something. You and Sophia have lots of paperback books lying around. I really do want to borrow a novel, if you don't mind, and if we're quick..." I felt her hand down there.

I stopped her, holding her hand. "Let's go to the couch."

She got up, took my hand, and led me to the couch.

When we finished, she got up and went to the bathroom. I heard the toilet flush, then water running in the face bowl.

Regina came out and stopped at the end table by the couch where we kept a stack of paperback novels. Some we brought with us from New York, and previous tenants had left some. Regina selected *To Kill a Mockingbird, Rosemary's Baby, Cat's Cradle, From Here to Eternity, Sister Carrie,* and *As I Lay Dying.* "Can I take these?"

"Sure. Come back for more whenever you like."

"I'll come back for more all right."

"I bet you will."

I walked her to the door and kissed her goodbye. She turned back and said, "You should come to the rodeo with us tomorrow."

I knew about the rodeo. I'd read about it in one of those tourist brochures left in the apartment, but did I want to sit with Cedric and Regina in the hot sun, watching men on horseback roping and bringing down wild horses? It was a charreada, a public fiesta. The cowboys competed in seeing how fast they could rope and bring down an untamed horse or bull or cow. They would be using young wild horses. Thinking back to the bullfight, I said, "Thanks, Regina, but I don't think I'm up to going."

I would feel uneasy sitting there in the hot sun with the two of them.

"Okay, suit yourself," said Regina.

I watched her go down the steps. I kept the door open till I heard her close her door downstairs. I went back to the typewriter, but I couldn't write. I typed the word "deception" and gazed at it. What did it mean? What about my deception? How was I living with it? Was there a poem here?

I was trying to own my deception. In the privacy of my mind I felt I was facing it, but more importantly for me, I was forgiving myself for deceiving Sophia and Cedric, and forgiving myself by having these meetings with Regina.

I made excuses. I reminded myself that in nature deception was a tool of survival. The lion hid behind a rock the color of its coat and when the zebra was close enough, it leaped out and brought down the zebra. In winter, for better camouflage, the snowshoe rabbit changed its color to white.

The caribou also changed colors according to the season. The weasel, the arctic fox, wolves, the hamster, lizards, all changed colors for protection or seasonally, and all the changing was done in the name of deception.

All of these changes were acts of deception in the interest of self-protection or survival. Nature was rampant with deception, and human beings, I told myself, were part of nature—not apart from it. There was no morality in nature. Perhaps nowhere in the universe was there morality except in the affairs of human beings.

My deception was not about survival. It was about pleasure.

My Christian conscience needed forgiveness, so I forgave it. I had no priest to go to. I was not religious. Absolved, I might be able to now write a poem about "deception" and continue living with deception itself, but wouldn't I, in the future, need to forgive myself again and again? The prospect was grim.

It was seven a.m. and I was still in bed but not asleep when I heard the apartment door open. As far as I knew, only two other people had keys to this apartment, Señor Perez and Sophia. I shouted out, "Who's there?"

No answer. There was a thud. I heard footfalls coming toward the bedroom.

I sat up on the side of the bed.

Then Sophia's face appeared around the doorframe. She was smiling. "It's only me. I'm back!"

I felt relief and resentment at the same time. She was back, and it was true I wanted her back. I loved her, but I had no idea where our relationship would go from here. I was mad at her. I thought going to Yelapa alone was a reckless and foolish thing for her to have done.

I consoled myself with the artificial idea that everybody had something they were not proud of. I told myself there was always a price to pay for the pleasures of a secret rendezvous. There was a price to pay for foolish decisions. There was also a price to pay for spending so much time at the typewriter. I was losing Sophia. I was possibly accomplishing one thing, and in the process, losing another, both enormously valuable to me.

Seeing Sophia, I wasn't sure she was back to stay. I had to wait and see. Perhaps she'd returned to pick up more of her things. Most of her belongings were still here in the apartment. She'd taken only a toothbrush, toothpaste, a hairbrush, a comb, soap, tampons, deodorant, underwear, socks and two pairs of jeans, two shirts, plus the clothes on her back when she left.

Sophia had lost weight, and she was deeply sunburned. She didn't tan; she burned.

She left the bedroom.

I got out of bed, showered and dressed.

I found her sitting out on the balcony, and I saw how unhappy she looked. Her eyes were bloodshot. She'd been crying.

I sat down in the chair alongside her. She reached for my hand. I hesitated to extend it. She withdrew her hand. She said, "I don't blame you for not wanting to touch me."

"How are you?"

She said, "I feel so stupid, so very stupid."

"What happened over there?"

"I went over thinking it would be an idyllic life, and it turned out to be anything but idyllic." She inhaled and exhaled. "I was so naïve!"

"You couldn't tell what they were about when we went over there?"

"No, I couldn't."

"What did you find out?"

"The whole encampment is just one big ego-trip for John Sharp. All the women are at his disposal. Apparently, years ago, he and Betsy Mae were married, but they're divorced now. He's legally married to Jean now, but she's into women. She and Janice spent a lot of nights together."

"What's Roy's role?"

"Roy is apparently homosexual. He's not involved with any of the women. He may also be celibate. He spends a lot of time off meditating by himself, and when he's in camp he walks around looking very pious."

"Is Sharp bi?"

"I don't know. I hadn't thought about that. Maybe he is."

"I guess the kids are Sharp's?"

"Yes. They look like him, too. The women take turns sleeping with Sharp."

"Did you sleep with him?"

"No!" She sounded indignant. Her voice cracked, and her eyes blinked several times and she looked down at the floor.

"He never asked you to sleep with him?"

"Sure, he asked me, but I refused. I slept in a tent with Janice and Louise, that older woman."

"What did you spend your time doing?"

"I helped with the kids and cooking and the sewing and keeping the camp clean. Sanitation and the outdoor toilet situation are big problems. I had to clean the toilet, too. All the women took turns cleaning the toilet."

"That must have been fun."

"Very funny. Going there was the dumbest thing I've ever done."

Around ten that night, I got into bed to read a bit before going to sleep. Across the bedroom, Sophia was undressing and getting ready to join me in bed. I said, "Are you going to sleep on the couch?"

She looked surprised. "Huh? You don't want me to sleep with you? Okay, if that's the way you want it, I'll sleep on the couch."

She grabbed a couple of blankets and a couple of pillows from the closet and quickly left the room.

The next day Camille and Miranda came. They were delighted to see Sophia. She embraced Miranda, who, by now, had become very attached to Sophia. When they finished cleaning, Sophia sat at the counter with Miranda and together they ate ice cream. Camille was putting the cleaning things away in the closet.

After Camille and Miranda left, I went out on the balcony to watch the morning mist lift as the sun was burning it away. The morning fishing boats were still far out on the bay. As usual, they'd been out there since before daylight. Construction workers nearby had their portable radio up loud playing mariachi.

Sophia came out and stood beside me.

I looked at her. "Why did you leave Yelapa?"

"I told you yesterday why I left."

"I mean, was there an incident…?"

She pondered the question, then said, "I guess I got fed up with the women."

"Not Sharp?"

"Huh? Oh, yes, him too, but the women kind of ganged up on me, some of them did. Betsy Mae and Lea mainly led the attack on me. They resented my coming there."

"Sharp forced you on them for his own benefit."

"What? No! What do you mean 'his benefit'?"

"He wanted you there; they didn't."

She didn't respond to that, but I could see she was considering it, perhaps for the first time.

I thought about Sophia's Mexican lover. Had she broken off relations with him while in Yelapa? Or had she kept up that relation while living there by coming over by boat to see him? If not, was she planning to resume that affair?

"Now what, Sophia?"

"If you'll take me back… I mean, I'm sorry. I know you're mad at me for going away like that, but if we can be a couple again…"

I felt completely numb and speechless. I didn't want to be difficult, but I didn't feel like touching her. I knew I still loved her, but for the moment no longer felt close to her, not the way I had felt before we came to Mexico, but in the abstract I still loved her, and I still felt kindly toward her.

"If we could leave Puerto Vallarta and start over fresh somewhere, I mean, somewhere else here in Mexico…?" she said.

I didn't answer. While she was gone, I'd wanted her back. Now that she was back, I had no idea how to respond to her proposition. I hesitated.

Sophia came into the kitchen while I was making myself a cup of coffee. She was dressed to go out.

She looked at the calendar on the wall. "Oh, look, it's August 22nd already. August is almost over."

"And in America, flower children are sowing peace and love."

"What?"

"Forget it," I said. "It was nothing."

She sighed. "Say, listen, Regina and I are going shopping this morning. I don't know how long I'll be gone."

She slammed the door and ran down the steps. I heard Regina's voice in the hallway. Then I heard the downstairs door slam. Then they were gone. I thought, this is probably not a good idea.

I was at the typewriter when Sophia returned three hours later. She was carrying a large flat box. "Want to see what I bought?"

"Sure," I said. I got up and met her by the counter. She flopped the box on the counter and opened it. Then Sophia held up a fancy cotton poncho, white, with a painting on the front. "What is the painting about?"

"It's the Blessed Virgin of Guadalupe healing a man whose spine was broken while executing the death leap on horseback."

I didn't want to know any more. I said, "So what did you guys do?"

"Let's go out on the balcony. It's interesting. She's an interesting girl."

Out on the balcony, we sat side by side. It had rained for about twenty minutes an hour earlier, but now the sky was clear, and out beyond the bay the mountain range was turning from ultramarine to turquoise. The sky all the way down to the horizon was cerulean.

Sophia said, "We walked around window shopping, stopping in all the little shops along the way. She bought a scarf and some sandals and earrings, but what I wanted to say is…" and Sophia lowered her voice to a whisper, fearing that somebody downstairs on the sidewalk might hear. "Regina came on to me."

"Are you sure?"

"I'm pretty sure. She kept telling me how much she was attracted to me, and was stroking my hair, right in public, stroking my hair. Imagine that?"

"I'm trying to." Actually, I was not surprised to hear this. Regina had said she was bisexual, that she liked women maybe even more than men. "What did you say?" I said.

"I let it pass, till she asked me if I wanted to get together."

"Get together?"

"Yes, she said 'get together,' leaving it ambiguous." Sophia was truly amazed. "I told her I like men. Then she pretended she didn't mean get together sexually, just get together as friends, she said."

"Interesting." I laughed. I couldn't help laughing. Life was funny. People were funny.

Four days later, around ten in the morning, Sophia was sitting on the couch reading a novel. Her legs were crossed. I was at the typewriter trying to decide between

> Pastel light luminous in morning haze

or

> Luminous pastel light in morning haze

when suddenly Sophia screamed at the top of her voice. She'd jumped up on the couch and threw the novel on the floor.

I leapt up, not knowing what was happening. I shouted, "What is it?"

Speechlessly she pointed to the floor. There was a small green iguana on the floor near the couch standing with his head raised, looking up at her. He had spikes on his upper back, a double chin, and the face of a Hollywood monster with bulging eyes.

Sophia had thrown the book at him, but it had missed, and he didn't seem frightened by her screams, but he was curious. He kept watching her.

The task was to make him leave the apartment, but how?

I got the broom and went toward him. That was all it took. He shot around the couch and headed for the balcony. That was what I wanted him to do. I chased after him to keep him going.

On the balcony, he crawled out along the stucco wall of the building, stopped, and looked back at me. I hit the wall with the broom, then he jumped down to the sidewalk and disappeared around the corner.

After the iguana was no longer in sight, I wondered why I had thought of it as a "he" rather than a "she" or an "it." The iguana might have been female. It was unsettling to realize that I tended to think of monsters as male, rather than an "it" or female. In the end, I was comfortable with personifying the iguana, rather than identifying it as a thing.

To calm my nerves, I went to the kitchen to pour myself a cup of coffee. I turned on the radio. In Spanish, the newsman said Mayor Daley in Chicago had just opened the Democratic National Convention, and that Vice President Hubert Humphrey was being nominated for president.

Sophia came over and said, "God, my heart is still beating like crazy. That thing scared the living daylights out of me."

I sipped my coffee and watched her pour herself a cup.

She said, "This place is so open, those things can just come in here anytime. Now I know I'm going have nightmares."

I wondered, how did she survive in Yelapa, sleeping in a tent on the ground with a bunch of people she didn't really know?

The next day, there was a knock at the door. I got up and opened it. Cedric was standing there, smiling. "Hello, sport," he said. "May I come in, or were you busy working? I hear the typewriter all the time. I don't want to take you from your work, but..."

"It's all right," I said. "Come on in. What's up?"

"The screen test fell through. I don't know exactly when we are leaving, but I didn't want to leave before having a chat with you."

I grew tense with anxiety and fear that he might want to talk with me about Regina, but I kept calm. "Sure, let's go out on the balcony. You want a beer?"

"Oh, no thanks."

We sat side-by-side looking out toward the bay.

"I just wanted to again wish you good luck with your poems. Are you having any luck getting them published individually?"

"Oh, yes, in fact just yesterday I got an acceptance letter from a magazine in Mexico City called *Nuevo Mundo*. I've published there before."

"Congratulations. Well, good luck with the book of poems you're working on, and I wanted to let you know that my wife is sweet on you. I love her, you know. She's a very beautiful, sexy woman. I'm madly in love with her and I know she's a flirt. She can't help it. Are you attracted to her?"

"Not at all," I lied. I felt a great need to protect his feelings, to give him the answer he wanted.

"I didn't think so. You're a good person, James. I can tell. Maybe that's why she's sweet on you."

"How do you know she's sweet on me?"

"She called your name in her sleep last night; she went, 'James, oh, James!,' and we don't know anybody else named James." He was smiling, sadly smiling.

"Cedric, there are so many people named James. How could you know for sure she was dreaming about me? Plus, dreams don't mean anything. Could she have been saying 'Jane, oh, Jane'? Sometimes a dream is about fear."

"It was 'James,' all right. I guess you're right. Say, let me get your address in New York so we can stay in touch."

"Sure," I said, "I would like that."

He took out an ink pen and his little black address book and looked at me, poised to write.

I gave him our address and phone number, but I didn't expect to ever hear from them again; people always said, "Let's stay in touch," without really meaning it.

I wondered why people impose on each other promissory obligations they have no intention of keeping. A promise assigned a moral obligation. A bond of trust was made. It was not so different from an oath in a courtroom or a pledge in a secret society. A social contract was established.

Yet it was widely believed, I'd learned in my philosophy class in college, that throughout virtually all cultures people believed that a promise was something to be honored, and that to break a promise was akin to bringing upon oneself a curse.

So I'd agreed to something I didn't particularly want to agree to. I'd told another lie, a lie to keep the peace. It was deceptive.

Cedric stood up. "I'd better get back downstairs and get back to reading that script. I'm going to be going to Boston for the lead role in *A Raisin in the Sun*. I like to know all the parts by heart."

"That's great, Cedric! Congratulations!"

In another context, Cedric and I might have become close friends. I had great respect for him and his steadfast devotion to his craft, but instead, my affair with Regina complicated any possibility of a true friendship.

I'd read that in some other cultures and places, like France or England, such friendships with the spouse of one's lover were sincere and common. Were we Americans too puritanical for such an arrangement?

My poetry manuscript was now finished. A couple of weeks ago, I'd walked up to the post office and sent off twelve typewritten formal letters to university presses, asking their editors if they'd like to consider my collection for possible publication.

A day or two earlier, I'd heard from and responded to Mr. Graham Rosamond, editor at Kensington & Livingston University Press in Middletown, Pennsylvania. They specialized in publishing high quality books of poetry. They put out about twelve a year. Rosamond said he'd like to consider my manuscript, titled *Rendezvous in the Rain*, for possible publication by the press. My cover letter was brief: Thank you for your interest in considering my collection. I look forward to hearing from you when you have had a chance to read the poems. Thank you.

I put the manuscript in a manila envelope with the cover letter, and went to the Puerto Vallarta post office and mailed it to him. I'd also sent my editor, Cynthia Bellringer at the *Brooklyn Daily Observer*, word on a postcard that I would be returning to New York before long. I said, "I'll be ready to resume doing editorial work." I told her that my phone number would remain the same as before.

After breakfast, I said to Sophia, "Let's do something together!"

"Wow! You really mean it?"

"Sure. What'd you like to do?"

"Let's go up the hill and explore the galleries and the little craft shops."

"Let's go," I said, feeling suddenly elated, glad I was making an effort. I'd put my work aside and out of mind.

In ten minutes, we were in the business district of vendors and shops and galleries. We'd open a door and a little bell over the door would ring, letting the proprietor know we'd entered. For about two hours, we wandered in and out of shops and galleries, looking at mostly tourist junk.

Then we came to Galeria Mateo. With a smile, the proprietor introduced himself. He was Mateo Cartillo, a little man with a toothy smile and a potbelly. I said, "¿Podemos mirar alrededor?"

Señor Cartillo said, "Ser mi invitado, por favor."

Here, Sophia was especially interested in the colorful pottery in the front room. Then we wandered to the back room for more pottery, shirts, and straw hats. Sophia picked among the items. We said thank you to Señor Cartillo. We left that shop without buying anything there.

In one shop, Sophia spotted a bright red and yellow poncho. She tried it on and looked at herself in the wall mirror. "How do I look?"

I said, "You look beautiful. Buy it!"

She bought it.

We wandered in and out of several other similar shops and stopped also at a few kiosks near the bay before going back.

On the way back down Hidalgo, Sophia took my hand and smiled. She was happy we'd done something together. I was happy that she was happy.

Cedric got a telegram from the well-known Boston producer/director Robert Ogden Miller, giving him the final confirmation he'd been waiting for. He wanted Cedric to play the part of Walter Lee Younger in *A Raisin in the Sun* at the Wilbur Theatre.

Cedric was excited. He said, "Miller is a great director! And he managed to get Clara Deloris Ellison to do the production design. A few years ago, I met her in New York. She's the greatest ever! Everybody calls her C.D."

I said, "Sounds like you're on your way!"

So Cedric and Regina said their goodbyes to us and to Puerto Vallarta. We had lunch with them the day before they left.

I said to Regina, "Any word from the people at *Hair*?"

"No, but there's a chance I may get an important part in another musical yet to be determined. I've heard from the great Vivian Wayland. She directs the Terpsichore Dance Troupe at the Odella Theater in Southampton. She's seen my work and I know she's serious about hiring me. So I'm hoping! Fingers crossed!"

Sophia and I wished her well. Sophia hugged her, then I also gave her a good goodbye hug. I was both sad and glad to see her leave.

A few days later, Estelle and Grant also said goodbye and took a taxi to the airport. They were returning home to Iowa.

We also wished them well.

While I worked, Sophia resumed her late morning walks, but now she always came back by lunchtime.

One day I was standing on the balcony, as I often did, to relax and to clear my mind of poetry chaos and, I guess, too, to wait for inspiration. I remembered the words of Socrates: "It was not wisdom that enabled poets to write their poetry, but a kind of instinct or inspiration." As usual, Socrates was right, but probably more instinct than inspiration.

All day one day, on the other side of Hidalgo, men were digging a hole. I was curious, but I had no idea what it was for. They finished around five in the afternoon.

Sophia had been sleeping on the couch for about a week. Then one night, around two in morning, she crawled into bed beside me. I felt the weight of her body as she settled. She turned her back to me and she slept like that the whole night, keeping her body as far from mine as possible.

This continued. We were living under the same roof without having physical contact. It felt like a waiting period. I didn't think of it as a standoff. I wasn't punishing her. She may have thought of it as my attempt to punish her. I believed I enjoyed sex with her more than she with me. So, if anything, I was punishing myself. Why? I simply was not ready.

One day, I was sitting on the balcony gazing out at the bay, thinking of nothing in particular, while, hopefully, a poem was developing in my unconscious mind.

Then, below, on the other side of Hidalgo, a truck drove up and stopped beside the hole that the men had dug a few days earlier. On the truck was a large pole. It looked like a telephone pole. Now I understood what the hole was for.

I shouted, "Sophia, come out here!"

She came running out to the balcony.

"They're getting ready to plant that telephone pole." The men were singing corridos as they lifted the pole from the truck.

"Oh, this is the kind of thing I came to Mexico to see," she said.

The men got the pole upright and walked it over to the hole.

Sophia said, "Oh, my God, they're going to place it. Oh, my God!" She sounded excited.

The singing was louder and louder as they got the pole over the hole.

"This is amazing," Sophia cried out.

The men got the pole into the hole and stood it upright, and in unison they shouted in triumphant and absolute victory. They poured cement into the hole to seal the pole in. They stabilized the pole with props, apparently till the cement had a chance to harden.

Sophia sighed. "That was fun to watch!" She laughed. "It was straight out of classical antiquity! The ancient Americas! Even ancient Egypt! And ancient Pompeii!"

Thursday afternoon I got up from the typewriter, stretched my arms, yawned, and walked out onto the balcony.

I said, "Let's move to San Miguel de Allende."

Sophia was already out there reading *The Razor's Edge*, a novel. She looked up. "Wow! You really mean it?"

The idea of San Miguel de Allende had come to me a few days earlier while looking through a travel magazine a previous tenant had left in the apartment.

"Absolutely."

"That's a wonderful idea. Leaving this place is what I've wanted for a while now," she said.

My optimism about our relationship was gone, yet the relationship was continuing. Somewhere in the back of my mind, before coming to Mexico, I had thought there was a possibility that our relationship might deepen, become deeper than romantic love, deepen into a lasting lifetime attachment, one with complete trust, that we might eventually marry and spend the rest of our lives together. Shortly after arriving in Mexico I began to see signs that the possibility for those things were quickly eroding.

Now we were planning to move to San Miguel de Allende rather than separating. Why? Habits were difficult to break. We had drifted into this relationship. Trust was gone. Yet some amount of loyalty remained.

No matter what, I would continue to write. I remembered the writer Jean Rhys somewhere saying she had to write because if she didn't, she would not have earned her death, her right to die in peace. That was how I felt about writing poetry. I didn't want to have to choose between Sophia and poetry.

At least that was the way I was feeling as we prepared to leave for San Miguel de Allende. At the same time, I felt we'd reached an impasse.

I went across the hall and told Señor Perez we were planning to leave soon, to move up to San Miguel de Allende.

He said, "Ah, you'll be there in time for the Mexican Independence Day, September 16th."

"We'll rent a car and drive there," I said.

"You can't rent a car here. No, not a good idea. The roads are too bad for driving. You'd run into animals and farm equipment on many of the roads. Some of the roads are not paved. No, best to fly."

The next day, Friday, September 13th, we walked up to the travel agency on Hidalgo across from the bank and bought airline tickets for San Miguel de Allende. The clerk was a young woman with an apple-shaped face with dimples and a halo of black hair.

While smiling, she said, "There's no direct flight to San Miguel de Allende. There's a stop and layover in Mexico City. Then you fly to Guadalajara. You will arrive too late for the flight to San Miguel. You must stay overnight there and fly to San Miguel the next afternoon at 4:15 p.m."

On the wall behind the clerk there were red and blue posters advertising the bullfights and the rodeos. The bull shown on the poster was suspended in midair, having leapt up trying to dislodge the banderillas. The clerk stamped our tickets and stuck each into its own separate sleeve. She said, "Enjoy San Miguel!"

Saturday morning, around 10 a.m., I walked up to the square in front of Our Lady of Guadalupe where there were always a few taxis parked along the curb. That morning three old black and yellow taxis were there.

Observing the protocol, I approached the one first in line and I told the driver we wanted to go to the airport. He said, "Entra en el taxi." I got in and directed him to our place. Our plane was due in at noon.

E LEVEN A.M. WE WERE THERE WAITING, watching for the Mexicana airplane's arrival. It was late.

Finally, we saw it coming toward the airport. Three other people were waiting with us. They were in suits and I assumed they were businessmen.

The airplane was an hour late when it finally landed. I watched the propeller as it kept turning after the motor was turned off.

Okay, I thought, we're in no hurry. Who knows? We might like Guadalajara and decide to stay there. It was a big city with lots to offer. We might listen to some mariachi music, drink a little tequila, and even go to the zoo. Sophia liked zoos.

We might visit the ornate neoclassical cathedral with twin gold spires. I thought since we have to spend time there, we might as well look around. Maybe we could also see the Jose Clemente Orozco murals at the Palacio de Gobierno I'd seen advertised.

When the propeller stopped, the agent at the gate told us it was safe to go out to the plane. The sun was bright, and it was already hot, especially as we walked out onto the sticky and steamy hot tarmac. The odor of tar was sharp, and the sun was so bright it was blinding.

A worker threw our baggage on a pushcart and pushed it past us out to the plane and loaded it in the baggage compartment.

We then climbed the metal steps up into the plane. The three businessmen followed. The five of us, plus about six or seven other people already there, were the only passengers.

Sophia said, "We may die in this thing."

I laughed, but I was thinking that what she said was possible. Yes, possible, but unlikely.

During the flight, the businessmen talked loudly and continuously about the local economy, politics, and Mexico's troubled relationship with the United States. The stream of air from the ceiling didn't do much to dispel the stuffy hot plastic smell of the interior.

When we reached Mexico City an hour and ten minutes later, Sophia and I remained seated. The three businessmen and half the others got off. The plane then quickly filled up with new passengers.

Sophia was sitting by the window and gazing out, apparently at nothing in particular. I was reading a little book of Emily Dickinson's poems I'd found in our apartment in Puerto Vallarta, apparently left there by some previous tenant.

One hour and twenty-five minutes later, we landed in Guadalajara. I was tired and Sophia looked tired, but we got in a taxi and were delivered to two-star Hotel Diego Santiago. We then found nearby a little taco place, ate dinner. Back at the hotel, we both showered and went to bed.

I slept soundly most of the night. I was dreaming I was searching for a misplaced key. Apparently, the key was for a door to a house I desperately needed to enter. Then morning came. I woke, and I was relieved to be free of the problem.

Because it was Sunday, we couldn't go to the Chamber of Deputies to see the Orozco murals or do most of the other things I'd thought about back at the airport in Puerto Vallarta.

We walked around the commercial district till lunchtime, then we ate lunch.

Back to the hotel we collected our luggage, paid our hotel bill, got a taxi back to the airport where we waited. I felt like we were in a kind of twilight zone.

The little white, blue, and green twin-engine Otter plane taxied in at about 3:30 p.m. In less than an hour, we were climbing the steps to the plane, followed by three other passengers: a middle-aged woman with hair tinted purple, and a teenage girl with curly light brown locks who were traveling together, and a young man in a cheap, ill-fitting suit came on next. He was alone. Then the uniformed flight attendant closed the door.

We were ready.

Over the loudspeaker, the pilot said, "Las nubes pueden causar algunos baches."

Sophia grabbed my arm in fear. "Oh, God," she said. "I'm scared, and now he says we're going to fly through bad weather."

"Just a few clouds," I said. "It'll be all right. Don't worry."

Soon we took off, climbed into those dark grey clouds the pilot promised us, and sure enough the little aircraft started bouncing and wobbling. It was very unpleasant. If we weren't zigzagging through a thunderstorm, it certainly felt like it.

We landed finally in a recently cleared area outside the city. It was serving as an airstrip. Trees and shrubbery were still green and piled up around the edges. Beyond the area in the distance were two or three farmhouses and pastures.

The luggage was quickly taken from the plane and placed on the ground, not on the usual four-wheeled flatbed.

Two taxis and a couple of private cars, one a fairly new metallic white Buick, the other an old dark blue Chevy, were parked at the edge of the field where the dirt road ended. The woman and the teenage girl got into the Buick. The young man got into the Chevy. Both cars backed up, turned around, and left the area.

One of the taxi drivers came over to the plane and picked up our luggage. He was a big man with bushy eyebrows and bowlegs. "Bienvenido. ¿Primera vez?" Then he said in English, "Welcome. First time?"

We were now walking to his taxi, an old green Ford with a black stripe around it, and the word 'Taxi' printed in black letters on the passenger door.

"Yes, first time." He clearly had us pegged as gringos.

"You're just in time for the festival. It starts tomorrow. Do you have a place to stay?"

"No, we were hoping you could recommend a hotel?"

"How long are you staying?"

"We don't know. Maybe a long time."

"Then why go to a hotel? How about an apartment? I can take you to a very nice place where you can rent an apartment. A very nice señora runs the place. She would be happy to rent you a nice apartment. Okay?"

I realized we hadn't thought about lodgings.

I looked at Sophia to get her reaction to this proposal. She nodded approval, and I said, "That sounds good. Let's go there."

Sophia and I got into the back seat, and our driver climbed into the driver's seat. I looked at his license on the dashboard. His name was Carlos Acosta.

Sitting there in the back with Sophia, I thought about what we'd gone through in Puerto Vallarta. During this transition period, leaving Puerto Vallarta and arriving in San Miguel, I was hopeful that this move would be a turning point to lay the foundation for a fresh start for us as a couple. I was also still thinking that we needed to do something that we rarely did, talk to each other about us.

Then we entered the city, and stopped at the top of Calle Nemesio Diez with the city stretched out below us. Carlos pulled over to the curb and stopped the car right there, parking alongside a large stucco apartment building with a courtyard. He said, "Amigos, estamos aquí. My friends, we are here."

The place was a Spanish Colonial mansion converted to an apartment building. From down on the sidewalk, we could see up into the courtyard. In the center was a fountain spouting recirculating water. Alongside it was a large succulent plant standing at least ten feet tall, growing out of a circular area of earth about the size of a car tire: The rest of the courtyard, like the fountain, was concrete. There was serenity to the place that pleased me.

Carrying our luggage, Carlos led the way up the two or three steps into the courtyard and put down the luggage by the office door. He rang the doorbell of the landlady, whose name, he said, was Señora Angelica Fatima Flores.

A woman, maybe fifty years old, opened the door and she greeted us with a big smile. She had white hair and she was rather plump and wearing an apron. She said she was Señora Flores.

We introduced ourselves.

Carlos apparently had some kind of ongoing arrangement with her. He probably brought foreigners to her all the time and got a kickback for doing so. He explained that we needed an apartment.

She said, "Ciertamente es posible."

I paid Carlos and tipped him generously, and he waved happily to us and skipped down the steps back to his car.

Now we were in the hands of Señora Flores. She led us across the courtyard to a door named and numbered Apartamento 1. We picked up our luggage and followed. She said, "This one just became vacant yesterday. The girls finished cleaning it this morning."

Aside from her apartment door and the one about to be ours, four or five other doors faced the courtyard.

Inside the apartment, Señora Flores took us to the small kitchen. Sophia said, "This is nice. I can work with this."

Then Señora Flores showed us the small bedroom. The bed was large with flanking bedside tables holding small lamps; there was one window. From the bedroom window I saw the city below with its crowded jigsaw puzzle of colorful orange rooftops, many church steeples, and the grand steeple of the Archangel cathedral looming above all.

Then she led us to the living room that contained a green wool couch with two matching chairs, and a large fireplace with a stack of wood alongside it.

I said, "We'll take it. How much per week?"

"En dólares estadounidenses doscientos, in U.S. dollars, two hundred," she said with a smile.

I took out my wallet and peeled off two hundred dollars.

"Just one week?" she said.

"Yes, we'll pay one week at a time, if that's okay."

"Eso estará bien."

The truth was I wasn't sure how long we'd be there, or how long we wanted to be there, or for that matter how long Sophia and I would be together. The relationship had become like a bad smoking or drinking habit. For your health's sake, you know you should stop, but you keep putting it off.

We thanked Señora Flores and we walked back with her to the courtyard to get our luggage.

She said, "Have you been to Guanajuato before?"

"No," we told her.

Señora Flores said, "The state is very old, and famous for silver mining in the old days. San Miguel is an old colonial-era city. It's been here since 1541. We're very high above sea level. We have many, many churches, too, maybe twenty or more. I lose count. The bells ring constantly. You will like it or you will hate it."

"Oh, I like the sound of church bells," said Sophia.

Señora Flores smiled and sucked her teeth.

After Señora Flores left, I said, "Sophia, we need to talk about where we are going with this relationship, or even if we have a relationship."

We were in the living room. Waiting for her to respond, I sat down in one of the armchairs. Sophia was standing by the window that looked out on the city below. Her back was to me. She looked back over her shoulder. "Where do you think it's going?"

"I'm asking you. Are we in a committed relationship?"

"I guess we could be."

"What I'm hearing you say is that we are not at the present time in a committed relationship." I was looking directly at her.

"I didn't say that."

"You said, 'We could be.' That implies that we are not in a committed relationship."

"Then I guess we're not." She was avoiding eye contact.

"I can see we're not getting anywhere." I stood up and went and stood beside her. She turned to me. I said, "I love you," trying to believe it beyond the abstract.

"I love you, too," she said, glancing up quickly at me.

"We came to this place with two different agendas: you wanted to have a good time, and I came to try to finish my book. Maybe coming here was a bad idea."

"You mean coming to San Miguel?"

"No, I mean coming to Mexico. We were not on the same page."

"No two people are ever on the same page," she said.

"That's a pretty grim observation."

"Think about it. It's true." She placed her arms around me and kissed me on the mouth. "I'm hungry. Why don't we go out and find something to eat? I want some fried fish."

It was true: Sophia and I were tired but also hungry. Hunger won out. We left the conversation that was going nowhere, and we left the apartment and walked down Calle Nemesio Diez, a narrow street of ancient grey and rounded cobblestones. On both sides were casas of one and two-story stone or brick or stucco. They were painted various colors from bright green to blood red.

This was clearly the historic district. I felt we'd lucked out by getting a place, unknowingly, in the historic district.

Many of the casas had iron bars on the windows that looked out onto the narrow sidewalk. Many also had gardens on the rooftops. I imagined most of the cooking and eating and the general living went on up there.

We walked till we found a little restaurant on the right side of the street. It was getting dark, so they turned on the outside lights. We sat outside in the garden area enclosed by a high stone wall. It was getting late. We were the only customers. No fish on the menu; we were far from the ocean. We ate chicken tacos, rice and beans, and drank beer.

When we returned, the apartment was very cold so I built a fire in the fireplace, and we stretched out on the shag rug in front of it. We made love for the first time since her return from Yelapa.

The next morning when we woke, we heard celebratory sounds: singing, drums, fireworks, the Grito de Independencia. It was Monday, the sixteenth, Independence Day. Mexico was celebrating its independence from Spain.

We lay side by side listening to the sounds.

Sophia said, "They've started already. This is the day in 1810 when a priest named Father Miguel Hidalgo y Costilla shouted, 'Independencia!' Eleven years later, Mexico was free from Spain."

"Took a long time."

"Everything takes a long time," she said. "It takes a long time for love to grow."

She was making an interesting point, one about another kind of love, one we didn't have. I looked at my watch. It was five minutes after seven.

The bedroom was still cold from the night. I resisted making a fire. We took our time. We made love again. We showered. We dressed.

Sophia got her purse and we left. By the time we got outside it was almost noon. We felt the difference in altitude: the air was colder. We were in the mountains.

We headed down Nemesio Diez along the narrow sidewalk, headed for the plaza, the place of that grand 17th century neo-Gothic cathedral, La Parroquia de San Miguel Arcángel, with its massive pink façade. We'd read about this one in a travel brochure. In front of it would be the Jardín Allende, a carefully manicured public garden.

On the way down, the crowds were so thick along the narrow sidewalks that the going was slow, yet we were making progress, weaving our way through spectators watching orderly children marching in the street dressed in colorful dresses, and men in cowboy outfits parading on horseback. The sounds were loud and dense. They were the sounds of great and joyous excitement.

Now we were in the crowd in front of the old cathedral.

Then I felt a hand tugging at my sleeve. I looked around. The hand belonged to a little boy with red hair. He had a tough face and he was dressed in raggedy clothes. He was maybe eight or nine or older. He was standing behind me, and he was trying to get my attention.

In English, I said, "What is it?"

"Señor, I be your guide for the festival? I no trouble."

"We don't need a guide," I said. "Thank you."

Then suddenly he grabbed Sophia's purse and ran. Sophia screamed and shouted, "My purse! My purse!"

Still running, the boy was bumping into people in the crowd, but he didn't get far. In his effort to get away, he nearly knocked down a big fat local man with a handlebar moustache. The man threw his arms around the boy and held him, and the man kept saying over and over to the boy, "¡Chico malo!"

The little redheaded boy was struggling against the man's grip, but it was an iron-tight grip. The boy was shouting, "¡Déjame ir, déjame ir!"

The ruckus attracted the police on the outer edge of the crowd. Now they were coming through the thicket of people toward the boy and the man.

People cleared the way for the police.

The man held the boy till the two policemen got there.

The boy then dropped the purse and he was red in the face with anger as the two policemen took hold of him.

One policeman, "¡Recoger el bolso!"

The boy said, "¡Policía, no hice nada, no hice nada!"

Again, the policeman said, "¡Recoger el bolso!"

So the boy stooped and picked up the purse.

The policeman said, "Délo a la señora."

Angrily, with tears in his eyes, the boy handed the purse to Sophia.

The policeman said, "Dile a la señora que lo sientes."

In English, the boy said, "I am sorry, lady."

Looking at Sophia, the policeman who made the boy pick up the purse said in English, "Señora, do you wish to press charges?"

"No, I do not. I have my purse back. Thank you, officer, thank you."

He said, "El placer es mío, the pleasure is mine." In Spanish, he said to both of us, "The boy's name is Santiago Angel Lopez. He does this sort of thing all the time. When he is older, I am sure he will land in prison. As soon as he is old enough, that is where he will go. He has no father; Sebastian Juan Lopez, his father, died in prison. The boy's mother, poor Isabella Viviana Marello-Lopez, she is at her wits' end. Santiago is beyond her control."

Both officers tipped their hats to us. Still holding the boy by his arms, the two policemen led him away.

Sophia said, "I feel so sorry for that boy." Tears filled her eyes. She blinked, and they ran down her cheeks. "Shouldn't we give him a few pesos?"

"Sure, why not?"

Sophia caught up with the policemen and the boy, and fishing in the pockets of her jeans, came up with a few pesos. I watched the transaction. Santiago held his little hand out and Sophia dropped the coins into it. One of the policemen smiled and tipped his cap, but the boy didn't say anything. As he pushed the money into his pocket, Santiago looked at Sophia with a fixed frown, squinting eyes and pouting lips.

As we wandered around in the area, watching the fancy children parading and the charros on horseback, we were approached by two young women and two young men. Immediately I took them to be Americans. The handsome one with friendly eyes, a full mouth, and a closely cropped beard, said, "Hi there! We saw what happened. You guys new to Mexico?"

"Not exactly," I said.

"The boy hangs out around the plaza all the time. It's unfortunate. He's had a rough life. It's rumored that his mother was a prostitute and his birth father a tourist from Ireland. His legal father died in prison."

Sophia said, "Oh, what a sad situation to be born into."

"Yes, it is. By the way, my name is Farley Kenton. I'm an art student here at Instituto Allende, down on Ancha de San Antonio." He turned to his friends with a wave of his hand toward them. "We're all art students from the Institute." He pointed to a young man. "Lionel here is an artist too and he lives with us, but he's not enrolled at the Institute."

I shook Farley's hand, then Sophia shook his hand.

We all exchanged names and shook hands. The others were Gwendolyn Williams, a quiet, soft-spoken girl with dark hair and green cat-eyes; Darrell Everett, a robust young man clearly full of himself with self-confidence; Ella Mae Gray, a young woman with very bad facial skin and unsteady, nervous eyes; and Lionel March, a scruffy-looking guy with bloodshot eyes and chapped lips, brittle blond hair, lots of freckles, and thick, stubby hands.

Farley said, "We all share a house with a great rooftop. When the weather is nice, we have parties up there. We're having one this coming Saturday night, starting around six. It will be inside because nights here tend to be too cold. Sometimes the music gets a bit loud for the neighborhood, but for the most part I think they like it. Maybe you two might like to come join the fun this coming Saturday evening?"

Sophia was quick to respond, "Yes, we'd love to!"

Farley wrote down the address on the edge of a cancelled ticket and handed it to me. Our eyes met. I saw that he was a painfully shy young man, maybe two or three years younger than I was. I had a hunch that he was extremely serious and driven.

"Well, James and Sophia, we'll see you guys Saturday around six."

Sophia and I bid them farewell and promised to come.

We stayed out in the crowds, listening to the music and watching the parades, soaking in the festivities most of the day, and around five, we headed back up the hill.

At the steps leading up into the courtyard we saw a woman and a man about to come down. Seeing that four people could not comfortably be on the steps at the same time, they politely stopped and waited for us to come up. I nodded a thank you, and we continued up. At the top, we were face to face with them.

The woman said, "You people must be the new tenants?" She was a short, plump, matronly woman. Her hair was cut short and fitted nicely around her square face. A little moustache was growing over her top lip.

Sophia and I spoke at the same time. "Yes, we are."

With a broad smile, she said, "Nice to meet you. I'm Barbara Hamlin -Frost, and this is my husband George Frost."

He said, "We're from Kenosha, Wisconsin. Where you folks from?" He was also short and stocky, with a little beard and a receding hairline. His ears were unusually large and so was his nose.

"New York," I said.

"Wow!" said Barbara. "The big city!"

They looked to be forty or fifty.

We said it was nice meeting them, and continued up and they continued down the steps. Looking back over her shoulder, Barbara said, "We're in Apartment 4. Come over and join us for a drink sometime."

"We will, we will," said Sophia.

Now, in San Miguel, I daydreamed about a future volume. I jotted down "New and Selected Poems." If I were lucky enough to live that long, I would be an old man by the time such a volume became a reality. At twenty-five, I could not imagine being an old man. In the best of worlds, I would have such a volume long before old age. Besides, old age may never come. I remembered that William Carlos Williams had his first "New and Selected" while still a young man. There was a precedent.

Saturday, we arrived at Farley's party around six-thirty, and the place was full of cigarette and marijuana smoke, and rainbow-colored strobe lights were casting colors around and around the walls, and the loud blasting sounds of the Bee Gees singing "Let There Be Love" were coming from the record player.

Farley led us in. "Get a drink, guys, and make yourself at home."

It was a big room, with a wooden floor and three windows on one side. Mattresses and large pillows were against all four walls all the way around the room. The center of the floor was big and empty. To our left, there was a door ajar to a dark side room, probably a bedroom.

Following the lead of others already seated, Sophia and I found our way to a big pillow on the floor.

A young man, already a bit plastered, asked my name. I told him. He wanted to know what I did. A question I dreaded! No way was I going to say I write poetry. I said, "I'm a freelance editor for a newspaper, but I'm on leave right now."

He nodded, smiled, and said, "I paint."

The apartment was already full of young guys and girls, mostly American, a few from Canada, many of them sitting or lying on the big fluffy pillows and mattresses, smoking and drinking. Some were standing with drinks and cigarettes in their hands, in little groups, deep in conversation.

Now the Beatles were singing "All You Need Is Love," and couples were starting to dance in that big empty space.

Lionel was drunkenly bopping around on the floor by himself with a drink in his hand. He was very smashed. Then suddenly he veered over to us and stuck his hand out to Sophia, in that gesture asking her to dance with him.

Being the gracious girl she was, she smiled and gave Lionel her hand, and he pulled her up from the pillow and spun her out onto the dance floor, wrapped his arms around her, pressing her body into his own, and proceeded to dance drunkenly and awkwardly around on the floor, trying to lead her in step to the music. The way he was handling her bothered me, but I wasn't going to get into a fight with this drunk among all of his friends. At the same time, it looked like Sophia was having a good time. She was smiling, even laughing. She was not pulling away. His hands slipped down to her bottom and he gripped her there, but laughingly she gently removed his hands.

Now suddenly Lionel danced Sophia off the floor and out of the room into the dark side room. I watched her face. All along she was still smiling. I felt a rush of anger as though a sudden danger was closing in on me. It looked to me like she'd gone willingly into that dark room. Smiling! It made me feel helpless. I was trembling with fury. It was like my world had turned upside down. The sound of the Beatles singing "All You Need Is Love" still filled the room, but all the conversation abruptly stopped. Everybody looked at me, obviously to see what I might do. There were no sounds coming from the dark room. My fury grew to rage. With a tightness in my chest and clenched fists, I stood up. This was a dilemma. Was this the way Sophia was ending our relationship? Why would she do this? She was not screaming or calling for help, and everybody was still silent and watching me.

After about five or six minutes back there, we began to hear sounds, bumping sounds and one loud grunt, and Sophia suddenly came out running, with her blouse opened and her skirt on sideways. She was out of breath and at the same time trying to smile apologetically, but it was clear now, as it wasn't before, that she felt terrified and embarrassed and humiliated.

I began to realize that she'd been whirled off the floor, smiling, before she knew it. Once back there she was probably prevented from leaving, but why hadn't she screamed or called for help? Maybe she couldn't. Lionel still hadn't come out.

On wobbly legs, she came over to me. I faced Sophia. She was red in the face yet she was still trying to smile, clearly trying to make light of what had happened. I could tell for sure now she was on the verge of tears. Yet I knew she didn't want to cry in front of these people we didn't know.

I said, "Let's go," and we left without saying anything to Farley or the others.

Without saying anything to each other, we walked up the hill. Sophia walked in front of me up the narrow sidewalk till we got to our place.

Inside, she said, "I'm sorry."

"What happened? Did he rape you?"

"I don't want to talk about it."

"Okay, but if I knew you didn't want to go back there with him, I would have done something, yet I had no way of knowing it wasn't your choice. In the end, I assumed it wasn't, given the way you came out of there."

"I'm embarrassed. I feel like dirt. I feel so humiliated. All those people looking at me, judging."

"Did you know he was taking you into a dark room?"

"I said I don't want to talk about it."

I wanted to comfort her, but since she was shutting me out, I had no idea how to begin. Later that night I said, "Sophia, I feel horrible about what happened to you. If I'd known—"

"I said I don't want to talk about it."

"It all happened so quickly—"

"I don't want to talk about it, James. Let's just go to sleep."

Yet we continued to do things together. We walked the city a lot, exploring its wonders. I still had a great appreciation for Sophia's passion for the anthropological understanding of people's lives. There were times when we stopped along the street to watch one activity or another.

At such times she would explain anthropologically exactly what, on a deeper level, was going on. For example, a couple of days after the disaster at the artist party, we were on a little street in the Santa Julia area, watching two men trying to get a stubborn donkey to move.

Sophia said, "The donkey senses a danger the men are not aware of. He won't budge until that dog over there is no longer in his field of vision."

There was a stray skinny dog sniffing at a garbage can alongside a little taqueria. We waited on the cobblestoned sidewalk to see what would happen as the two men continued to pull at the donkey's bridle.

Sophia said, "Those men think the donkey is deliberately disobeying them. They are taking his actions personally. This is a typical thoughtless human response. This is the sort of thing I love to study in human nature."

"You don't study donkeys in anthropology."

"That is true," she said firmly, smiling.

One of the men shouted, "¡Vámonos, burro, vámonos!"

The other one was offering the donkey a carrot, but he was not interested.

"See," Sophia whispered so they couldn't hear, "if they only knew why he was sitting down, they could try to reassure him that there was nothing to worry about."

I said, "How do you know so much about donkeys?"

"I studied animal psychology, too," she said. "The donkey doesn't run when he senses danger. Whether that's smart or dumb is debatable. But he's no coward. He stops and he often sits down and studies the situation to see what the best course of action might be. He's methodical."

I laughed. "I love it: a methodical donkey."

In the mail forwarded from New York, there was again a postcard, dated September 16th, from Amy Lawrence, saying, "Still waiting for that conversation about poetry— Best wishes, Amy."

Sophia read it over my shoulder. "Who is Amy?"

"A teacher at Warren Lowery."

"Oh. She sounds interested in you."

I turned and looked at her. "How do you infer that from this postcard?"

"I can tell."

"Well, I can't, and I don't think you're reading this postcard correctly. She teaches poetry."

"Sure, sure," said Sophia, with a smirk.

There was also a letter addressed to Sophia here in San Miguel from her friend, Ruth Klein. She went to the bathroom and closed the door to read it.

When she came out, I said, "How's Ruth? What did she say?"

"Oh, not much, just chit-chat, girl-talk stuff, you know."

That day I sent Agnes Ludovic a postcard saying, "We'll be coming back home at the end of September. You should plan on giving up the apartment before then."

I was actually looking forward to returning to life in New York, and this surprised me.

Sophia and I were sitting on a bench in the plaza around noon on the last Tuesday in September when we saw Santiago, the boy with red hair. He was entering the plaza and he seemed to be following an elderly couple that looked like American tourists.

He was wearing jeans too big for him and a red polo pullover also too big for his little body. He was so focused on the elderly couple, he had not yet seen us.

He walked up alongside the elderly man and put out his little hand, obviously asking for money. The man, surprised by the boy's sudden presence at his side, was startled. The couple stopped. The boy kept his hand out.

The elderly man reached into his pocket and pulled out a few peso coins and dumped them in the little extended hand. Santiago sang, "Gracias, Señor hombre Americano!"

When he turned from the elderly couple, he spotted us. I saw fear cloud his face. Sophia waved to him. She said, "Santiago, esta bien, ven a hablar con nosotros."

He hesitated, then smiled, and came across the plaza to us.

"Santiago, I forgive you for taking my purse. Do you understand?"

In English, he said, "Yes, I understand, Señora."

"Here," she patted the seat beside her. "Sit with us a while. It's okay."

Reluctantly, he eased his little body up onto the bench, and sat beside Sophia.

She said, "What do you want to be when you grow up?"

"I want to be astronaut and fly far, far away."

"Why do you want to fly far away?"

"I don't know. It is just what I want. I will fly over the moon."

"What about your family, your mother? Wouldn't you miss her?"

"I take my mother with me."

"I see. Would you come back to Earth to see people?"

He shook his head no.

"Why not?"

"People don't want to see me anymore. I will be far away, up in the sky." He raised his right arm and pointed at the sun.

"You know what might happen to you if you fly too close to the sun, don't you?"

"No, what?"

"You might melt and fall out of the sky. Then what?"

He thought about that for a while, then said, "I no fly to the sun."

Now he suddenly leaped up and walked away toward two women that had just entered the plaza.

They looked like American tourists. When they rebuffed Santiago, he spat at them and ran out of the plaza.

While we were walking back up the hill, Sophia said, "Let's buy our tickets tomorrow. I'm homesick. I want to go home."

She took my hand, and we walked like that all the way to our place. It was the first time we'd held hands in a while.

"Yeah, I think it's time." I'd finished my poetry collection. Thousands of people were writing poems and there were few outlets for publishing them, but I liked my chances. I was optimistic.

The next day, at the travel agency on El Cardo, we bought our Mexicana Airlines tickets: two coach seats to New York's LaGuardia Airport. Flight date: Wednesday, October 2nd. We'd left New York on July 5th and now, four months later, we were ready to return.

A couple of days later, we were eating lunch at El Lugar Feliz Taqueria, just off the plaza, when Farley walked up and said, "Well, well, hello! Didn't know you guys were still in town. May I join you?"

I said, "Sure, have a seat."

He was dressed in natty fashion with a long red scarf thrown around his neck though it was not yet cold. True, earlier that morning it had been chilly enough for the scarf to make sense and it would be cold enough again after sundown. I had to keep reminding myself that San Miguel was located high up in Mexico's mountains.

The fragrance of his cologne was that of green apple.

Farley crossed his legs and leaned back. "Sophia, I want to offer you my sincere apology for what happened to you. It was awful."

She nodded, apparently an acceptance of his apology.

Farley continued, "What happened to you is unacceptable. After you guys left, I threw Lionel out. He was no longer welcome in my apartment. I hear that he left Mexico and returned to the States. He said he drove down here in a 1963 VW bus with fifteen windows. It was a bus painted with 'Peace and Love' and flowers all over it. I imagine it was a carnival going down the street. The thing broke down and he junked it in Mexico City, then he found his way here. He said he was an artist and wanted to hang out with us. So we let him stay."

I said, "Did he ever rape a woman before?"

"I don't know, but he has a history. He's touched women who did not want to be touched and gotten slapped, that sort of thing. He talked a lot about holistic medicine and dharma glory, but he was always drunk and trying to get laid." Farley sighed. "I'm just glad, Sophia, that you kicked him hard in the balls. That is what you have to do with a guy like that. He was badly hurt, but he had it coming to him."

The kick was news to me. Sophia had refused to talk about what happened.

Farley said, "When a guy like that tries to force himself on a woman, she has every right to not only kick him in the balls but to de-ball him, if necessary."

I smiled at the image of a de-balled Lionel.

The waiter came out and said, "¿Señor, te gustaría ordenar?"

"Just a Dos Equis, por favor," said Farley.

The waiter quickly brought the beer.

Farley sipped his beer while we ate our chicken tacos. It was only 2:30 p.m. and already a cool breeze had just started coming down from the higher mountains. It was truly late September weather.

Farley said, "Why did you guys come to Mexico?"

I said, "To get away from the craziness of New York for a change." That was not really the reason, yet it was good enough for the occasion.

"You know, when I first came to Mexico," said Farley, "I didn't want to be in a touristy place like San Miguel, or Cancun or Puerto Vallarta or Oaxaca or San Cristóbal or La Paz or Puebla. I wanted to be in the real Mexico where real life was going on."

Sophia said, "Such as?"

"I come from Chicago, born and bred there. By the time I finished undergraduate work at Northwestern, I knew for sure I wanted to spend my life painting. It is my passion. I was optimistic, and last year the Summer of Love gave me renewed optimism. It felt like we were witnessing the birth of a new world. Everything was changing for the better. All we needed was love, or so it seemed. But at the same time, I was becoming disillusioned. The world no longer respected painting."

Sophia said, "Is that true?"

"Yes, absolutely."

"It's long been that way in poetry," I said.

"You're a poet?"

"I write poetry. I haven't yet earned the right to call myself a poet."

"I understand." Farley frowned. "So I became disillusioned. Like you, I too wanted to get away. I went first to Chapala and checked into a little hotel facing Lake Chapala, but it took me two days to see that I couldn't stay there: there were too many retired capitalist conservative Americans living there around the lake, and I'm such a liberal socialist, they would have banished me, so I saved them the trouble and kept moving."

"Is that a freshwater lake?" I said.

"I don't know," Farley said. "I liked the hills around there, but I had to get away, so I went to Tizapán el Alto, thinking there would be no Americans there. I was right: there were no Americans. The streets were unpaved and muddy when it rained. Starving dogs were wandering around sniffing at piles of garbage. Everybody was poor, no telephone service, hardly any electricity, but it was real, all right."

Sophia said, "Sounds awful."

"But these were the real people, this was real Mexico, not tourist Mexico. I was shown an apartment. The man who showed me the apartment was very kind, but there was a pile of hay in the living room. The family next door was using the empty apartment to store their hay. The kind fellow said, 'They will move the hay, of course.' I thought, my God, this is ridiculous. I can't live in the real Mexico."

Sophia again said, "Sounds awful."

"It was. I looked out the window: a poor pregnant girl, about twelve, and three or four old women, and six or seven farm boys were standing outside, waiting to see what I would do. I imagined they had never seen anybody like me, a gringo, come to their town. No, I thought, there was no way I could live in the real Mexico, so I came here to San Miguel and enrolled at the Institute, and the world still didn't want painting, but I said, 'Screw it.' It's what I do, and I will keep doing it."

"We Americans avoid the real Mexico?" I said.

"That's right. We couldn't stand it. Not for one day," said Farley. "I'm twenty-six, I'm a few years older than Ella Mae, Luke, Gwendolyn, and even Lionel, who's just twenty-two, and God knows I can take a lot, but even I can't take the real Mexico. I know they wouldn't be able to stand it."

At that point, two young American guys, both well dressed but anxious-looking, walked up to us. The one with a ponytail said, "Would you fine folks like to buy some Alcapulco Gold?" He was talking to the three of us.

The other one was nervously looking around.

Before we could respond, the speaker continued, "We're running out of money, but we got plenty of marijuana. It's like our credit card." He laughed at his own joke.

Farley said, "Sorry, I'm allergic to it. Once I tried to smoke a joint and almost died. I spent a week in the hospital."

The speaker said, "How about you, ma'am?"

Sophia said, "No thanks. It's against my religion."

"And you, sir?"

I said, "No, thanks."

The speaker sneered at us, then the two of them stalked off, apparently to try elsewhere to replenish their funds.

Farley said, "I'm not allergic, and I never spent a week in a hospital, but I'm not going to risk being arrested here in Mexico. The jails, from what I've heard, are awful. I've heard horror stories about Americans rotting in these jails just for selling or buying weed."

We talked a bit more with Farley and said goodbye.

With only two days left in September, we were focused on returning home to New York. Colder weather was coming soon to this part of Mexico. Sophia and I were in the apartment. I was trying to start a fire, blowing gently on the burning kindling and paper to get it to ignite and spread, when a knock came at the door.

My first thought: Señora Flores. I opened the door and Barbara Frost stood before me with a big smile. "Hi," she said, "we were just wondering if you and your wife would like to come over and have a drink with us, you know, get acquainted...?"

Sophia came up behind me and said, "Sure, I'll grab my sweater."

As we were walking over to their place, Barbara said, "Good thing you got your sweater. It's pretty chilly in our place."

"Yeah," I said, "I was trying forever to get a fire started."

Their furniture was arranged the opposite of ours, and their front window looked out onto the little courtyard with its fountain. Not a bad view.

George looked up from reading a newspaper when we entered. He seemed surprised to see us. I thought that was odd. He stood up from the couch and said, "Oh, you two came to visit." He had a high-pitched girlish voice.

I said, "Sounds like you didn't expect us? Your wife invited us over."

"I know, I know," he said hastily with a touch of irritation in his voice.

"Come in," Barbara said, and we followed her. "Have a seat, please. What would you like to drink? Sorry, no wine or beer. We have scotch and tequila."

We both said tequila. It was about six o'clock and we hadn't yet had dinner.

We sat down across from where George had been sitting. Barbara was now fussing around at the breakfast counter with crackers and nuts, dumping them onto a platter beside the bottles of booze, and there was a rack of whiskey glasses and a bucket of ice.

"I think we told you we're from Kenosha, Wisconsin," George said. "Have you people ever been to Wisconsin?"

We said no.

Barbara said, "George is from the corporate world where money is God. He thinks in dollar-signs." She laughed and came over with the two tequilas.

He said, "But now I think in pills. I've become a slave to my daily routine of pills: pills for my gut, pills for my high blood pressure, pills for aches and pains, pills for my prostate, pills for things I no longer remember."

I took one sip and put it down on the end table, determined not to take another sip. I felt the sharp burn of the alcohol going down my throat to my empty stomach. I preferred beer or dry white wine.

Barbara sat down in the armchair facing us. George now stood behind her chair, holding his glass of scotch on the rocks. His eyes were already glassy red from drink.

Sophia said, "So, Barbara, what kind of work do you do?"

"We're both retired. Doesn't it show? We're old folks!" She laughed. "I was assistant floor manager in a factory that made home supplies, such as kitchenware and the like. The good Lord blessed me with twenty-five years at that factory without even one day being off for sickness."

George said, "Now we're just tourist bums." He laughed and sipped his scotch.

"The good Lord knows you're the bum, I'm not," said Barbara, laughing. "George and I have been talking about pulling up roots and moving here. Not to San Miguel, it's too expensive. We'd move to maybe someplace like Morelia or San Cristóbal de las Casas or La Bahía de Navidad."

George said, "Yes, we've been talking about it, and that's about all. Talking, but truth be told, I don't like Mexicans very much."

"You just said yesterday you like Mexico," said Barbara.

"I like the country, but I don't like Mexicans."

"The country is Mexicans," said Barbara.

"Yeah, yeah," he said, irritated.

"You like Mexican food," said Barbara.

"Not as much as you think I do," he said.

"Well, you sure have been wolfing down a hell of lot of it since we've been here."

"Yeah, that's true. I do like the food. That's what I mean about liking the country. I like the food and the houses and the… and… you're just trying to confuse me, Barbara." He looked at me. "Let's change the subject. Get off my case, Barbara. What do you folks think of all the race stuff going on back home?"

Sophia said, "What do you mean by 'race stuff'?"

"You know, all the troubles the Negroes are causing. They're giving the police a lot of trouble, tearing up their own neighborhoods."

I was looking at him, but he avoided eye contact with me.

Sophia looked at me, then back at George. She said, "Most of the riots were caused by police mishandling the initial incident."

Barbara said, "Some white man killed that little colored boy down south everybody was talking about. Emmett Till was his name."

George said, "I don't believe for a minute that police caused even one riot and all that other stuff, and the damn hippies and all that crazy stuff they're doing, drugs and everything. All that anti-war stuff…"

Sophia said, "The flower children stand for peace and love."

George laughed. "Peace and love, my foot." He took a big gulp of his scotch. "They're just as bad as the Hispanic people. If we don't stop their proliferation, they're going to take over America. It's already predicted that they'll be the majority. That's pretty scary."

"George!"

"It's true, Barbara. It's true, and I don't like it. Some of them are white, some black, and some brown. How in hell you supposed to know who they are? I tell you, they don't fit in in America. They upset the way we see things. I don't like it and I don't mind saying so. The hippies, the Hispanics, the beatniks, the homos, and the…"

Barbara cut him off. "George, get off this subject. You always get yourself so upset when you start talking about race and stuff."

"Okay, okay. What should we talk about, Jesse?" He was looking at me.

"His name is James, George. James is his name, just like one of Jesus's brothers: James, James, James! Not Jesse!" said Barbara. She sounded exasperated.

"James, what should we talk about?" said George. He was ignoring her.

I didn't really want to hear any more, so I was trying to think of a graceful way to leave, but maybe George didn't merit our departing gracefully. No matter how unpleasant and rude George was, my upbringing didn't permit me do otherwise.

"Actually, we're leaving." I stood up, and Sophia also stood. "So you guys can talk about anything you'd like."

Barbara said, "See what you've done? You've upset our guests. Good Lord, I swear, George, you are so boorish!"

We walked toward the door.

Barbara leaped up and followed us to the door. "I apologize for my husband's behavior. He can be offensive, I know, but he's not really a bad person. We're good Christian people. We were both brought up in the Baptist church and we try to live by the teachings of Jesus. I'm so sorry, so sorry…"

We both said good night and left.

Outside, crossing the yard, Sophia said, "That guy was awful."

"Well, I'm sure he believes he has a valid point, and nothing is going to change his mind. He believes he's a victim."

"Only so many slices of the pie to go around?"

"Exactly. He's worried that the status quo is going to be upset."

We then entered our apartment and closed the door.

Back in our apartment, Sophia said, "Can you believe that guy? What a rude, racist jackass!"

I was familiar with bigotry. While working in the bank my father managed, I occasionally had face-to-face encounters with angry people, and even bigots of one kind or another. Once a customer wanted to cash a very large check. I was not qualified to cash a check that large. I had to call Dad to okay it. The customer cussed me out using racial slurs for not immediately cashing the check.

I sometimes fetched keys for customers who wanted access to their safe deposit boxes. Once or twice, I noticed that the signature did not match the one we already had on the card. On those occasions, when I questioned the discrepancy, I was sometimes the target of anger or even slurs. One woman said, "Go back to the jungle where you came from."

I was called the n-word more than once. We even had drunks and bums coming in, shouting and cussing at everybody. Dad always told me to keep my cool and remain professional. It was difficult, but I followed Dad's advice. George Frost was a familiar type of person.

That night Sophia and I made love. Maybe we were grasping for the way things had been before..

It was close to noon. We hadn't yet decided where we'd go for lunch. We were once again at the central plaza of Parroquia de San Miguel Arcángel, relaxing on a bench when Farley's friends Ella Mae and Gwendolyn entered the plaza. They were wearing jackets and jeans.

The day was unusually chilly and windy: it was about 65 degrees Fahrenheit. We'd heard that normally here in mid-September, it was about 77. We knew by nightfall the temperature would be in the mid-fifties.

Ella Mae waved to us, and they came over. They were carrying sketchbooks.

"What're you two lovebirds up to?" said Ella Mae.

I said, "Trying to decide where to have lunch."

Gwendolyn, in her usual quiet, soft-spoken manner said, "Sophia, I am so sorry about what happened…" She opened her sketchbook.

"Thank you, Gwen, but it's okay. I'm over it."

Gwendolyn said, "I don't think I could get over something like that very quickly." She shook her head. At the same time, she was making a sketch of us looking up at her.

Ella Mae said, "Sophia gave him a quick kick where it hurts the most, and he was out for the rest of the night and could barely walk the next day. I think you may have put his thingy-wingy out of commission for a while."

She and Gwendolyn laughed.

Gwendolyn said, "We were planning to just get something quick at El Lugar Feliz. We'd be delighted to have you guys join us for lunch?"

"Sounds good," I said, looking at my watch. It was a quarter to twelve.

The four of us walked out of the central plaza and over a few steps to El Lugar Feliz Taqueria, south of the plaza. We got a table outside. Not many people were around. This time of year, there were not many tourists in the city. Locals were already home eating the noon meal or in neighborhood restaurants. El Lugar Feliz catered to foreigners and tourists. It was not a bad place to eat.

After we'd ordered and started eating, Ella Mae said, "Something like that happened to me once."

Gwendolyn said, "Oh, I think I know what you're referring to."

"It's similar to what happened to Sophia," said Ella Mae. "I was only seventeen. I'm from Pittsburgh. At that time in Pittsburgh, street gangs were really bad. I was coming home late from the library. I'd gone to the library after school. Four street hoodlums, boys really, grabbed me and forced me into an alley. One covered my mouth with his hand, so I couldn't scream. Two of them held me down. One pulled off my shoes and pants. I was kicking and trying to scream."

"Oh, my God, Ella, that's awful," said Sophia.

"I've heard this before. It is awful," said Gwendolyn.

Ella Mae said, "But a man who was passed out farther back in the alley behind a garbage dumpster heard the commotion and woke up. He came at the boys with a big stick, something like a baseball bat. They turned me loose and ran for dear life. That drunk chased them out of the alley. He saved me from being raped. I got back into my pants, and he walked me home. I thanked him. No telling what would have happened to me. That helpful hobo was my hero."

"Boys sometimes act like wild dogs," said Gwendolyn.

"Where are you from, Gwendolyn?" I said.

"Boston. Outside Boston, really. Canton, Paul Revere's town. He rolled copper there. I grew up there. Nothing like what happened to you, Ella, or you, Sophia, has ever happened to me. Thank God!"

"You're lucky," said Ella Mae.

We finished eating, and pushed our plates away.

Then Ella Mae looked at her watch. "We've got to go. We promised to help Farley clean the damn place. It's a mess."

They stood up and bid us farewell. I watched them walk away, two nice young women. We hadn't bothered to tell them we were leaving Mexico, but I was sure it didn't matter.

Just then I saw Santiago walking quickly toward Central Plaza. "There he goes," I said.

Sophia said, "Who?" She turned and saw the boy enter the plaza.

"Santiago, the astronaut." I looked at my watch. "I wonder what will become of that kid?"

"Unfortunately, he'll probably end up in prison."

IV

WHEN WE FINALLY ARRIVED BACK IN NEW YORK, it was eight o'clock at night. The transition from Mexico was sudden. It felt like one minute we were in the world of Puerto Vallarta with its dreamy slow pace and blue skies, and the ancient world of San Miguel de Allende with its high mountain air, and the next we were back home in New York where everything was at once familiar yet oddly new.

Somewhere in the building, somebody was playing Bob Marley's song "Simmer Down," from the *Wailing Wailers* album.

When I unlocked our apartment door, we were shocked. The place was a pigsty. It was filthier than a pigsty. There were empty wine bottles, cigarette butts, and empty beer cans everywhere. There were old pizza boxes, cake crumbs, crushed crackers, and used syringes with dried blood in them. I opened the refrigerator. It was empty. The floor was crusty with spilled soda pop, cheap wine, and beer. I had no idea what else. The bottoms of our shoes stuck to the floor when we tried to walk anywhere in the place. There were used condoms and dozens of used plastic cups thrown all around the floor. The cushion in one chair was burned black. The kitchen sink was full of dirty dishes and cooking pans and a skillet with old food caked in them. In the bathroom, the toilet bowl was black with scum and a pile of feces and paper. It was unflushable. Had I tried to flush it, all the mess would have spilled out onto the bathroom floor that was already dirty beyond belief. A leg was broken off one of my chairs. It was leaning sideways on three legs. My books and records were gone.

Sophia, with both hands pressed against her cheeks, said, "Who could live like this?!"

This was the mess that Agnes Ludovic left for us. It was clear that while we were gone, our apartment served as a shooting gallery for junkies. Agnes was herself obviously a strung-out junkie. That pretense of smoking occasional marijuana was such crap, and she evidently had had her junkie friends in here with her, and they were all shooting up, fornicating, eating, vomiting, and doing who knows what else.

I'd left our luggage out in the hallway with the door ajar, so we could watch it. I didn't want to bring our luggage into this filth. Now we could hear the loud blasting of Bob Marley singing "Lonesome Feeling," and the sound was coming from somewhere upstairs.

I immediately went upstairs to the apartment where Agnes and her roommate lived. I knocked and an elderly man with a scraggly beard opened the door. I was surprised. I told him my name. He said he was Reuben Quinn. It was clear that the music was coming from the apartment next to his.

I asked for Agnes. He said, "The two girls who used to live here, they're gone. This is my apartment now." He didn't know how to contact them. He said, "The damn people next door are driving me crazy! I've asked them to turn it down, but they refuse. I can't get any sleep around this damn place! And I got to go to work tomorrow."

I said, "Yes, it is loud. Do you know who was living in the apartment down on the first floor, on the right side?" I explained that I had sublet my apartment to Agnes, and that I had been in Mexico since July.

Quinn said, "I don't know. I know there always was a lot of thuggish-looking people in and out of that apartment all the time, day and night. People called the police on them, but they'd clear out before the cops got here."

Sophia and I turned off the lights in the apartment, took our luggage, and walked up to First Avenue to get a taxi. It took a while, but we got one, then we shot over west to a little hotel just off Washington Square Park. We got settled in the room, took a shower, and went immediately to bed and to sleep, and we didn't wake till noon the next morning.

I thought now would be a good time to end this relationship. Old habits are hard to break. By now, we were well into the habit of being together. How could I ask her to leave? She had no place to go. How could I leave? At this point, I just didn't have the will to end the relationship, but half-heartedly I was hoping it would somehow end.

I got up, dressed, walked down to 5th Avenue and 8th Street, and bought a couple of newspapers. I took them back to the room, and Sophia and I sat on the bed and searched the Classified section for apartments available. We wanted to stay in lower Manhattan.

"Here is one on East 10th Street," Sophia said.

On paper, it looked perfect. East 10th Street faced Tompkins Square Park. The whole block was well kept and clean. The building was in the middle of the block. It was 10:30 in the morning when we got there. I pressed the door buzzer.

A young man with an angelic face opened the door and his blue eyes stretched with surprise as though he'd seen something shocking. "Yes? Can I help you?"

I said, "We are here about the apartment you have listed for rent."

He suddenly flushed with embarrassment, then said, "Come in."

We stepped inside.

"I don't know how to tell you this, but the owner of the building doesn't want me to rent apartments in this building to colored people. The whole block here, 10th Street, has an agreement to keep colored people out, but maybe since your wife is white, the owner might make an exception."

"You know what you are doing is illegal?"

"It's not me, it's the owner," he said, touching his chest with all ten fingers.

"But you are complicit," I said.

"Never mind," said Sophia. "We wouldn't want to live on a block that has such a policy."

And we thanked him for his candor and left.

Later that day, back at the hotel, I said, "Here's one on St. Mark's Place at First Avenue, for $250 a month."

On the first Monday in October, I settled the business of the 12th Street apartment with the rental agency. They were just one block over on 11th Street. They knew I'd sublet the apartment and they were sympathetic. They understood why I needed to move.

There was no lease to worry about. I'd been on a month-by-month basis. I paid the final rent—rent Agnes had neglected to pay—and paid to have the place cleaned.

That same day, we moved into the St. Mark's Place apartment. It was in a three-story building, with two apartments on each floor. Our apartment was on the second floor. The ceiling throughout the apartment was high, and I was pleased that it was. Our front door opened into the kitchen. That was unusual, but nothing in lower Manhattan should have surprised me. People with lots of money or good jobs lived next door to people on welfare. Old World immigrants who spoke no English lived next door to hippies, flower children, poets, novelists, dancers, painters, small-time thieves, and conmen.

The landlady lived up on the third floor, in the apartment on the left side.

Our apartment consisted of a large living room, a bedroom, and a small kitchen, all in a straight line, shotgun-style, with a big window up front looking out on St. Mark's Place, and if you looked sharply to the right, you could see First Avenue and the continuous traffic.

Right away we bought a bed, a couch and chairs, a kitchen chair set, and an assortment of other necessities from the trusty used furniture store near 14th Street. They delivered everything at once and I paid with a check. Then, from a small shop down on Orchard Street, we bought silverware, plates, glasses, a skillet, two pots, new sheets, pillows, and pillowcases. I paid with a check.

I called Cynthia Bellringer, editor of the *Brooklyn Daily Observer*, and told her I was back in town. She said, "Okay. Welcome home! I'll soon send you some copy to edit."

That following Thursday, around noon, I opened the mailbox downstairs in the hallway, and there was a package of manuscripts from Cynthia and a letter with the Kensington & Livingston University Press address in the upper left corner. I felt a rush of excitement and anticipation—but also fear of disappointment. Standing right there, I ripped opened the envelope, unfolded the letter, and read:

Dear Mr. Lowell:

It is my pleasure to inform you that the peer reviews for your manuscript are in. Both are very positive, and I am happy to inform you that we are going forward with plans to publish your poetry collection, 'Rendezvous in the Rain.' The title may have to be changed, but that can come later.

Congratulations, and I look forward to working with you during the production process. We here at the press are all excited about the prospects for this fine book.

Sincerely yours,
Graham Rosamond

To myself, out loud, I said, "Wow!" Then I did a happy dance around the hallway, and for days I walked on a cloud of reassurance.

When I calmed down, I wondered: do we live for these brief moments of reassurance, while much of life is routine? I remembered a poem I read as an undergraduate, Ben Jonson's famous but grim "On My First Son." Jonson is bidding farewell to the son of his "right hand." The boy, seven years old, has died. Then Jonson concludes that his son is lucky to have died so young. In this way he has avoided the miseries of life, and especially the task of growing old. It was an oddly pessimistic position for Jonson to have taken.

I remembered my English class had a passionate discussion about the poem, and most of us, myself included, agreed that despite the "miseries" of life, dying was not a good alternative, certainly not better than living, even living for rare moments of joy, euphoria, delight, exuberance, bliss, or just plain happiness.

That afternoon my phone rang. I picked up. It was Cynthia Bellringer. "I sent you some feature articles to edit."

"Yes, I got them."

I thought of telling her that I may have to resign if I get a teaching job, but I felt it wasn't the right time to say that. I had to try to calm down, calm down, and stop thinking about my forthcoming book. I needed to edit some feature articles to earn money, and maybe start writing new poems.

I'd heard poets in interviews say that the most disquieting period of time was between having the manuscript accepted and the long stretch leading up to the moment when they started working with their editors. They felt great relief, they said, when that time came, because they were seeing and making progress. Misgivings vanished. Once that period was over, the next long, anxiety-ridden period was the stretch from there to the finished book. The moment of glory came when the poets could hold their finished books in their hands. At this point, they said, anxiety ended and joy spread like a summer shower.

It was the middle of October when Sophia's sister Belinda came to see us in our new apartment. As usual, she sat on the edge of the chair with her knees close together and her hands folded on her lap. She had not bothered to take off her coat.

She said, "Sophia, Poppa told me to tell you, now that you're back from Mexico, you can make a fresh start. He says he will pay for you to start seeing a psychiatrist, a very good psychiatrist on Fifth Avenue. He told me to tell you that if you move and find your own place, he will pay your rent until you find a job. All you have to do is find your own place. Poppa wants you to leave this situation."

"Belinda, that's obvious."

I was watching Sophia's reaction. I saw that she was considering it. The idea of seeing a psychiatrist interested her. As before, Belinda's demeanor toward me was offensive. My feelings were hurt, but I also had known for a while that maybe it was time for Sophia and me to seriously consider separating. It was clear that we both were unhappy with our relationship, but clearly had not yet had the courage to break away. Change was difficult, even if you knew it would be for the better.

For the next several days Sophia and I talked about her father's proposal. I said, "If it's what you want, so be it. He obviously believes that you are crazy to be living with me."

"I'm not sure what I want."

"He wants you to leave me. He's willing to pay to make it happen."

"I know, I know. I just need to think about it."

That night, Sophia woke me at 3 a.m. and said, "I'm going to give it a try, James. That's the least I can do. He's my father."

"Sure," I said, still half asleep.

Without admitting it at first, her leaving was also what I wanted now. Ironically, Sophia's father had solved our problem. We were holding on to a relationship that was in need of new energy or abandonment.

On the eighteenth, Sophia was ready to move in with her sister in the Bronx. The plan was she could stay there till she found her own apartment. Belinda was working as a receptionist in midtown somewhere. She was also going to help Sophia find work.

Belinda's boyfriend, Saul, came with his car. Saul avoided eye contact with me. I kept trying to meet his eyes, but he refused. I helped him load Sophia's belongings into the back of his beige 1966 Ford Country Squire station wagon with side panels.

Just before Sophia climbed into the front passenger seat, we stood together on the sidewalk and hugged for a long time. I said, "Take care of yourself. I hope this is a good move for you, Sophia."

"I'm just going to try it for a while," she said. "Okay?"

"Okay," I said, knowing that our relationship was about to end, and probably it would be best for both of us.

She started crying. She blew her nose on a tissue, then turned and climbed into the passenger seat of the station wagon.

When she looked out at me, she started crying again.

Saul started the engine and pulled away from the curb into traffic.

Sophia was gone, but I had both a hopeful and a dreadful feeling that our relationship was not completely over. Her words, "I'm just going to try it for a while," had given me pause.

I wanted to move on, and at the same time, part of me was not completely ready to give up the habit of our troubled relationship, but the saner part of me said, "Move on!"

Monday, I called Kenneth Jeremiah at the Warren Lowery School of Fine Arts. His secretary, Rosalie Washington, said, "I'm sorry, he's on another line right now. May I give him a message?"

"Sure, tell him James Lowell called. Tell him my book has been accepted for publication by Kensington & Livingston University Press!"

Rosalie Washington said, "Congratulations! He'll be happy to hear the good news! He'll call you as soon as he can."

I hung up, and ten minutes later, the phone rang. It was Kenneth Jeremiah. He said, "Congratulations, James. I heard the good news."

"Thank you, Mr. Jeremiah."

"Call me Kenny. All my friends call me Kenny."

"Okay, sure."

"Are you free to have lunch with me tomorrow?"

"Yes, I am—free all day."

"Great! Meet me at noon at Tea for Two? It's on 8th Street, about two or three doors up from Fifth Avenue, on the north side of the street. You know the place?"

"I certainly do. See you tomorrow at noon."

Tea for Two was a very busy restaurant, but Kenny had reserved a table far from the front door, back where potted plants hung above our heads and large lobster tanks lined one wall. Waiters rushed about in white shirts, black vests, and black slacks.

We ordered. While we waited for our food, Kenny drank tomato juice and vodka. Just to be safe, I sipped apple juice.

"As I told you back in March, we'd love to have you join the faculty, and now that you have a book in-press, going forward with this idea should be easy, but unfortunately, we will have to put those plans on hold for a while. Our board of directors has ordered a hiring freeze, and I have no idea when it will be lifted. I'm sorry." He paused and gazed at me, then he said, "But don't be discouraged. Our board of directors is made up of academics, scientists, artists, writers, and actors. We have all kinds of creative people. I have complete confidence in them. They will lift this thing as soon as possible. It's just a budget snafu."

I was disappointed. A hiring freeze could go on for years.

While glasses all around clinked, and silverware against china clattered, and polite chatter filled the room, I gave him my best 'I'm impressed' expression: lifted eyebrows and a slight back jerk of the head. I said, "Well, I'll try to keep a positive thought!"

"Good, very good!"

And so went our conversation during lunch.

On the way out, at the exit, Kenny said, "So, when the time comes for you to fill out a formal application, you can stop in my office and pick up the packet of paperwork that we require you fill out to start the application process. It's a formality that we must follow."

"Of course."

He stuck his hand out for me to shake, and I grabbed it and we shook.

I said, "Thanks, Kenny."

"My pleasure."

Outside, at the corner of 5th Avenue and 8th Street, we shook hands again. He then headed down 5th Avenue at a brisk pace.

That afternoon, while I was unpacking the things from the Mexico trip, I came across two postcards from Amy Lawrence. I'd forgotten all about her. I liked her and was interested in seeing her, but I wasn't excited to talk with her about poetry.

I never liked talking about theories of poetry or its meter. It seemed pointless. Poetry was made with words that used metaphor, that made allusions, that sometimes dealt in repetition or used metrical feet such as anaphora or dactyl or trochee or heptameter or iambic pentameter or any number of other metrical feet or poetic devices, but its essence lay beyond words, beyond its basic units of measurement, the foot, or its metrical feet, the iamb. Most talk about poetry was barking up the wrong tree since the poem, if it was any good, like a quick and energetic squirrel, had already leaped on from that treetop across dozens of other treetops and was a mile away from where it started.

Criticizing student poems, on the other hand, had nothing to do with theories. That was all about craft and technique.

Diplomacy told me that, since Amy was going to be my colleague, I'd better make an effort to meet with her and to be friendly. I dialed her office number. There was no answer, so I left a message: "Hi Amy Lawrence, this is James Lowell. My apology for not getting back to you earlier. I was in Mexico and I just returned a few days ago. I hope you can forgive this delayed response. If you're still interested in having lunch, please let me know," and I left my phone number.

The marketing department at Kensington & Livingston University Press sent a questionnaire for me to fill out. They wanted me to write a brief description of the book so that the promotion and salespeople would have something to work with in constructing their jacket and advertising copy. One of the questions: "Who is the audience for your book?" I had no idea, so I said, "Everybody."

They wanted me to suggest noted poets to receive advance copies in the hope that they might read the book and give us blurbs to be used on the back cover. I didn't know any noted poets. Since I was unknown, my only hope was that my poems were good enough to attract the attention of established poets who might endorse the book. The publisher, I guessed, would have to send the manuscript around to see who among those famous poets might like it.

The marketing people also wanted names of periodicals that might review the book. I suggested the current best-known literary periodicals and newspapers. I believed in aiming high. I did this doubting that any of them would review the book.

Then they said, "Anything else you can think of to help us sell your book would be much appreciated." I thought hard about this. I guessed I needed a hook, a gimmick, something to grab the attention of the busy, uninterested public, but I couldn't come up with anything respectable. All I could think of was some audacious public prank that would get TV, radio, and news-people talking about me. That would do it, but doing such a thing was not in my nature. I knew of a few poets who got attention that way. There were many ways to get attention. The less such a prank had to do with poetry, the better.

Getting arrested while protesting the Vietnam War would work. A picture of the author naked on the front of the book might also do the trick.

An unknown poet with a book coming out had sent out word that he would be reading with a famous Nobel Prize-winning poet at such-and-such address. Hundreds of people and reporters showed up to cover the event. The unknown poet took the stage and said the Nobel Prize-winning poet had taken ill and would not be coming. It was a clever ploy. Reporters wrote about the event anyway, and the unknown poet became well known.

The marketing department also requested a good quality black and white photo of me. I dug up what I thought was a good photo, and spent three hours working on the questionnaire.

By now I was so excited about my forthcoming book, just getting a book published period, that I hardly noticed that my birthday, October 20th, had come and gone. I was now the ripe old age of twenty-six.

Amy and I had agreed to meet at Tea for Two. She had office hours till 1:00 p.m. It would take her twenty minutes to walk from school to 8th Street. We agreed to meet at 1:30.

I waited in the waiting area just inside the front door. When she came in at 1:20, I hardly recognized her. She was shivering from the cold, holding her leather coat together at the collar.

I stood up, and we shook hands. She said, "So nice to see you again!"

"Good to see you, too."

I was seeing her afresh. With a soft and controlled voice, she was a good-looking young woman with dark brown hair and brown-grey eyes and a chin that protruded a bit too much. She was slender and moved gracefully.

The maître d' led us to a table for two against the wall. Of the three tables available, it was the best. Even this late, the restaurant was still very crowded.

Once we were settled with menus in front of us, I said, "I guess it was some time ago that you were teaching Whitman?"

"Yes." She laughed, showing small, even teeth. "I'm happy to say the students wrote good papers on Whitman. Our focus at Lowery, you know, is on the arts, but we also focus on historical aspects of the arts, hence Walt Whitman becomes a fitting subject for our literature students. I also teach Emily Dickinson. I love her work. I also teach Sylvia Plath, H.D., E.E. Cummings, Randall Jarrell, Robert Frost, Wallace Stevens, Gwendolyn Brooks, Langston Hughes, T.S. Eliot, and William Carlos Williams."

What a lineup.

She said, "Kenny tells me that, after the hiring freeze, you're going to be joining us?"

"That's right. I guess I'll be teaching the poetry workshop."

"Yes, I think that is the opening that we have right now. I'm so thrilled you're coming to Lowery!"

I said, "Are you a native New Yorker? Did you grow up here?"

"I grew up out on Long Island and here in Manhattan. Out there, our house is on the north shore, Huntington in Suffolk County, to be exact. It's mostly our summer home; it's an old 19th century house that never seems to ever be warm enough, even in summer, but we are in walking distance of the beach and the bay, a great harbor view. My dad and mom love boating and all kinds of water sports. Out there, we have Caumsett and Heckscher and Gold Star Beach."

"Sounds like a good place to have come of age."

She narrowed her eyes and looked sharply into my eyes. "How about you? Where'd you grow up?"

"Brooklyn. Do you go back to Long Island often?"

"Actually, I have to. My parents are presently in Brazil on an extended stay. They're in Rio. Dad is doing some kind of diplomatic work there. I never understand exactly what he's doing. They love it there, and are in no hurry to come home. I am charged with keeping an eye on the Long Island house and my parents' Manhattan apartment. My brother, Billy, is away at Yale, and my sister is in Boston attending Emerson. They're both younger than I am."

"You commute in on teaching days?"

"No, I have an apartment here in the city."

The waiter came, and we ordered. Amy ordered the Special: baked chicken breast and noodles in a white sauce. I ordered Beef Wellington with wild rice.

When the food came, for a while we ate in silence, then Amy said, "You like to dance?"

"I'm not very good at it, but I'm game to try."

"Do you have a car?"

"No, I haven't had any need for one in the city. There are plenty of taxis around, but I do have a license to drive."

"I have a car, but it's out on Long Island and I'm not even sure it will start, it's been sitting so long."

"I'd love to go dancing with you," I said.

"We can go to the Dom in the East Village."

"It's in my neighborhood. That place gets pretty crowded. There are people lined up every Saturday night all the way out onto the sidewalk and down the block, waiting to get in."

"Oh?" She smiled. "We could go to the Electric Circus on St. Mark's Place."

"I live on St. Mark's Place."

"Oh! That's great! What a terrific street to live on! You're right in the heart of the action."

"Where do you live? I mean, in the city?"

"My apartment is in the 300 block up on West 57th Street."

"Third floor?"

"Yes, how'd you know?"

"Just a lucky guess. Doorman?"

"Yes, a doorman, of course." She was smiling. "Are you teasing me?"

"Not at all."

"We could go tomorrow night," she said. "Tomorrow is Saturday, right?"

"Day and night."

"I could take a taxi downtown, and meet you at the Dom, if that's where we want to go. If it's crowded, we can go somewhere else."

"That sounds fine. So, is it a date?"

"It's a date to dance."

Nice title, I thought. *A Date to Dance.*

I said, "Another option is jazz. We could go to the Village Vanguard. I think Coltrane is there tomorrow night, or we can go to the Blue Note on West Third Street, or Mezzrow's or Small's, both on West Tenth. I don't know who is performing at any of those places; we can play it by ear, or we can go to any number of downtown Saturday night cafes with live music."

"Yes, or if all else fails, we can go to St. Mark's Church and listen to poets read their work. But let's try the Dom first," she said.

I reached across the table intending to shake her hand as if sealing the agreement, but she slipped her hand softly into mine, and our eyes met, and our gaze stayed fixed. I felt a rush. She was clearly sending me a message.

She giggled a bit and fanned her face as if to cool off.

When Amy and I got to the Dom, the line to get in was all the way down the block, almost to First Avenue. People were standing in the dark, shivering in their clothes.

Amy said, "This does not look good."

We turned around and looked at crowds on both sides of the street. St. Mark's Place was aglitter with the colorful electric lights of the various businesses strung along both sides of the street.

As usual, the foot traffic was thick. My guess was most of them were young people from other boroughs looking for excitement or just to be part of the bustle of St. Mark's Place and the East Village.

Since moving from Brooklyn to Manhattan, I'd become familiar with this long-standing Saturday night tradition. I was now in it, but didn't particularly feel part of it. I loved the friendly noise of the crowd, but rather than as a participant, I almost felt myself to be there as an interested observer.

I hadn't felt that way on East 12th Street, but St. Mark's Place, only a short distance from East 12th Street, was a different world.

Now with Amy, two years younger than I was, I wondered if I shouldn't try harder to blend in, but ironically, we both were better dressed than the people I saw around us. She was wearing a trench coat over a purple dress. Her tall oxblood boots were striking and stylish. Under my tweed jacket, I was wearing a pullover, a blazer, and dark slacks.

"So, what do you want to do now?" she said.

At that moment, I heard somebody calling, "James! James!"

I looked across the street. It was Abbie Hoffman. Jerry Rubin was with him. They came across the street, and I introduced them to Amy.

Abbie said, "Where's the happenings tonight, man?"

"I wish I knew."

Jerry said, "The scene is dead, really dead tonight."

"Nice meeting you, Amy. See you later, James," said Abbie.

They continued east along the crowded sidewalk, weaving and side-stepping their way through the revelers.

I said, "We can go to The Vanguard?"

"Where is the building you live in?"

"You can see it from here. It's the second one from the end, down near First Avenue. See the grey one there?"

"I see it. Why don't we buy some Chinese food, a bottle of wine, and go to your place? I'd love to see where you live."

A little Chinese restaurant, Shanghai Gourmet, was around the corner on First Avenue, two doors down from the laundromat and a wine shop. McGovern's Liquors was across the street from the restaurant. With food and wine in hand, we were set.

I opened the door and led Amy inside the kitchen. She put the bag containing our Chinese food and the one with the bottle of white wine down on the kitchen table. We'd bought shrimp fried rice, egg rolls, and a bottle of Chablis.

I took off my coat and jacket, and placed them on the back of a kitchen chair.

While I uncorked the wine, Amy looked around. "You have lots of room here. It's larger than I expected." She was looking up the hallway, past the bedroom, toward the living room.

She took off her coat and threw it on the back of a different chair.

I got two glasses and filled them halfway with wine. I handed her one and I took the other. We clicked glasses together.

She said, "What should we toast?"

"Our first date? Getting to know each other?"

"That sounds good to me," she said. "Here's to getting to know each other."

We clicked glasses again.

I watched her sip the wine.

She said, "This is a good one. I like Chablis. I'm hungry. Shall we eat?"

"Sure, we can go up to the living room. It's more comfortable up there."

We sat together on the couch, with the food and wine on the coffee table before us, and we started eating the shrimp fried rice, the egg rolls, and sipping the white wine.

I turned on the radio. It was already at a classical music station. I left it there. A pianist was playing Chopin's *Fantaisie-Impromptu*.

I said, "How long have you been at Lowery?"

"I started last year. I'd just started shortly before you read there. I'm an adjunct. I have only a master's degree."

I nodded approval.

"I teach two days a week: Tuesdays and Thursdays."

"Good schedule," I said.

"Kenny says if I go back to school and get my Ph.D., they can put me on as a lecturer. Eventually I might be able to move to a tenure track."

"Terrific!"

"Kenny and my dad were roommates at Princeton."

"Good school," I said.

"You have an MFA, right?"

"Yes."

"That's why he'll be able to put you on a tenure track, because your degree is terminal."

"Yes."

We finished the food and continued to drink the wine.

Amy said, "Are you in a relationship?"

I could see asking this question was difficult for her; blood rushed to her cheeks and ears.

I didn't answer right away.

She said, "I know it's a personal question. I probably shouldn't have asked you such a ..."

"It's okay, it's all right. I was in a relationship till just recently. We were in Mexico from July to October. The relationship started falling apart in Mexico. When we got back, her father paid for her to see a psychiatrist. Apparently, being with me, in his judgment, was a sign of mental instability."

"What was her name?"

"Sophia."

"That's a pretty name. I always liked the name Sophia. It has so much old-world charm. In my mind, it conjures up a young woman wearing a long dress and a white apron, going to the village well with a clay water jug. Painted on the water jug, in a line strung all the way around it, are little bright flowers and birds balanced on thin branches."

"She's nothing like that. She aspires to be an anthropologist."

"Well, my parents would love you. My father's name is Robert, people call him Bob, and she's Alice. We used to call her 'Alice-in-Wonderland' just to tease her. They are very liberal. In fact, my mom once had an African lover, a Kenyan professor."

"You mean before she was married?"

"No, she had an affair. This is just between you and me. My dad never knew about it." She laughed. "I told you they're living temporarily in Brazil now. I wouldn't be surprised if Mom has a Black Brazilian lover by now."

"She's pretty adventurous, huh?"

"I admire my mom. She's so alive and smart. Yes, she intends to live her life. In fact, it would be all right with her if Dad would have affairs, but Dad is too straitlaced, too morally conservative."

I said, "What are your sister and brother like?"

"Billy is a nice boy, he's nineteen. He's quiet and rather studious like Dad. Judy is twenty, and becoming more and more self-confident. For a long time, she had low self-esteem issues. She's very self-conscious about her weight. She's not fat, but she still has her baby fat, you know. She's really a pretty girl, she just needs to start believing it."

"And your dad?"

"I told you, Dad's a diplomat. He served as ambassador in Kenya for three years. He served three more years in Ethiopia. We went to school in Kenya and Ethiopia. They were schools for children of people in foreign service."

"That must have been very interesting, living in Kenya and Ethiopia."

"It was. I still have friends from those days that I keep in touch with. Mom does, too."

"What does she do?"

"Mom was always a homemaker. Dad wanted her to stay home and raise us kids. He had some pretty old-fashioned ideas, but it was fine with us." She sipped her wine. "How about you, any sisters or brothers?"

"Nope! I'm an only child!"

"What about your mom and dad?"

"Dad's a retired bank manager and Mom was a librarian. I grew up in Park Slope, Brooklyn. Brooklyn born, bred, and Brooklyn-educated." I sipped the wine. "What about you? Are you in a relationship?"

"Me?" She shook her head, and looked down at her knees and sighed. "No, not now. I was involved with the son of a diplomat. His name was Kofi. He was from Ghana. We started going together while I was in school at B.U. Then when I left and got the job at Lowery, that sort of ended our relationship. I think we both were ready to break it off."

She put her glass down on the coffee table.

When she placed her hand back on her knee, I touched the back of her hand. We looked into each other's eyes.

She lifted my hand and placed it against her cheek and closed her eyes. She said, "Your hand is so warm, so nice and warm."

When she returned my hand, I turned her hand palm-side up and gently ran the tips of my fingers along the veins in her wrist. She shivered, took a deep breath, held it. She let it out. I leaned toward her. She leaned toward me. She wet her lips. Our lips met. Her lips were warm and soft and moist. She closed her eyes.

At that moment, the phone rang once, then again, and again. I said, "I'm not going to answer."

"Maybe it's an emergency," Amy said. "Maybe you should answer it."

I reached over to the end table and picked up the phone. "Hello?"

"Hi, James, it's me, Sophia. How are you?"

"I'm well."

"Hope I'm not calling at a bad time. It's just that I've been in these stupid sessions with Dr. Abraham. It's just been an awful brainwashing. He keeps asking me about our relationship. Why was I attracted to you and why were you attracted to me? Really stupid! He keeps telling me I should be with a different boyfriend who is more appropriate. Can you imagine that?"

"No, I can't. Sophia, this is not a good time for me to talk right now."

"Oh? I'm sorry. You have company?"

"Yes."

"A woman?"

"Listen, Sophia, I've got to go. It's rude for me to keep my company waiting. We'll talk another time."

"Okay, James. Sorry I called at the wrong time."

I hung up.

Amy was smiling. "That was Sophia, huh?"

"Yes, and she's not happy with the way things are going with the psychiatrist."

"Poor girl. She must still be in love with you to call when she has a problem, and on a Saturday night too, or maybe she's just checking up on you."

"I doubt it. Our relationship is over."

"What happened?"

"We had different agendas. That's all I can tell you. She went to Mexico to have fun, to be affirmed, and I went to get my book finished. I knew it was unfair, but I guess I worked all the time, and she went out looking for ways to entertain herself."

"I see. You got your book done, but was she affirmed?"

"At one point, she was almost raped." I stood up. "Let's not talk about Sophia anymore. Okay?"

"Does it bother you?"

"No, it doesn't bother me. It's just that I'd rather talk about you." I felt annoyed by Amy's questions.

I walked back to the kitchen, opened the refrigerator, and looked in without knowing what I was looking for.

Amy walked up behind me. "I'm sorry. I ask too many questions." She slid her arms around me and pressed herself against my backside. "Do you mind if I spend the night here with you? It's kind of late and…"

"Sure, spend the night." I turned around and took her in my arms. We kissed again. This time it was a sustained kiss, with our tongues doing a kind of dance.

The next day, Sunday, we stayed in bed till almost noon. We'd made love off and on most of the night, and were both sleepy by the crack of daylight.

She showered first. After we were both showered and dressed, we walked out onto the street. St. Mark's was quiet. All the revelers had gone, except for two or three drunks sleeping in doorways. I was glad Chicken Man was nowhere in sight.

"After breakfast, let's go up to Central Park," I said.

She said, "What a lovely idea, Sunday in Central Park!"

It was fifty-two degrees, not too cold. We walked holding hands, over past Cooper Union and Astor Place, to a little breakfast restaurant on 8th Street called Smarty's Breakfast & Lunch Grill, and we sat in a booth. The place was full of people with red eyes drinking tomato juice or coffee, trying to get sober.

Amy ordered a soft scramble with toast and orange juice. I ordered pancakes and orange juice. The elderly waitress, in a starchy pink uniform with a starchy white apron, had dyed blond hair with purple tint, and she fancied herself a comedian.

Her name tag said she was Liz, but she said, "Today I'm Lola, so be nice to me because, remember, Lola gets what Lola wants."

She kept coming by to check on us.

"You two lovebirds need anything else, just whistle. You know how to put your lips together and blow, don't you?"

She was fun.

As we were finishing, I thought about the irony of how little I knew Central Park. Growing up in Brooklyn, grand old Prospect Park was my Central Park. It was my getaway place. As a teenager, I'd go there, sit on a bench, and write poems or just daydream.

The expansive boathouse, with its white façade and pink roof, was majestic. South of the boathouse, there was mystery for me in walking under the Cleft Ridge Span bridge with its old terracotta design. There was a sense of freedom during summer in strolling along the path in the green Long Meadow.

I wrote a poem about the old 1869 well house, reflecting on its pumping of water throughout the park's waterworks. It was not a good poem. Things I wrote in the park often failed. It was a good place to daydream.

Amy and I walked back up to Astor Place to try to catch a taxi coming up Broadway. Empty taxis with their available lights on kept shooting by, both up and down Broadway.

Amy said, "It's weird. I never have this much trouble getting a taxi. Why aren't they stopping?"

We stood there twenty minutes before one stopped. We climbed in. The driver was a handsome dark-complexioned young man, with a mop of thick black hair. Judging from his ID, he was of Iranian descent.

We shot up Broadway, and somewhere in the twenties crossed over to 5th Avenue, then up to the southern tip of Central Park, and got out at the corner of 5th and West 59th Street.

We entered the park right there, walking past Kate Wollman's public ice rink. About six or seven skaters were out there doing fancy turns. Then we stopped briefly at the zoo to say hello to the animals. The park was already crowded with Sunday folk, but it was still green, and the day, though cold, was refreshingly clear and sunny. Even the air here smelled better.

We walked over to the Loeb Boathouse office. The iron gate was already opened, and plenty of boat renters were coming and going along the cobblestoned walkway to the entrance. We made reservations for lunch at the boathouse restaurant.

We rented a rowboat. In the boat, we sat facing each other. Amy was very familiar with boats from having grown up on Long Island near the water. The boat-keeper gave us a push, and we were out on the lake in an instant.

We both did the rowing. We rowed out by Bow Bridge and turned around. People on the bridge, leaning on the stone railing, waved to us. We waved back. A few high clouds were receding, and the sun was beginning to feel warmer, and the sunlight was clearer and brighter.

Here we were. We'd known each other just a short time and already I felt comfortable with Amy, and she seemed completely relaxed with me. We stayed out there about an hour, then turned in the boat.

Now it was lunchtime. It was a fancy restaurant, and it was more expensive than I anticipated, but to myself, I said, what the hell. We requested a seat by the window, and it was granted. People, mostly in groups, were coming in and being seated. The waiter, tall and stern, was pleasant. I ordered a bottle of Sauvignon Blanc. The waiter poured the wine into our glasses, then said he would return to take our orders.

Amy said, "I'll be teaching Walt Whitman again next week."

"Any particular aspect of Whitman's work?"

"Yes, the way he expanded the line. I'll give them examples, and I'll show them how he enlarged what a poem could be, and I'll also talk about his use of repetition. I want the students to understand how important Whitman is to the idea of America. He was out to make a poetry as big as America."

"Sounds like a good plan, Amy!"

We talked a while longer about Whitman, then the waiter returned. "May I take your orders now?"

"I'll have the honey-glazed pork loin," said Amy.

I said, "I'll have the seafood picatta." It was a dish of pasta, vegetables, and shrimp with a garnish.

We took our time over the food and wine, and I was thinking, Prospect Park, though made by the same men who made Central Park, was never like this, but it would always be my Central Park.

Amy said, "This is so nice, being here like this with you. I'm having a wonderful time."

I said, "I'm glad." I reached across the table for her hand, and she slid her hand into mine. I kissed the back of her hand.

"Are you enjoying yourself?" Her smile was radiant.

"I'm loving it."

After lunch, we walked around and stopped at the edge of the pond. We walked along the cobblestoned walkway surrounding the pond. There were no ducks there, no kids sailing toy sailboats. I thought of the fictional character Holden Caulfield in *The Catcher in the Rye* wondering where the Central Park ducks went in winter when the water froze over.

The lake was not yet frozen, and still there were no ducks. It was October. The ducks had gone south. They would be coming back soon enough in the spring.

We walked over bridges following paths, and we walked in the Conservatory Garden and around ponds. It was warm enough that day for the fountain to be on. We stopped to look at Schott's *Three Dancing Maidens* sculpture holding hands in a circle around spouting water. I felt like a tourist. We were both acting like tourists.

Amy said, "I once saw a stream of this water frozen in midair. It was a big curved icicle. I was just ten years old and it amazed me." Her eyes sparkled with the memory.

"I think I was about that age when I first came here," I said.

Mom, the librarian, brought me here when I was a little boy. She had said, "A German gentleman made that sculpture in 1910. You must learn to appreciate things like this, Jimmy."

I now thought of Sophia. As an anthropologist, she would see it as a fertility rite: three maidens dancing around an explosive orgasm. My mother never saw it that way, I was sure. For her, it was romantic and pretty.

Amy and I walked between the well-manicured hedges along more cobblestoned paths, and out onto the mall. We walked past the sculptures of Sir Walter Scott, William Shakespeare, and Robert Burns along the Literary Walk. These were figures people hardly noticed anymore. They'd become too familiar to be truly seen.

That night, after dinner in a midtown restaurant called Sadie's, we walked rather aimlessly, or rather carefreely, enjoying Manhattan's nightlights and bustle. All the lights were aglitter. We entered a nearby movie theater. *Funny Girl* with Barbra Streisand was showing.

Coming out, Amy said, "Did you like the movie?"

"I loved it." I was thinking I never did anything like this with Sophia. We never spent a string of days together like this. Now, in retrospect, I felt badly about it. Had I spent more time with her, perhaps our relationship, our love, would have blossomed and flourished. I was old enough by now to realize that the failure of the relationship, along with my regret, was, in retrospect, one more thing I would have to try to forgive myself for. The difference, though, was that I was not now trying to finish a book. I felt untroubled and open to adventure.

Amy and I also spent all day Monday together, mostly in her apartment, just hanging out. We read together. We danced to dance music on her turntable. We ordered pizza. We ate together. We talked about poems we loved. We watched TV together and we made love and we napped together. It was a blissful Monday!

These three days with her had lulled me into a state of comfort I hadn't felt in a long while. It was a relief to get out of my own head where I had spent so much time.

Tuesday morning, we caught the subway back downtown together. She was going to Lowery to teach her classes. I was going back to my apartment. To do what? I was in limbo now, waiting for my book's production process to begin. I'd heard that some poets and prose writers called this period one of "post-manuscript depression," but I didn't feel depressed.

Later that day, I took my laundry around the corner to the laundromat on First Avenue. As I approached, I saw a woman tying a little nondescript angry-looking dog to a parking meter in front of the laundromat. The dog fretted and barked as the woman walked away into the laundromat.

She and I entered with our bundles at the same time. I got to it first, but I let her have the only available washer. It was steamy and hot in there. While waiting for a washer to be free, I went back outside and stood on the sidewalk where it was cooler.

A woman and a little girl, about three years old, were coming along the sidewalk. Seeing the cute dog, the little girl broke free and ran to pet the dog. The second she touched the dog's head, he snarled, leapt at her, and took off her whole ear in his mouth. Blood spilled from the side of the child's face.

At first, the child was so shocked, she was frozen speechless.

I was stunned, watching the child scream with blood running down her neck, and there was the dog with an ear hanging out of his mouth, not sure what he should do with it.

The owner of the dog came rushing out of the laundromat looking confused and annoyed. Then, when she saw what had happened, instead of rushing to help the child, she rushed to her dog.

The mother of the little girl, hysterical and screaming, shouted to the dog owner, "Why did you leave a vicious dog out here?"

The dog owner snapped back, "My dog wasn't bothering nobody. You should have kept your daughter away from my dog."

As she and the mother of the little girl continued to argue, I went back inside, to the public pay phone at the back on the wall, and dialed 911. I said, "A little girl just got her whole ear bitten off by a dog. She needs help fast. She's bleeding profusely." Then I gave them the address.

The medics and the police got there quickly.

I was inside doing my laundry, so I didn't see what happened after that. I finished my laundry and went home and sat by the window with the radio on. Life was full of unpredictable random events. I felt bad for that poor little girl. I couldn't stop thinking about it.

While I was sitting in my armchair reading the local newspaper, the man on the radio was talking about something, types of wood, maybe. I wasn't paying much attention to what he was saying, not till I heard him say, "…the difference was slight…," and just as he said those words, I was reading the same words in the newspaper: "…the difference was slight…" This sort of thing had happened countless times over the years, but was it anything other than coincidence?

First day of November, Herbert Griffin called everybody and said there was an emergency editorial meeting for *Up Against the Wall*.

The meeting, he said, would be at Darius Wright's apartment the next day, Saturday, at one o'clock in the afternoon.

Herbert was the managing editor and the treasurer. Of all of us, he was the one most invested in the quarterly. The bank account for the magazine was in his name.

When I arrived at 1:30 p.m., Darius was there with his wife, Josephine. She was also a member of the board. Alvin Johnson, Glen Harrison, David Williams, and Maurice Neal were there. Herbert came in about ten minutes after I arrived.

Maurice said, "Are you on C. P. time, man?"

Herbert said, "Don't get me started, Maurice."

Once we were all settled in Darius's living room, from the couch Herbert said, "Well, I'll get right to the problem. We have no money to print the next issue, our spring issue. It is supposed to go to the printer in two weeks. We have the material, a strong issue: twelve outstanding poems, two outstanding short stories, an essay on Richard Wright and Existentialism. Our balance is thirty-five dollars and twenty cents. Our usual donors have not been coming through lately. So I called this meeting to ask you: what do you want to do? Do we discontinue the magazine, or do we suspend it till we can raise the money, or do we want to pay for this issue out of our own pockets?"

Darius said, "An equally serious problem is that we have no distribution system. For a distributor to take us on, we need to produce a professional-looking product every time and have it come out on a regular basis. So far, we've been at best irregular, meaning each issue has come out late."

Maurice said, "Either we get behind this publication or give it up. It's become an important magazine to the literary community, and I mean far beyond New York."

Darius said, "Maurice is right. University libraries are our biggest customers. Just about every major university in the country has a subscription, but we can't depend on subscriptions alone. They don't bring in enough money to cover paper, envelopes, and postage."

Josephine said, "We need at least a thousand dollars to print the spring issue, and that would cover the cost of a modest version of what we want the magazine to be."

I said, "I'll donate a hundred dollars."

David said, "I got a hundred also."

Glen said, "I can put in two hundred, too."

Maurice said, "I'm putting in two hundred."

Herbert said, "With my two hundred, we should be close to what we need!"

Josephine said, "I'll put in five hundred."

"I think we're getting there," said David.

At this point, beer and wine were passed around, and the gathering became more relaxed. At such times, when we were all together, we often engaged in literary gossip—but it was never malicious. We were like upper crust ladies at a tea party.

"I heard that you-know-who called you-know-who a you-know-what," said David.

"It was not to her face," said Glen. "Do you guys know about this? It was during an award ceremony. You-know-who and some other men were looking through photos of previous winners. He saw a photo of you-know-who, and you-know-who said, 'Who is the you-know-what?' The other men were surprised and made to feel uncomfortable. Of course, you-know-who uses words like that in his poetry, too."

Glen said, "It didn't happen like that. They were at the ceremony, and you-know-who was on the stage, and you-know-who was in the audience, and the one in the audience asked of the people at the table with him, 'Who is the you-know-what?' and mind you, she was one of the judges who had fought to give him the award, the biggest literary award in the country. That's how it happened."

"Okay," said David. "It happened. It happened, and it was stupid and crass on his part."

"And he's such a fine poet, too. Too bad he's that kind of person," said Glen.

Maurice said, "You think that's bad? Recently, I was in the audience at the Fillmore East when you-know-who came out on the stage drunk and started arguing with the audience about who was the enemy. I thought he was going to talk about the Vietnam War but, no, he called us, in the audience, the enemy!"

David said, "I was at the New School not long ago when a different you-know-who was the guest speaker. He made the crass statement that you-know-who was the only accomplished Afro-American writer. Then he went on to say that it was because you-know-who was influenced by you-know-who. Well, man, I tell you, the audience challenged you-know-who about that statement, and the backlash was not only from Black people in the audience, but from most of the white people there, too."

Despite the fact that these guys gossiped, argued, and even fought sometimes, they were the friends I'd gravitated to after leaving Brooklyn and my job at the bank, and upon going to work for CUI and settling on the Lower East Side. In a way, they had replaced my now-defunct group of poetry-writing friends at Brooklyn College.

The first Monday morning in November, I walked into the Strand bookstore on the corner of Broadway and East 12th Street, and I went straight to the poetry section. One of the clerks, my friend Joe Allen, came over and asked me to do a sketch of myself for a book of self-portraits of poets and writers he was editing. I dashed off a quickie and handed the sketchbook back to him.

Just then, Joe was called away to help a customer.

I'd selected five thin paperbacks, books by Sylvia Plath, Walt Whitman, Robert Hayden, William Carlos Williams, and Emily Dickinson. I took them to the checkout counter, paid, and with my bag of fresh books to read, I headed for the exit.

Just as I stepped out onto Broadway, I saw Regina and Cedric about to enter the store. Of all people! Imagine! It took me a second or two to recognize them.

Cedric said, "James, my good man!" He threw his arms around me.

I said, "Cedric! Regina! Wow! What a pleasant surprise to see you guys here! I thought you were in Boston."

Regina then hugged me. It was a stiff hug, but done with a wink and a half-smirk. "We were in Boston," she said.

Cedric said, "*Raisin in the Sun* had a good long run, but it's done now and here we are, back in our city of choice."

Regina said, "Not just choice, my home, Spanish Harlem. We're staying uptown with my parents till we find a suitable apartment, hopefully down here somewhere, or in midtown."

I said, "Did you get the part in *Hair*?"

"No, unfortunately," said Regina. "They said I was too classical."

"Oh, well. When'd you get in town?" I said.

"Just last week, actually." Cedric looked around. "Do you have time to sit down with us and have a cup of coffee? Look, there's a coffee shop up the street on the other side. See it?"

"Yes," I said. "Sure, let's grab a cup of coffee."

We crossed the street and walked up to Ludwig's Quick Fix Coffee Shop. Beneath the blinking name, in smaller neon, Breakfast & Lunch Served All Day. It was eleven-thirty.

While walking, Cedric asked about my book of poems. I told him it was finished and already accepted. They both congratulated me.

We were lucky, we got the only empty booth left. It seated four people. Regina sat next to me facing her husband. I shouldn't have been, but I was surprised. I was against the wall. She was on the outside. I placed my bag of books on the seat between the wall and myself.

I could see the street through the front window. The traffic of cars and trucks was dense and intense, and I remembered sitting on a balcony not long before, gazing at the calm of the Bay of Banderas and the mountains beyond. In memory, that was a more peaceful time than it actually was.

A waitress, about forty-five years old, in a light blue uniform, came over. She was wearing eyeglasses shaped like cat eyes and she had a gold front tooth. She said, "My name is Nona. Can I get you fine folks some coffee to start?"

We said yes, and she went away to get the coffee.

Cedric looked up from the menu at me. "You want to have lunch, James? Let me treat you to lunch! I never had a chance in Puerto Vallarta. How about it?"

"Sure, it's almost lunchtime. Why not?"

Regina looked at me and smiled, and while Cedric was studying the menu, I felt Regina's left hand under the table grab my crotch and give it a hard squeeze. All the while, she was looking at the menu and talking, "My, my, everything looks so good. Maybe I'll have scrambled eggs and bacon and call it lunch. I didn't have breakfast this morning."

The waitress brought the coffee and said, "I'll come back in a minute to get your orders."

"So, tell me," I said to Cedric, "how was it in Boston? Did you enjoy doing the play?"

"It's such a serious play that gets at the delicate issue of manhood, but it was great fun to do. Having to do it so often, of course, got a bit tiresome, so I tried to vary it a bit each night just to keep myself fresh, to keep the energy level up."

Regina said, "He was wonderful, James. I wish you could have been there."

Cedric said, "I think I, too, will just order breakfast and call it lunch."

I'd had a toasted bagel and orange juice at home, but I was hungry enough by then to eat again. I said, "Scrambled eggs sounds good." I closed the menu and put it down.

The waitress came back, and we ordered. She thanked us and took the menus away.

"How's Sophia?" said Cedric.

I said, "She's fine, I hope. She's seeing a psychiatrist."

"Oh?" said Cedric.

"We separated."

Regina said, "Where is she now?"

"She's living in the Bronx with her sister. Her father is paying her bills. I think she's also trying to find a job and an apartment."

"Oh, so sorry to hear you guys separated. You seemed to me like the perfect couple," said Cedric.

Regina smirked. "Mexico makes people look happier than they are."

"That's an odd thing to say, honey," said Cedric.

"It's true. You're in this dreamy idyllic place. Why wouldn't everything seem perfect?" said Regina. "Everybody thought Connie and Clifford in *Lady Chatterley's Lover* were an ideal couple, but behind his back, as he sat crippled in a wheelchair, she was unhappy and screwing another man. Doing so made her happy, and when she was happy, Clifford was happy too, at least for a while."

I said, "Well, obviously our relationship was not perfect. What relationship ever is?"

Cedric said, "Regina and I have a perfect relationship."

She laughed. "You've got to be kidding."

Cedric said, "I am. I was being ironic." He gave her a hangdog smile.

When we finished lunch, we walked out together. At the corner, we stopped. Cedric and Regina were about to cross the street to go to the Strand. We exchanged contact information and promised to stay in touch. Regina winked at me and said, "Don't forget!"

With my bag of books, I started walking the short distance back to St. Mark's Place. Halfway home, it occurred to me that I probably would never see either of them again. I didn't know how I felt about that. On the one hand, I was glad my risky dalliances with Regina were over, and on the other, I regretted that Cedric and I would probably never be able to establish any basis for a lasting friendship.

I spent Thanksgiving and Christmas with my parents in Brooklyn. The weeks and months seemed to pass quickly. I was keenly aware that 1968 was about to end, and I knew it would be a year I would never forget.

Shortly after Christmas, Kenneth Jeremiah called and said, "Good news! The hiring freeze was lifted this morning!"

"Bravo!" I was both happy and surprised that it had happened so soon.

"So, James, the need is upon us. Professor Kirkpatrick is on sabbatical. Can you start teaching workshops at the start of the winter semester in January?"

"Absolutely!"

"Great!"

That night I had a first-day-of-class dream, or call it nightmare. I arrived in class and greeted the students, but suddenly I realized I had forgotten to bring the syllabus copies that I had so carefully printed and assembled, stapled, stacked, and placed in a manila folder. Had I left them in the mimeo copy room, or in my office, or at home? In a panic, I told the students I'd forgotten something, not saying what, and that I would dash out and retrieve the forgotten item and be back in a jiffy. I ran out of the room and down the hall. After running for several minutes, I realized that I was running in the wrong direction to get to the copy room and to my new office, but when I turned back, the hallway had changed and everything looked unfamiliar. I told myself I needed to go outside and get reoriented, then reenter the building, but when I got outside, the building itself was no longer Lowery. It was a building I'd never seen before. At this point I concluded that my only hope was that I had left the copies at home. Of course, I knew how to get back home but, unfortunately, the minute I formulated that thought, I realized that I was no longer in New York City. I was in a neighborhood in a city I'd never been in before. The houses were like Park Slope, Brooklyn, neighborhood houses, yet they clearly were not Brooklyn houses. On the hunch that I had simply walked in the wrong direction, I started running down a side street, believing that if I kept running, I'd surely reach St. Mark's Place. Time was running out. I was already at least a half hour late for the start of class, and students were waiting. Some may have already left. Perhaps all had left by now. I was in a panic. My best bet was to simply return to school and try to conduct the class without a syllabus. Surely the students would understand, but given my predicament at this point I had no idea how I would ever find the school. I was lost and I had to admit it.

I woke with a pounding heart, and lay there sweating and remembering the dream. The emotional content of the dream took me back to when I was a first-year graduate student about to teach my first undergraduate poetry workshop. I was panic-stricken. I had no idea how I ever got through that first class.

I started teaching my first creative writing workshop at Lowery in January 1969, and I was glad to not have to wait seven months till September, the usual time new faculty started. I was ready to get started and I needed the money. I would also go on a health insurance plan, something I hadn't had since I left my father's bank.

And there was no first day panic! My twelve undergraduate students were all brilliant, highly motivated young people: ten young women, in their early to mid-twenties, and two young men in the same age range.

In my graduate workshop, I had eight: four men and four women, all second year. Two of them, Mabel and Lotus, had transferred recently from New York University; Wesley and Vaughn had been undergrads at Lowery. The other four, Vivian, Eunice, Willis and Yardley, came with BAs from CUNY.

I had taught many undergraduate poetry workshops while in graduate school so the routine and format were already very familiar. Yet this was my first time teaching a graduate workshop, and so far I was enjoying it. Most of them seemed ready to take on the world with their words and their imaginations.

But it was funny how poetry workshops tended to attract more women than men. I'd noticed that in college while I was a student in workshops, and it was true of both graduate and undergraduate workshops.

I called Cynthia at the *Brooklyn Daily Observer* and told her that, for the foreseeable future, I would no longer be editing feature articles for the newspaper. I explained that my schedule would now be full because of teaching and reading student manuscripts. She said, "Congratulations on your teaching job! It's what you've wanted. I'm so happy for you, James."

Now it was already March. My book was scheduled to be in bookstores before the end of the month.

Amy and I had planned to spend a weekend together again. Actually, we had four days free, from Friday till Monday. So she and I took the train out to her parents' house on Shoreview Place in Huntington. On the train, she said, "You know, the house Walt Whitman was born in is in Huntington. If my car will start, we can drive by there."

In town, we stopped at the local grocery store and bought eggs, cheese, rye bread, bacon, steaks, peas, pears, apples, grapes, two large bottles of spring water, cooking oil, and two bottles of dry white wine.

We took a taxi out to the house.

On the way, she said, "My family spends only summers out here. In the winter months, they live in the apartment in the city, on Park Avenue South. It was an apartment that my grandparents bought way back when the street was called Fourth Avenue. It's in one of those landmark buildings, just north of Union Square."

"So your hands are full taking care of everything while they're away?"

"Yep."

"So you really grew up in the city?"

"As I said before, half and half."

It was dark by the time we got there. The house was a big two-story, wood-framed house set slightly below the road, with a three-car garage.

We entered through the garage. "That's my car," she said. The car was covered with a red tarp. She lifted the tarp. It was a white 1965 Ford Galaxie convertible. Then she re-covered it.

Parked alongside her car was a late model black Cadillac and a green Ford station wagon.

I said, "I assume those are your parents' cars?"

"Yes, Dad asked me not to try to drive them while he's gone. He's very fussy about those two cars. He doesn't trust my driving. Mom drives the station wagon."

When Amy unlocked the door, we could smell the stale air of a place long closed, and there was even a faint smell of mildew.

There was a big old television console sitting against the wall facing the sectional arrangement. I turned it on, and in progress was a rerun. It was already midway through an episode of Leonard Bernstein's *Young People's Concerts*. When I was younger, I loved that show! I turned off the TV.

In the living room, the sectional couch was clearly the source of the mildew. Amy said, "That smell is from years of us coming in from a swim and sitting there in damp swimsuits to watch that TV." She looked around in frustration. "Let's sleep in the tree house. It's not so cold. The temperature will be about fifty-five tonight. This time of year, by this time in the evening, it's usually in the forties."

"A tree house?"

"Sure, come here! Look!"

I followed her to a side window and looked out.

There it was, perched high in a great old oak tree growing out at the edge of the yard where it dropped off sharply into a ravine. The ladder to the tree house looked sturdy enough.

"We can take a pile of blankets up there and it will be cozy." She kissed my cheek. "Okay?"

"Where are the blankets?"

"Right here in this old trunk." Amy pointed to a large steamer trunk around which the sectional was arranged. It was serving as a coffee table.

I opened the trunk and saw about a dozen blankets and comforters neatly folded and stacked.

She climbed up first. I stood on the lower slats of the ladder and handed things up to her: the blankets, pillows, sheets, her nightgown, my sleep shirt, and a jug of water and the wine. We were a short-term assembly line.

She said, "Dad built this house for Judy and me before Billy was born, but by the time he was old enough to come up here by himself, we no longer had any interest in it. It became his playhouse."

"It's cozy, and sturdy-looking, too."

Amy said, "During the summers, my childhood was spent between the beach and the pavilion, between the picnic area and the boardwalk, between the dock and the wharf, between the bulkhead and the dinghy racks, and between the pier and the boat ramp and the boat."

The tree house was one big space about the size of a large bathroom, with windows all around, and on the side facing the road, there was a deck overlooking a thicket of bushes. On the backside, there were bushes and trees and undergrowth where the Lawrence lot ended at the beginning of the ravine.

In the moonlight, I took off my shoes and belt, pants and shirt. I put on the long heavy white cotton t-shirt I'd brought with me. I'd bought it and three others like it two years before from a New England catalogue selling supplies for rural living. I liked sleeping in it in cold weather better than sleeping in pajamas or my underwear.

Fog had come inland, and night smells were of damp weeds and trees and the sharp tanginess of wet earth, and some distance away an owl or a mourning dove was saying "hooo hooo" over and over. I quickly adjusted to those sounds and to the denser sounds of other night creatures croaking and burping.

Amy got naked and quickly into a heavy wool nightgown. She shivered. "Ah, that was invigorating!"

"Being naked, or getting into the nightgown?"

"Being naked just for that second!"

I just looked at her and smiled.

"In the night, if you have to pee," Amy said, "just pee over the railing down into the ravine. It's better than making the long trip back into the house. That's what I do. It's good fertilizer for all that shrubbery down there."

The bed was just a mattress on the floor. Once we were under the covers, I turned my back to her. Instantly, I felt her cuddling up behind me spoon-fashion. She had her arms around me, and her hands were resting against my stomach.

"Are you warm enough?" she said.

"Yes, how about you?"

"I'd be warmer with your arms around me," she said.

I turned around and pulled her to me, with her breasts against my chest. I felt her hand down below checking the state of my interest. The interest was growing.

We did it without dislodging our blankets. In the process, we actually generated some heat under there.

After we made love, she said, "I feel much better now. I'm a lot warmer. I'll be able to sleep. How about you?"

"Yes. I didn't know how much I needed that. I'm more relaxed."

We fell asleep with our arms around each other.

At the first crack of daylight, I woke.

I got up and relieved myself over the railing down into the undergrowth. My getting up apparently woke Amy. I looked back at her. She was squinting, looking up at me, with one eye opened.

"I need to do that, too," she said.

I finished, and she got up and lifted her nightgown, and standing at the railing, with knees apart and bent, and with her torso pushed out and up, she shot a long golden stream out through the railing and down into the ravine.

Later, in the house, I warmed a skillet and poured some oil into it. I cooked bacon and scrambled eggs for us. Amy was making the toast in the toaster. She placed fruit in a fruit bowl on the dining room table, and she got plates down from the cabinet alongside the sink.

We ate our breakfast on the deck looking out on the yard and the trees through which we could see the bit of ocean known as Long Island Sound in the far distance. From this angle, you couldn't see the bay because of the land and houses, but the ocean was very visible because it was higher.

Later, Amy tried to start her car. Nothing. It was dead.

We spent most of the next day in the tree house making love. Later we walked to town and ate pizza in a pizza shop. We visited the Huntington Rural Cemetery where Amy's grandparents were buried. She placed flowers on their graves. We walked the boardwalk at Gold Star Beach Park. We visited the Main Street Nursery, and we walked around in Heckscher Park. We stopped at the cannon. "It's the Soldiers and Sailors Memorial," she said.

Saturday morning, Amy said, "Let's go check on my dad's boat. It's out at Mill Dam marina. We can get the bikes out of the garage and ride there in about ten minutes. We can also ride the bikes to the Whitman house, if you want to."

"Is it open?" I said while pumping air into the tires.

"No, but we can see the outside."

"Sure, let's go take a look."

I finished inflating the tires.

It took twenty minutes. I was on her brother's Schwinn Panther II, and Amy's Schwinn Hornet was for boys. She said she didn't like girl bikes. "I don't need a girl's bike since I never wear dresses when I'm riding a bike. I've always been something of a tomboy."

We got to the marina and parked the bikes.

The anchored boats were gently rocking in the breeze. She led the way to the boat shelter.

Amy pointed, and said, "That one there is ours."

It was a Hacker Craft Runabout, with an Evinrude outboard motor. It looked like it could seat eight people. It was built for speed and appearance. It was of highly varnished oak and cedar. It looked too pretty to use.

Amy said, "Dad has the bank send a check every month to pay for docking it here."

"It's a good-looking boat."

Sunday afternoon, we were walking along the beach. Two young men out on the water were talking in low voices, but the water carried the sounds of their voices to us. They were about Amy's age. One said to the other, "Isn't that Amy Lawrence with a nigger?" His companion said, "Looks that way."

Amy looked at me to see if I heard. I knew she was concerned and worried that if I had, I might be upset, but I didn't let on that I had heard, and truly I was not upset. The conversation on the boat said something about the speakers and nothing about me.

Monday night, we ate dinner at Jon Scott's, a five-star restaurant in town. While eating dinner, I said, "When are your parents coming back?"

"Probably coming back in a few months. They've been down there now for almost a year. I think I told you Dad is on some kind of diplomatic mission. I think they're getting a bit homesick. Besides, his assignment there seems to be coming to an end."

We biked to the Whitman house out on Old Walt Whitman Road. We left the bikes in the little parking lot, and walked over to the house. I'd seen pictures of the house in books, so I knew what to expect. It was a neat little log cabin situated in a plush yard of well-kept trees and lawn. No one else was there. In the yard, there was an iron sculpture of Whitman's likeness, and a red brick patio with six wooden benches. We sat on a bench facing the house. I said, "It amazes me how small it is."

We returned to the city.

At home, I opened my mail. There was an invitation to read from my new book at St. Mark's Church-in-the-Bowery. I knew the poetry reading program was relatively new, having just started in 1966. The invitation excited me.

St. Mark's Church, at 131 East 10th Street, had long been a magnet for me. As early as 1961, I first started going to the free jazz concerts in the west yard. I knew none of the people who organized such programs, but the church had become one of my favorite cultural stops.

At the same time, from 1966 on, the church was also a magnet for all the various poetry groups. I noticed that the basis for poetry groups tended to be gender or age or sexual orientation or race or social class, but at the church most of the groups came together for readings, if not to socialize.

From then on, when I could, I came to the St. Mark's Church poetry readings, but long before '66 I was coming to the Lower East Side to hear poetry. At that time in lower Manhattan, poetry was being read in coffeehouses such as the Tenth Street Coffeehouse, and later, Les Deux Magots on 7th Street, then Café Le Metro on Second Avenue and 10th Street.

At first, a cup of coffee cost a dime. It went up in some coffeehouses to as much as a quarter. I often sat for hours in those coffeehouses, usually at night, listening to poets read, wondering if someday I might be able to stand before a group of people and read my own poetry with as much self-confidence as those poets obviously had.

This invitation meant a lot to me. It meant I had arrived. I was now experienced at reading in public, having done it countless times while in college and later. I now had a book coming out, and was beginning to feel comfortable thinking of myself as a poet.

At school, I was getting to know my undergraduate students better: Leo, Sue, Estelle, Donna, Karl, Fanny, Babette, Gladys, Beryl, Carmen, Dena, and Christel. I was past the stage of having to match names with faces and to memorize the matches. In that way, I had been able to call on a student without checking my roster.

Fanny Mortimer, a big girl, twenty years old, with a large head full of auburn hair and pleading grey eyes, daughter of a famous literary critic, I could tell had a crush on me. She was smart and talented. I knew I had to be careful with her. No matter how flattering her interest in me was, there was a line not to be crossed.

At the same time, I did not want to lose her attention or anger her. I wanted to keep her focused on her work and on the class, not on me. It was a tightrope to walk. Fanny came to see me in my office during office hours, and even when I was not holding office hours.

She came when she had issues to discuss and when she had made up issues. I was nice to her, but I had to be nice in a way that she would not interpret as a response to her obvious flirtation. When she talked about being disappointed in her ex-boyfriend, I did not respond. I knew this was her way of trying to give me an opening.

The poems my undergraduate students were writing fell into three categories: 1) introspective and confessional: this was the largest category; 2) nature poems: poems that defended or revered the natural world; and 3) poems about social and political issues: anti-war poems, and poems in support of women's struggle for equal rights under the law.

Fanny and Beryl were writing introspective poems. Estelle and Donna were writing confessional poems. Sue, Karl, and Leo were writing anti-Vietnam War poems; Christel, Carmen, Dena, Babette, and Gladys were alternately writing in all three categories.

How I criticized the poems in class also required diplomacy. Invariably, I liked some poems better than others, and it was necessary to talk about those poems, along with the weaker ones, as "works-in-progress."

I also always tried to find something good to say, even about the worst poems. I wasn't lying, but there really was always something good to say, even if that positive thing was only subject matter, which usually was irrelevant because it could be anything.

My relationship with Amy from the beginning felt easy but tentative. I was stunned when, ten days into April, she stopped me in the hallway, and said, "I'm going to Rio to visit my parents. I won't be back till school starts in the fall. By then, they'll probably be ready to come back, too."

I didn't know what to say.

Then she said, "Can you come with me?"

"Sorry, Amy, can't do it." Why did I say no? I might have said yes had she, instead, said, "Let's go to Rio! We can visit my parents."

But no, she said, "I'm going to Rio," and "Can you come with me?" seemed like an afterthought. I understood what the answer should be, and I gave her the correct one.

April 10th was also the pub date for my poetry collection, *Rain*, with its new title suggested by my editor, which I liked better than my working title.

So the big day was here, and there were no bells, no whistles. No parade. Nobody called to congratulate me. It was just another day!

I knew the score with poetry. You were lucky to get a book of poems published. Having it celebrated on the day of publication, as though it were the birthday of a saint, was asking a bit much.

For someone to notice would be a miracle. If a little magazine ran a review six months or a year after the book appeared, you could consider yourself lucky. I knew from friends and from reading interviews given by well-known poets that the audience for poetry was very small, mostly other poets and a few English majors.

But one could get a lot of academic mileage from just the book's existence alone, and especially if it was published by a highly respected university press such as Kensington & Livingston.

Sunday, May 11th, I was awakened at 7 a.m. by the telephone. It was Sophia screeching into the phone, "Have you seen the *New York Times Book Review* yet?"

"No," I mumbled, only half-understanding her.

"Your book is reviewed in the *New York Times Book Review*! Your book got a front page review!"

"What? What're you talking about?"

"Wake up, James! This is no joke!"

I was beginning to understand.

"This is big, really big. You're going to be famous. This can make your career. The famous critic, John Hugo, wrote it! He reviewed your book with three other books of poems. It's a group review."

I sat up on the side of the bed and I realized I wasn't dreaming.

"Do you want me to read it to you?"

"No, Sophia, that's okay. I'm not even fully awake yet. I'll go out and get the *Times*."

"By the way, I'm moving back to the Lower East Side next week. I've already found an apartment. It's on Eleventh. We'll be neighbors."

"Are you still in therapy?"

"No, I'll tell you all about it when I see you. Let me give you my address. You have something to write with?"

"Wait a minute." I picked up a pencil from the bedside table. There was a notepad there. I always kept a pencil and pad by the bed because many of my best ideas for poems came in the middle of the night. At such times I could quickly scribble a phrase to help trigger the idea during waking hours. "Okay," I said, "now I'm ready."

She said her address and phone number, then said, "I'll be in Apartment D, on the third floor. It's the usual walk-up type building. You know the neighborhood."

"Sure." I paused. "You working? You got a job?"

"I will have a job soon. I'm hoping to be working in the public school system as a substitute teacher, but I'm also going back to school to get my master's degree in anthropology. I've decided to be practical. My goal is to teach junior college or high school anthropology."

"I hope it all works out for you."

"Are you coming to see me in my new apartment?"

"Sure." I saw no harm in being friendly. Besides, I'd once loved her, and now I wished her well.

"I'll call you once I get settled. Now run out and get the *Times*!"

I showered and dressed, and walked up to Second Avenue and bought the *Times* from the corner newspaper vendor. I was excited, but it was my temperament not to show excessive excitement. I couldn't explain it. It was just the way I was. Even in a crisis, I remained calm. Once the crisis passed, I often looked back in amazement.

If you knew a review was going to be positive, you could allow yourself to be excited, but judging from what I'd heard published poets and writers say, if you had no idea what was in the review, you might feel apprehension. I never believed the poets, in interviews and elsewhere, who said they never read reviews of their books.

I'd seen Maurice Neal get very upset over negative reviews of his novel, *Dominican Woman*. He wrote angry letters to editors of newspapers and magazines where negative reviews of his novel appeared. He once told me, "I don't take that crap! I fight back!"

I knew I would not be inclined to complain about a negative review. I might feel depressed about it for a few hours, then move on. I would chalk it up to the opinion of one person whose critical judgment was different from my own. If I thought the review was deliberately mean and untrue, I knew I would dismiss it as unfortunate on the part of the person who wrote it.

Back in my apartment, I took out the book review section and placed it on my kitchen table.

There was that black and white photo I'd sent to Kensington looking back at me from the first page of the *New York Times Book Review*. Photos of the other three poets appeared with mine in a line at the top of the review.

I did not expect this ever.

I read the review of the four books through twice. The other three poets were Kathy Hargrove, Jack Golden, and Paul Murphy. Kathy Hargrove: Boston-born and raised, was now living in Paris, married to the French novelist, Michel Vere, author of the celebrated séries policière Ferdinand Roubad. She and Michel had two small boys. It was well known in literary circles that Kathy had had mental problems and had been hospitalized several times for treatment. Sylvia Plath was her idol. Plath had committed suicide in 1963 and was now fast becoming widely known. This was Kathy Hargrove's second book of poems. Hugo thought it better than her first. In fact, he said it was "brilliant." He thought she might win the Pulitzer Prize this time around.

Jack Golden: born in Vermont, at age nineteen lost one arm in a car accident. He was now teaching at the University of Mississippi. It was known in literary circles that he bought a farm near Jackson and was raising ducks. He was now divorced from poet Flower Chilton, editor of Rake, a highly respected poetry small press.

Paul Murphy: born in Ireland, now an American citizen and teaching at Brown University. Not much was known about his private life. His poems were short and written in short lines and always with simple one or two-syllable words. He was said to be "inimitable."

Jack Golden and Paul Murphy were famous. Each had published more than ten books of poems and won many prizes. Critic Hugo thought these two volumes were among their best works. Both men had won all the top American literary prizes. According to Hugo, they were likely to win again with these new books.

Then I read the review a third time to pick out good phrases to try to remember. Hugo said Rain was "compassionate and deeply felt…", "brilliant, sensual, and lyrical…", and "vivid and confident…" And he said it had "immense clarity…" And, finally, he said, "Remember the names Kathy Hargrove and James Eric Lowell. They are here to stay. Each of them is already an accomplished poet with a promising future."

I said out loud, "Thank you, John Hugo. Bravo!"

A few days after the front page review appeared in the *New York Times Book Review*, I received in the mail at Lowery invitations to read at three universities on the West Coast and two in the Midwest.

In telephone conversations with each, I discovered that none of the reading programs had enough money to cover the travel cost of a round-trip ticket. Even the honorariums they were offering wouldn't have covered expenses.

So, after considering the tour, I scrapped the idea of going. I would have ended up spending more than I brought home. Had I been better known, the schools might have managed to come up with better offers. I would have to confine myself to the New York, New Jersey, and New England areas.

The month of May went quickly. My graduate and undergraduate classes were going well, and I had tons of manuscripts to read and edit every weekend.

I'd done all of this before at Brooklyn College when I taught undergraduate workshops. Teaching creative writing workshops meant giving up weekends. It meant almost giving up any real social life.

I saw Amy occasionally, usually for a quick hour or two for dinner in a downtown restaurant or we caught a movie together, but she too was busy, especially on weekends, grading papers. It was the life we'd bought into. It meant very few free weekends. Lately, whenever I saw her, she had a stack of student papers under her arm. She'd take them with her to lunch and grade as many as she could while eating.

On a Thursday, at six in the evening, I went to visit Sophia in her new apartment. She was expecting me. I knocked at the door and she opened it. Her face was flushed with emotion, and she was wearing a flimsy bathrobe over pajamas.

I said, "Oh, did I wake you?"

"No, come on in. I was just taking a nap." She was smiling and she kept a fixed sleepy smile.

After closing the door, she walked quickly to her couch and flopped down as though she was exhausted.

I followed her and sat beside her. I said, "How are you? How have you been?"

She looked into my eyes and said, "You sure took your time coming to see me."

"I apologize. I've been busy, overwhelmed really. Teaching two classes and editing student manuscripts is taking up all my time."

"By the way, congratulations on getting the teaching job. You're on your way up."

"Thank you. I feel lucky, but it's hard work. Are you back in school yet?"

"I start classes in the fall. My focus will be cultural anthropology, not in the old racist way, but the new ethnology. I want to study similarities between cultures, explore how they evolve, and how they are different from one another. Are all people more or less alike, or are there distinguishing cultural characteristics? I don't mean to go on and on about this..."

"Oh, that's all right." I gave her a warm smile. "So why did you move back to the Lower East Side?"

She sighed and shook her head. "I got sick of that psychiatrist, Dr. Abraham, sick of my dad trying to orchestrate my life, sick of my sister trying to do the same thing."

"I see."

"They seem to think they know what's best for me. That is such bullshit. My dad is still pissed because I went to Mexico with you. They all thought I was losing my mind."

"I see."

"I just got sick of it all, sick, sick, sick! And that's why I moved back to the Lower East Side. Here I can be around people who are not trying to tell me what is best for me."

"I see."

Suddenly she kissed me on the mouth. I kissed her back. Then the kiss got more sensual. I felt her tongue reaching for my tongue. She whispered, "I missed you."

I said, "I missed you, too." I surprised myself by realizing, as I said it, that I meant it. I had missed her. Time had passed, and I'd come to mainly remember what was good about our relationship.

"I want you right here on the couch," she said.

We lay down on the couch, side by side, still kissing. One of her legs was thrown over my hip, and her naked belly was against my shirt.

Just then there was a knock at the door.

Sophia's eyes stretched. "I think that's my boyfriend." She smiled, watching my reaction. She laughed. I thought she was joking. It was the kind of joke Sophia would tell.

She got up and opened the door, and a young man with light brown skin, curly hair, and dimples came in with an alarmed and curious look. He was dressed casually in a cotton shirt and jeans and tennis shoes. He looked to be about eighteen. He looked at me with his mouth open as though he was about to speak. He seemed puzzled.

Sophia closed the door and returned to the couch. Still smiling her secret smile, she said, "Melvin, this is James Lowell."

He stood looking down at her, then at me, and back at her. Finally, he said, "Yeah, I know who James Lowell is. He's your ex-boyfriend. What's he doing here?"

"He came to see me, Melvin."

His ears and cheeks and neck were turning red with nervousness.

"James, Melvin is my next-door neighbor."

"I thought I was more than that," Melvin said.

She laughed. "You are more than that. You're a friend, Melvin."

He said, "I thought I was more than a friend."

"You are more than a friend, Melvin. You are a very, very good friend."

He snorted with disgust.

I said, "Sophia, I think I'd better go, and let you and your friend have this discussion in private."

"Oh, you don't have to go, James."

I stood up. "I'll see you in a day or two. Okay?"

"I'll walk out into the hallway with you," she said.

"Okay."

She followed me out into the hallway and closed the door so that it did not lock.

She said, "I'll be home in the daytime. I didn't get the substitute-teaching job. I'm going to be working nights in a restaurant over on Fifth Avenue near the corner of 9th Street. It's called Bill Miller's American Cuisine. I'll be hosting, you know, seating people as they come in."

"It's hard for me to see you in that role."

"It's just temporary till I save up some money and get back in school. I've got to pay bills some kind of way."

"Understood."

"Listen, James, Melvin is a kid. He's just eighteen, just turned eighteen, actually. He's from a well-to-do family in Hoboken. He's a dropout and a runaway. He's of age, so his parents can't make him come home. They wanted him to go to college. He was accepted at Harvard, but decided to come to the East Village for his education. He's also trying to discover what it means to be Afro-American."

"What's his family's name?"

"Woodrow. He's Melvin Lee Woodrow, son of Walter Yates Woodrow, the congressman."

"He's in love with you," I said.

"He thinks he's in love with me."

"Okay, Sophia. I'll give you a call in a day or two."

"Promise?"

"I promise."

She kissed me on the lips. "Bye!"

"Bye, Sophia."

A few days later, I was coming down the steps of my apartment building. I was headed to Second Avenue to eat breakfast at the Sunny Side Up diner when Melvin Lee Woodrow accosted me. His forced smile did not conceal his agitation.

"James, may I talk with you a minute?"

I stopped at the bottom of the steps. "What is it?" All my senses were alert to danger. I had no idea what this boy might do.

"Can we go somewhere and talk?"

"No. Tell me what you want to say."

"Sophia. I want to talk about Sophia."

"What about her?"

He scratched his head and looked down at the sidewalk. Frowning, he said, "I think she's passive aggressive."

"She's what?"

"Passive aggressive."

"Okay, so she's passive aggressive."

"Don't you find her passive aggressive?"

"No, I don't."

"I mean, she wants me to make the decisions, but they have to be what she would decide."

"She wants you to make decisions?" I laughed. Then I realized I had inadvertently insulted him.

"She says, 'Tell me what you want to do,' but it always has to be what she secretly wants to do."

"That's interesting."

He said, "In other words, she wants me to lead her, but I have to go where she wants to go. Didn't you find her to be that way?"

"No, just the opposite, actually." I looked at him now with sympathy. He was just a sensitive kid. I could now see that. "Listen," I said, "I have to go. Take care. Good luck with Sophia."

And I walked away, leaving him standing at the foot of my steps.

Halfway down the block, I walked past a boy sitting on the top step of a brownstone with a portable radio on his lap. It was turned up to maximum volume. It was blasting the song "Age of Aquarius" by the 5th Dimension. I didn't know if the moon was in the seventh house yet, but if it was, the alignment wasn't doing me any good.

One day, early at school, I was on my way to class when Amy stopped me in the hallway and said, "As soon as I finish finals and get my grades in, I'll be going to Rio."

"Yeah, I know. You told me."

"The whole family will be there together. They wanted my brother and sister and me to come down and spend the summer so we, as a family, would have the Brazil experience together." She sounded apologetic.

"That's nice," I said.

"They haven't set an exact date, but they are coming back here to stay, probably sometime early next year."

"Well, thanks for telling me."

"Let's get together before I leave. We have a few weeks. Okay?"

"Sure, okay. Call me."

One morning, my phone rang. It was Joyce Smith, director of the National Book Awards programs, calling. She said, "James, your book *Rain* has been nominated for a National Book Award. Isn't that exciting?"

"Wow!" It didn't seem real.

"Congratulations, James! The poetry committee loved your book. You will be getting an official letter, but I wanted to personally congratulate you. Okay?"

"Thank you. I'm speechless. Thanks again!"

After I hung up, I stood at the window looking out at St. Mark's Place and the people. I wasn't thinking about the street or the people. It'd been a while since the Hugo review. There had been a few other reviews since. The best ones were in the *San Francisco Chronicle, Boston Globe, Denver Post,* and the *Washington Post.*

Despite all this good luck, I didn't feel that I had suddenly leaped forward into a new life. Not that my life was so bad, but back when I was a college student, I somehow innocently believed that such reviews would change a poet's life from ordinary to sublime. How I'd gotten that impression, I didn't know. I knew enough now about academic life to realize those reviews and this nomination might have a positive effect on my eventually being considered for tenure at Lowery. Job security was something I longed for. That would be payoff enough. It would mean progress of the best, most stable kind.

The semester was going well. I was on a Tuesday through Thursday schedule, with office hours on Tuesday morning and Wednesday afternoon. I required my students to come to office hours to discuss their work privately with me, usually before it was discussed in class.

The poems kept coming. Karl wrote a poem about his dog's protracted illness. Donna wrote one about her broken heart after breaking up with her boyfriend, a math major at another college. We critiqued Leo's poem about his inexpressible inner life. Babette's poem was in

couplets and about her trip with another girl to Paris and why they parted ways. Fanny's was a quatrain and it dealt with her battle with her hair,
which was long and often tangled. The poems kept coming and coming.
They kept my weekends busy.

Also, the new issue of *Up Against the Wall* finally appeared in my
mailbox. The cover was disappointing. It was amateurish. It was from
a drawing of imaginary animals climbing all over each other by Camille Armand. The reproduction was not very good, and the two-color
scheme was off. Each of us had excellent poems in the issue. The short
story by Alvin and the essay on Richard Wright by a professor of English at Temple University were both first-rate.

Beyond the university libraries, we still had no serious long-term
subscribers; putting out an issue was almost a private matter. A few copies would be available in St. Mark's Bookshop, the 8th Street Bookstore,
the little bookshop down on Avenue C near 10th Street, a few other
bookshops, and two or three newsstands, also downtown.

These places would never take more than two or three, maybe four,
copies. Copies would be mailed to our handful of individual subscribers.

We had about fifty of those, but we'd printed five hundred copies,
the minimum we could get a printer to do. Lots of copies were always
left over. Maurice said, "Someday scholars will study and write about
this magazine." We gave away more copies than we sold, but putting that
magazine out was worth the effort.

One day after the semester ended, that Wednesday night, Amy and
I had dinner together at an 8th Street restaurant called Mr. Shapiro's.
She didn't say, "I'm going to miss you;" I didn't say to her, "I'm going to
miss you." I wanted to say that I was excited for her, but what I ended up
saying was, "Have a great trip and a great time in Brazil."

She said, "I'll send you a postcard, many postcards!"

She talked excitedly about her upcoming trip. She'd never been to
Brazil and she was an adventure junkie. She and her brother and sister
would be travelling together.

I thought I might feel sad about her leaving, but all I felt was a kind of numbness. I wanted peaceful closure to a relationship that at first seemed promising. She seemed to be leaving with the sense that we would remain friends, and I couldn't say for sure that we would not.

She left for Rio the next day.

I knew Sophia was now working nights. How late, I didn't know. How many days per week, I didn't know, but I suspected she was sleeping late into the morning.

Saturday morning, I stopped by Sophia's place. She opened the door dressed in her nightgown. I stepped inside, and she closed the door quickly and quietly. I followed her back to her bedroom. She climbed in bed, face down, and didn't pull the cover over her. The room was small and in semi-darkness because the curtains and shade were closed. The bed was also small, a single, and pushed against the wall. Sophia's right foot was touching the wall.

I sat down on the side of the bed and looked at her backside. I said, "Are you okay?"

Talking into her pillow, Sophia murmured, "Sleepy, tired."

"Maybe I should go and let you sleep. I can come back another time."

She raised her head and turned her reddened face toward me. "No!"

"No?" I said, confused.

She stretched her left hand toward me, reaching back with the fingers wiggling. I took her hand.

"Come here," she said.

I didn't think about it. As imperfect as our relationship was, we knew each other; her body remembered mine, mine remembered hers. I just did it. Undressed, I went to her.

When we finished, she looked back at me and said, "That was our best yet."

I sat on the side of the bed again and got dressed. As before, the new terms of things going on between us were undeclared. Yet it didn't seem to matter now.

Sophia! There was her eighteen-year-old playmate next door. What was his name? Melvin? She was no doubt now involved with Melvin Lee Woodrow. Poor kid, he was probably in love with Sophia and headed for a broken heart.

I continued to write poems. I hadn't really ever stopped, but teaching and editing student manuscripts now kept me very busy. On weekends, I tried to distract myself by getting out of my apartment and going someplace, any place, to the Strand bookstore, or to St. Mark's Church to listen to poets read their poems, or to just sit on a bench in Tompkins Square Park and admire the flower children at play.

It was a Friday or Saturday evening. I wandered into Cooper Union Theater. The place was full.

I sat down in the first empty seat I came to. It happened to be on the aisle. After sitting there a while, my eyes adjusting to the dark, out of the corner of my eye I noticed that I had sat beside a young woman almost as tall as I was.

I hadn't noticed her till she glanced at me and smiled. She had freckles, grey-green eyes, dark brown hair, and the point of her nose was slightly tilted up. Her eyes were big and moony. She had a kind of dreamy inwardness. She also had full lips and a pouty but friendly smile. She was wearing a light blue blouse, jeans, and sandals.

The Alvin Ailey Dance Troupe was performing on stage. They were dressed in red against a grey background. This was my first time there. I'd known about the free performances, but had never before now bothered to take advantage of one.

I knew that Cooper Union Theater also featured interesting speakers on a variety of subjects. Abraham Lincoln spoke here February 27, 1860, on the question of slavery in the territories. I'd read that speech, with its long loopy sentences, while in college.

When the dance performance ended, I walked out. In the lobby, I looked back and noticed that the young woman was right behind me. Again, she smiled. So I returned her smile.

"Hi," I said. "My name's James."

In a soft voice, she said, "My name's Rachel," and she extended her hand for me to shake. Her pear-shaped face was crowned with thick brown curly hair cropped short. Her moony eyes were wet, and she blinked often. I suspected she was wearing contacts. I liked her freckles, but now I noticed that her cute upturned nose seemed a bit too small for her large face, yet she was pretty because her eyes emitted kindness.

I said, "How about letting me treat you to some ice cream?"

"Sure," she said. We walked over to Second Avenue and entered that famous little ice cream parlor, Screaming Delicious, and ordered at the counter. As we came from the hot fumy night air into the brightly lighted parlor with its sweet sugary smells, the air conditioning felt good.

High on the wall were pictures of the various ice cream dishes.

Rachel ordered a strawberry sundae with vanilla ice cream, topped with sliced strawberries, drenched in red syrup, and garnished with peanuts and whipped cream. It came in a tall, thick glass.

I ordered a fudge sundae. It consisted of vanilla ice cream with hot fudge poured over the ice cream, with walnuts and a cherry on top.

We took our tickets and sat in a booth, waiting for the server to bring our sundaes to the table. That was the way they did it there.

"Tell me," she said, "Who is James Lowell?"

I told Rachel where I was born, where I went to school, what kind of work I did and was now doing. I didn't mention Sophia or Amy.

"How about you?" I said.

"I live here in the city, but I grew up in a small town called Antwerp; it's near Albany, New York. You want me to tell you my whole life story?"

"Everything!"

"I recently graduated with honors, with a BA in math from the State University of New York at Albany. My father is a surgeon, a pretty good one, too, I must say. My mother is a nurse. They both work at the same hospital, Albany General. Right now, I'm working as a receptionist for a doctor-friend of my father's, Dr. Meyer, on Fourteenth Street."

"That's it?"

"Well," she said, laughing, "I want to one day get married and live on a farm and have a house full of kids running in and out, and I will bake lots of cookies for them, and we'll have a bunch of pets, cats and dogs, and maybe a talking parrot or two."

I smiled. "You grew up on a farm?"

"Sort of. Antwerp's population is about seven hundred. We lived in an old farmhouse, but my parents didn't do any farming. Oh, my mother had a garden, sure. She grew squash and carrots and tomatoes. That was all the farming we did."

"So, in the future, when you have a house full of kids and your farmhouse, are you planning to grow your own food?"

"I'm sure I'll have a garden, like my mom. Food is better when you grow it yourself, don't you think?"

"Sure, I've never grown any food, but yes, I suspect it's better that way." She smiled, then said, "Tell me more about James."

I knew it was coming. "You want the short version or the long version?"

"The long one."

"Okay. I was born and raised in Park Slope, Brooklyn. I attended Brooklyn College, have a BA and MFA from there, in English. I write poetry and I'm teaching creative writing at the Warren Lowery School. That's about it."

"Have you published any poetry?"

"Yes, one book. It's called *Rain*."

"Poetry, huh? Are you related in any way to the poet Robert Lowell?"

"None whatsoever. I'm descended from a long line of Black Lowells of Springfield, Massachusetts."

"You have a long history in America. My ancestors came here around the end of the 19th century. They were escaping persecution in Europe."

The server brought our sundaes to the booth, along with napkins and two long-stemmed spoons. The sundaes looked just like the pictures up on the wall behind the counter.

We started eating right away. It'd been at least a year or longer since I'd eaten anything as sweet as that sundae. I immediately got a sugar high. The coldness of the ice cream also gave me the jitters.

I'd smoked cigarettes for a couple of months when I was nineteen. Fearing that I would become addicted, I gave up smoking. I never learned to properly inhale. I'd also smoked marijuana once, didn't like it, and never tried it again. I didn't like the drowsy feeling it gave me.

Because I enjoyed ice cream, around the same time I promised myself I would not become a sugar addict, and from that time till now I'd been mostly successful in my effort to keep away from both cigarettes and sweets, but salty things, like french fries, I was still hooked on.

When Rachel and I finished, we walked outside. She turned to me and said, "Well, it was nice meeting you." And she stuck her hand out for me to shake.

I shook her hand and said, "I'd love to see you again."

She smiled. "I'd like to see you, too." She took out a notepad and wrote down her phone number, and handed me the piece of paper. "May I have your number?"

"Yes, of course," I said.

She tore off another sheet of notepaper, and handed it with her pen to me. I quickly jotted down my number. I returned her pen and gave her the sheet with the number.

"Well, goodbye," she said, and started walking toward St. Mark's Place.

Walking alongside her, I said, "I'm going that way, too. We can walk together. I live on St. Mark's Place."

As we entered my street, she said, "I live down on Tenth between A and B."

"Oh," I said, "That's not far. May I walk you home?"

"Sure, I'd be happy to have you do that. It's pretty dark down my way. I get scared at night walking home. The streetlights are far apart and dim. A girl in my building got raped one night, around midnight, about a month ago."

"Oh, no!"

"They raped her in the hallway behind the stairway, you know, in the stairwell."

"Did they catch the rapist?"

"It was four or five guys. They were just young boys. A gang, probably. She didn't scream. She said she was afraid they would kill her."

"Did she report the rape?"

"I don't think she did. She told me about it quite by accident. We happened one morning to be walking together from our building to the subway, going to work. She was just telling me to be careful coming home at night."

When we reached Rachel's building, we stopped at the bottom of the ominous stairway. I said, "Well, I think you'll be okay from here."

"Yes, but it would be rude of me not to invite you in after you've walked all the way down here. Would you like to come in for a cup of tea?"

"Okay, sure. I'd like a cup of tea."

Rachel's apartment was the first one on the first floor, Apartment 1A. It was on the right side of the hallway. I stood beside her as she, using two different keys, unlocked the door.

She looked around at me and laughed. "I know this looks ridiculous, but these locks were here before I moved in."

I shrugged. "Maybe they're there for a good reason."

"Being a first-floor apartment," she said, as the door swung open, "it's easy access. I'm learning these things, farm girl that I am. At home upstate, we never had to lock our doors. Everybody in our town knew one another."

I followed Rachel into her apartment. The place had a Lysol smell. She hit the light switch and the dull ceiling light came on. She'd covered it with one of those Japanese paper lantern shades. It was pink and green.

The tiny apartment was dark and typical of the Lower East Side apartments I'd seen. The furniture, couch, chairs, kitchen table with its two chairs, all looked like things she'd bought at the local used furniture store on First Avenue.

Her taste was expressed everywhere. She had spread an inexpensive Indian textile with colorful images of dancers, across the back of the couch, and another one over the cushions. Same with the armchair: she'd covered the back and cushion with textiles. Each had its own colorful mandala design. Hanging over the paper-shade window was a fifth textile with an elephant pattern.

"Have a seat. I'll put on some hot water for tea."

"I can help you," I said, and followed her into the tiny kitchen. It smelled clean to the point of mania.

The small table was covered with a plastic tablecloth with a red and white pattern. I sat down at the kitchen table and watched her at the sink filling the kettle with water. "This is herb tea, it's German chamomile. I'm trying it for the first time. Do you like chamomile?"

"Yes, I do, but I haven't had it often."

"I usually drink rosehip at night or peppermint or just plain American chamomile."

When the tea was ready, we sat across from one another at the kitchen table with our cups of hot tea steaming in front of us. I said, "It's too hot to drink right now."

"It'll cool quickly." She smiled. "So, tell me more about James."

"Didn't I say enough?"

"Well, you didn't say a lot."

"Let's see. I recently spent a few months in Mexico. I finished my book there." I paused. "I also recently got a good review in the *New York Times Book Review*."

"I thought I recognized your name."

"You saw the review?"

"Tell me again the name of your book?"

"*Rain*."

"I'm going to buy it tomorrow. Do they have it at the Strand?"

"I'm sure they do, but don't bother. I'll give you a copy."

"Oh, great! You're peachy keen! I can't wait to read your poetry!"

I felt a little embarrassed by her enthusiasm.

"Didn't you get nominated for something?"

"The National Book Award. Many are called, few are chosen."

"Very funny. I bet you'll win."

"You have more confidence than I do." I sipped the hot tea and burned my tongue.

Smiling, Rachel said, "All good things come to those who wait."

"I'm waiting." I was watching her toothy smile. "So, why did you move to New York?"

"It was time. I needed to get out of Antwerp."

"Why?"

"Why? Because it was all I knew, and I needed to know something else. I now realize that Antwerp is a nice quiet town and I don't regret having grown up there. The Indian River runs through town right under Main Street, and there are Amish people riding through town in their buggies pulled by horses."

"Sounds idyllic."

"It's quaint. After I read every book at Crosby Public Library, I left town for college. After college, I knew I could never live in Antwerp again."

"Did your folks approve your coming to New York?"

"Oh, no, no way! My dad almost disowned me, that is, till I promised to take the job in Dr. Meyer's office. You see, in that way Dad could get reports on me from his friend, Marvin. They think I don't know that Dr. Meyer tells them how I dress and how I look and if I look like I'm getting enough sleep and eating properly, all those kinds of things."

We drank our tea and talked for another hour before I stood and said, "Well, it's late, I'd better go. Wouldn't want to keep you from getting your sleep." It was a quarter to ten.

Rachel stood up, too. "It's Saturday! Tomorrow is Sunday! Why are you leaving so soon?"

She came around the table and kissed me on the lips. My arms slid naturally around her and pulled her closer so that I felt her body against mine.

"Wow!" I said.

"I've been a good girl too long. I have a right now, for a change... Don't you think?" She kissed me again.

"If you say so," I said, and felt the tip of her tongue touch mine, causing the last word "so" to come out muffled.

After we made love, we lay there on the couch side by side in the dark. At one point, Rachel said, "Do you remember your first love?"

"Sure, Adella Jones, high school, Brooklyn. Beautiful girl, people called her Mellow Yellow. She had a head full of curly red hair and pretty skin. Her eyes sparkled, and she had pretty teeth, with a small gap between her two front teeth."

"I bet she was very pretty."

"She was. How about your first love?" I said.

"I wasn't allowed to have a first love. I never dated till I was away from home in college. My parents were very strict."

I didn't know what to say.

Rachel said, "Did you keep in touch with Adella?"

"No, it's a long story."

"Give me the short version."

"Maybe it was puppy-love, but at the time it seemed profoundly real to me. I used to walk her home from school. I would carry her books for her. She was my goddess. Then another girl, Eudora, became interested in me. Having two girls wanting to be my girlfriend went to my head. Then, one day, Eudora caught up with me walking Adella home, carrying her books. She confronted us. She said, 'James, you have to choose. It's Adella or me. You can't string us both along.' So I chose Adella, and Eudora walked away in a huff."

"Oh, how sad for Eudora."

"Yes, it must have been painful for her."

"What was your courtship like with Adella?"

"We never went all the way, if that's what you're asking. She wouldn't let me. We just kissed a lot. I would walk her home, and we would sit on her couch and kiss."

"Where were her parents?"

"She lived with her mother in an apartment near school. Her mother liked me. She thought I was a nice boy and she approved of me seeing her daughter, maybe because she knew we weren't doing anything but kissing."

"Were you a nice boy?"

"I wasn't trying to be, but maybe I was."

"I think you were probably a nice boy, and handsome, too. I bet all the girls called you 'cute.' Or was it 'pretty boy'? Tell me what led up to the kissing."

"She and I would get to her apartment a little after three. Her mother didn't get home from work till around five, so we had plenty of time to kiss and kiss and kiss."

"Girls like to kiss. There was no father?"

"Her mother had a boyfriend."

"Oh, did he live there?"

"No, he didn't. I think he may have been married, and Adella's mother was his mistress on the side. I don't know, but he wasn't around often."

"Did you keep in touch with Adella?"

"No, that was a long time ago. High school. I don't even keep in touch with my friends from college these days."

It was 1:30 a.m. when I left Rachel's apartment, walking home. On the way, I thought about Rachel and my high school girlfriend. Rachel was a nice girl, but she wanted a house full of kids. I didn't. She wanted to live on a farm. I didn't. By now I was longing for a stable lasting relationship and even marriage, but I knew Rachel was not the girl to step into that role.

She was sweet and innocent and playful. I didn't want to lead her on or give her the impression that I was interested in a serious, lasting relationship with her. That would have been dishonest.

So, should I see her again? If there was no future in the relationship, why should I see her again? On the other hand, I wanted to. What was wrong with giving each other temporary comfort? I was beginning to realize that loneliness could do a lot of damage to a person. Human beings were social animals. We needed each other.

It would not be enough to teach my classes, correct manuscripts, then go for a walk in Tompkins Square Park or to go listen to poets read their work at St. Mark's Church. So, sure, I would see Rachel again, and she would be happy to see me. She didn't want to be alone either. Like me, she was probably waiting for the right person to come along. Till she found the guy who wanted to live on a farm and have a house full of kids and lots of animals, she needed to do something about her present loneliness.

When I reached my street, St. Mark's Place was still crowded with revelers milling about up and down the block. Many stores, head shops, and clubs were still open and brightly lighted and doing brisk business. The street was full of the voices of excited people and music from more than one portable radio.

The free St. Mark's Theater, with people living on the stage, was open continuously with a steady parade of people entering and leaving. I walked in and, about halfway along the aisle, sat down. On stage, one young man was arguing with another about a missing sandwich. He said he'd placed it in the refrigerator to have for tomorrow. The other young man kept shrugging his shoulders and saying he had no idea what happened to the sandwich.

After ten minutes of that, I got up and walked out. I was tired. I was on my way home to go to bed.

The Lower East Side clubs called Gas Station and Theatre 80 were also open. Crowds were gathered there. People were sitting on the steps of St. Mark's Hotel smoking dope.

Six teenage girls, probably from Long Island or New Jersey, were parading along the sidewalk, arm and arm. They were wearing tons of makeup and bright red lipstick. They were laughing hysterically at a half-naked man ahead of them walking along, shouting, "Emma Goldman lives! Long live Emma Goldman!"

As I approached my building, I saw Chicken Man sitting on the bottom step, talking to his chicken. He was an old Black man with unkempt white hair and beard. He had a mouth full of bad and missing teeth. He wore raggedy clothes and he smelled bad. It was widely known that at night he slept in doorways along St. Mark's Place.

Any time of the day or night you could see Chicken Man walking up and down St. Mark's Place with his chicken on his shoulder. He never begged or asked passersby for money. This, of course, caused people to wonder how he managed to feed himself.

Stepping around Chicken Man, I started climbing the steps to the entrance of my building. He watched me climb the steps. "Hey, Boss," said Chicken Man.

"Hello, Chicken Man."

"Ain't the stars pretty tonight?"

I looked up at the overcast night sky, and I couldn't see any stars. "I don't see any stars."

"I thought you had the third eye, Boss. You need the third eye, you got to have the third eye to see them."

I laughed. "Then I guess I'm out of luck."

I continued on up the steps. On the landing, I had to step around a drunken man sleeping near the doorway.

Inside, I took a quick shower and went to bed. In five minutes, I was asleep, with the Saturday night sounds coming through my widow.

Later in the night, a sound woke me. There was no wall between my bedroom and the kitchen. Lying in bed, I could see into the kitchen. It took a few seconds to get my eyes opened so that I could focus. Then, clearly, I saw the silhouette of a man outside my kitchen window standing on the fire escape at the back of the building. I had the window opened for night air. Just as he sat down on the sill and started hoisting himself into my kitchen, I shouted, "Hey!"

His legs were inside, but the rest of his body was still outside on the fire escape.

He called out, "Sorry! Wrong apartment! My mistake!" And he scrambled back out onto the fire escape, and I heard him jump down to the ground.

I got up and went to the window. I looked out, and in the dim light I saw a splash of blond hair as he was limping away down the alley. He'd obviously, in the jump to the ground, sprained his ankle.

New York, Sunday morning, 6 a.m. was local television's "ethnic hour." I was half awake and turned on the TV to see who or what they might come up with that morning.

I saw the face of well-known Black Nationalist proponent of "the Black Aesthetic," Merton R. Nestor, Jr. I caught him in mid-sentence saying, "...and Mr. James Eric Lowell has just published a book of poems called *Rain*, and in my opinion, it leaves a lot to be desired. I know it was well-reviewed in the *New York Times Book Review* and that it's just been nominated for the National Book Award, but that's just the problem: they nominate these Black authors who write like white folks. I want to see poetry that speaks to the Black experience, poetry that tells it like it is, not this imitation white-folk stuff. I want to see that poetry get the kind of recognition that they tend to give books like *Rain*. Why, you read those poems and you don't see anything in the poems that tell you the author is Black."

The camera moved back, and panning, it included the man Nestor was talking to. He was Professor Johnson from one of the Black colleges. Johnson said, "I tend to agree, Mert, but remember, this is a new generation of young Black poets, and Mr. Lowell is just starting. Maybe in time he will evolve and find out who he is, and learn to appreciate his Blackness and his great heritage."

Or, I thought, perhaps your definition of "Blackness" is too narrow, too limited, too restricted to stereotypes. Here again, like the Black Nationalist poets in Harlem who took issue with my poems, Nestor had a very narrow concept of Afro-American life. My poems were the product of my experience and I was a Black American. Period.

I turned off the TV and closed my eyes and tried to go back to sleep, but instead, I lay there fuming, thinking that Blackness, and its invention, whiteness, were two unhealthy social constructs constantly being used as political footballs. There was no end in sight.

A Monday early in July, I heard the mailman downstairs in the hallway at 10 a.m., his usual time. When I heard the outside door close, I knew he was gone, so I trotted down to collect my mail.

Back upstairs, I sat at the kitchen table and separated first class from junk. There was a piece of mail that caught my eye, a letter from Frank Garrick with this return address: Department of English, Willem Granville University. It was a small liberal arts college in Stamford, Connecticut. Wow, I thought, Frank is back in the States and it looks like he's teaching.

I quickly tore open the envelope and started reading.

Dear James,

I would have called, but you are apparently unlisted. So I got your address from your school. They didn't want to give it to me, but I told them I was a close friend and that it was an emergency.

First, let me congratulate you on *Rain*. I loved it! You've gotten off to a great start. Congratulations also on the National Book Award nomination, and I also congratulate you on that excellent front-page review in the *New York Times Book Review*. You are well on your way. I'm a bit jealous.

I am once again living in New York City. I'm on West 73rd Street. I commute to Stamford to teach. It was time to leave Mexico. Things were getting crazy there; the house was broken into several times. Americans were being kidnapped for ransom. It was too much!

Suzette, of course, is still there. She has her practice. My kids, Bonita and Selena, are up here right now visiting me, but for the most part, they still live with Suzette. She and I have a good arrangement. More good news: you remember meeting Carol Leland when you were visiting us in Mexico City? Carol and I got married just this past April. We're a legit family now. She's still working on her poems, trying to make sure they are as good as she can make them.

Aside from all of the above, I am writing to ask if you'd be interested in coming to Granville to read from your new book. By the way, we're on the quarter system. We can't pay a lot, but at least you don't have to get on an airplane and fly anywhere.

If you don't have access to a car, I can pick you up and bring you up here, and I'd be happy to deliver you safely back home. We can decide on a date and time as we get closer to the fall quarter.

One of the first things I did on returning to New York was to buy a pretty good used car, a 1966 Ford Fairlane. I kind of like the long front and short back. A muscle car! And, by the way, I brought *Nuevo Mundo* with me, and its new address is my apartment here at West 73rd. Send me some new poems. I look forward to hearing from you.

All the best to you,
Frank

He had written his phone number and apartment address at the bottom of the page.

That afternoon, I called Frank and he picked up. I said, "Hey, Frank! I got your letter! Good to hear from you ..." We talked for a while about Mexico, then I said, "Sure, I'd be happy to give a reading at Granville in the fall."

"Actually, James, I can give you a date now, and you can see if it works for you. How about Monday, October 13th?"

"As far as I know, I have nothing else going on at that time so, sure, I'll put it on my calendar." Then, before hanging up, for a while we talked about the joys and woes of teaching.

I wouldn't have to return to teaching till September. *Rain* got me the job. The nomination and the front-page review got me a pat on the back. I needed another book to be considered for any kind of promotion.

Tenure would mean job security. It would free me from financial worry. Short of winning the National Book Award, that second book was essential. Probably not even the National Book Award would be enough to propel me from assistant to associate.

I'd heard from various longtime associate professors in the department that they were having a hard time getting promoted to full. Even those with new scholarly books were only grudgingly promoted. The salary increase was not much. Jealousy and hypocritical backbiting were quietly rampant.

Part of the problem was Lowery was a prestigious small liberal arts school, and the powers that be felt that we should be contented with the privilege and honor of teaching at the great, historic Warren Lowery School of Fine Arts. Never mind the low salary. Money was a pedestrian subject. Creative people and intellectuals should keep their minds free of such base concerns.

Five-thirty in the evening, I got tired of struggling with words and went out for a walk. Impulsively, I found myself walking to Rachel's on

East 10th Street. I got there and knocked on her door. I was thinking I should have called first. What if she had company?

Inside, I heard her say, "Who is it?"

"It's me, James."

She opened the door, and I was glad to see a big smile spread across her face. "Come on in, I was just thinking about you. I just got in from work. You want some tea? I was just making some for myself."

"Yes, thank you."

I sat on the couch and Rachel went to her pretty ceramic teapot on the counter. It had pictures of hummingbirds in midair feeding at the faces of flowers. She lifted the top and looked in. "Not ready yet, still steeping."

She came back and sat beside me. "What've you been up to?"

"All afternoon I've been struggling with a poem that is not evolving the way it should."

"Bad, bad poem, misbehaving poem," she said, laughing. "You seem kind of tense. You want to… ?"

"Sure," I said.

On the couch, as before, we made love. Finished, I got dressed and she put on a robe.

"I'll get the tea," she said. "You stay right here and just relax."

She placed the teacups on the coffee table. As she sat down, she said, "Last night, I had a bad dream that something happened to you. My dream was pretty awful. I woke up sweating." She sipped her tea, keeping her eyes focused on me.

"Don't worry about me."

"Why not?" She paused. "Are you going to spend the night with me to keep me from having another bad dream?"

"No, sorry, I can't. I've got to get back to the typewriter, back to the sweet struggle. I'm working on a second book of poems."

"I assumed you were," she said, with a sad smile.

That following Friday, I opened my mailbox, and I immediately saw an airmail envelope with a lot of colorful foreign stamps: a blue one with a World War I airplane, one with a cowboy on horseback, one with a red and yellow parrot, one with a waterfall, one with a lighthouse, and one with a beautiful light-blue butterfly.

I thought of my stamp collection. When I was about fifteen, I started collecting stamps. I inserted them in little sleeves in my stamp scrapbook.

I remembered my greatest ones: Monaco Exposition du Centenaire 1847-1947; Danmark 200; Australia 1829-1929, three half-pence, with a profile of a graceful swan; New Zealand, 1½ Postage & Revenue Victory, with the face of an aboriginal man on the right side and the leaves of a plant on the other side; Portugal, 30, with a green and yellow parrot in the center; Hong Kong, 30 cents, in blue, red, and white.

I also had stamps from Cuba, Yugoslavia, Nigeria, Ghana, France, Liberia, Italy, and Spain, but most were United States stamps. To my way of thinking, the U.S. stamps were not as flamboyant, not as exotic, and therefore not as interesting.

Gazing now at the stamps on the envelope, I remembered my childhood daydreaming about those places and their peoples. Back then, it was my fifteen-year-old way of traveling the world.

Before I went to college, I sold the whole collection to a Brooklyn dealer, Orville's Stamps, Coins, Gold & Jewelry Company, Inc., for a tenth of what it was worth.

Now, these Brazil stamps would have been a delightful addition.

In the same instant, I noticed the name and the return address. It was from Amy Lawrence in Rio. I climbed the steps with the envelope and the other mail, mostly bills and junk, and walked up to the front and stood by the window where the light from outside was strong and bright. Then I sat down in the armchair with my back to the window. I opened the envelope, unfolded the letter and started reading:

Dear James,

I trust you are well and happy. I'm enjoying life here in Brazil. I'm no longer staying with my parents. I have my own apartment, or rather, Jordao and I have our own place now. I dread having to go back to teaching this fall. New York seems like a faraway, distant world.

Yes, I'm in love! And Jordao is teaching me Portuguese!

You would like him! He writes poetry, too. He has not published, but his poems are delightful. We do everything together. We go to the market to shop for our food every morning. We buy only fresh things. We hike together. We swim together, but my parents don't approve of our relationship.

They don't understand what Jordao and I have together, but I knew you would understand.

Affectionately,

Amy

The letter surprised me. I got a pen and paper and immediately wrote to her:

Dear Amy,

It was nice to hear from you. I am happy for you. I'm glad you are happily in love. I wish you continued happiness in the bright sun of Brazil.

Warm wishes,

James

The following morning, I got up, showered, dressed, and skipped down the steps to the sidewalk. St. Mark's Place was already getting crowded with Saturday people.

Chicken Man was walking up and down the block with his chicken on his left shoulder. He saw a pretty girl coming his way. He took off his old greasy hat and bowed to her. Then he shouted in her face, "Girl, you better get ready! Glory train a-coming!"

In the past, I'd seen him approach girls together and not only bow, he'd do a bit of a fox trot in celebration of their beauty. Girls who knew his antics would laugh. Those who'd never before seen him would run as fast as they could.

Now, as always, even as he danced, the chicken stayed on his shoulder. The chicken's head was bobbing in jerky motions as he was looking around.

I walked to the mailbox and dropped the letter to Brazil in the box on the corner. My neighbor, the poet W. H. Auden, came up behind me. He lived on the other side of the street across from my building. I had occasionally seen him in the neighborhood and at St. Mark's Church.

Holding an envelope bright with airmail stamps across the upper right corner, Auden, with a faint polite smile and nod, waited for me to finish with the mailbox. I returned his unspoken greeting with a nod and smile. After I stepped away, he dropped his envelope in the box. Then he turned and headed back across the street. As he walked away, I noticed he was wearing house slippers.

I walked up to Second Avenue and entered the Sunny Side Up diner. I took a booth by the window, and I could see Cooper Union with the morning sunlight shining on its dark red brick façade, and the summer school students on their way to classes.

I ordered bacon, eggs, an English muffin, orange juice, and coffee.

While I ate, I listened to the guys in the booth behind me. They were talking about Janis Joplin's upcoming appearance at Woodstock in August. They were planning to go. Then they were soon talking about Neil Armstrong in Apollo 11. They were speculating about whether or not the moon landing would be a success. "That's going to be some occasion," one of them said.

I was also thinking of Rachel. I finished breakfast and headed for East 10th Street. I figured since it was Saturday morning, she would be home.

Inside, I heard the whirring of a vacuum cleaner. After I knocked three times, the vacuum cleaner stopped, and I heard Rachel ask, "Yes? Who is it?"

"It's me, James."

She opened the door. She stood there with a slightly embarrassed expression. There was a red and green kerchief tied around her hair, and she was wearing an old faded white t-shirt, and faded and torn tan shorts. She was barefoot. I noticed for the first time how large her feet were. "Come on in. I'm cleaning! Saturday morning, I clean!"

I stopped in the doorway. "Oh, should I come back another time?"

"No, no, come on in, I'm almost done. You want to help?"

"Sure! Put me to work."

"Here's a dust-rag, go to work." I took the rag and started dusting surfaces everywhere I saw one.

Rachel turned off the vacuum cleaner and I watched her store it in the little closet by her front door. "Guess what?" she said.

"What?"

"My mother, my dear mother, went to the trouble to make duplicates of all my baby pictures and pictures of me when I was growing up before I went away to college, and this morning I got this album. Yes, she put them in a scrapbook for me, and sent it. This is one of the nicest things my mother has ever done for me. I was so surprised! Would you like to see me when I was little?"

"Sure." I sat on the couch and waited.

She sailed out of the room and returned from her bedroom with a dark blue photo album. When Rachel was excited like this, her voice rose to a higher pitch. "Here," she said. "I'll put it here on the coffee table, so you can see. I'm so pleased you want to see my pictures!"

"Of course."

She opened the album to the first page.

"This is a picture of Poppa and Mama on their wedding day. Her maiden name was Sturm. She was first to tell you that the Sturm people were very stern."

"Very funny. Is this you as a baby?" I was pointing to the next picture.

"Yep! That's me! Sometimes I think Mama regrets that I'm no longer her baby. We've had some conflict ever since I went away to college. Maybe her sending this album to me is her way of saying, 'See, this is the you that I like best.'"

I smiled, thinking of my own mother's regret that I was no longer a little boy she could pamper and dress in knee-pants.

"This is me at about age three on my little tricycle."

"Cute!"

"And this is me with Mama and Poppa at the carnival that came to town once a year. They put me on the merry-go-round horse. At first I was scared out of my mind, then I got used to it and grew to like it."

"You look scared."

"I was!" She turned the page. "I was about fifteen here. A local rancher, Morris Lothario, let local kids ride his ponies. He was a friend of Poppa's. This pony's name was Fergus. I always thought that was a funny name for a horse."

"When were these taken?"

"High school. This girl's name is Helen, this one is Jean, this one is Ruth, and the blond is Rebecca. We were just clowning around for the camera. I think it was the last day of school. We were happy summer was coming. It'd been a very cold winter."

"No college pictures?"

"No, I guess Mama didn't really have any. I don't think she was interested in pictures of me at that point, but I have a few. Do you want me to get them?"

"Sure, why not?"

She left the room and returned with a manila envelope. She sat down again beside me and pulled a handful of photographs from the envelope. She spread them out on the coffee table.

"Wow!" I said. "I like these. May I have this one?"

"Of course. I'm flattered you want a picture of me."

In the one I chose, she was sitting on the arm of a couch. She had a toothy smile and her eyes were glassy as though she'd had a couple of drinks, and she was wearing a short skirt and her bare thighs shone very prominently. I stuck the picture in my shirt pocket.

Rachel suddenly kissed me. "I'm so happy you wanted to see my photographs."

When I got back to St. Mark's Place, I saw Darius Wright coming along the sidewalk toward me. He waved and smiled, with sunlight shining on his front gold tooth.

I stopped at the foot of my stairway and waited for him. I hadn't seen him since the last editorial meeting for *Up Against the Wall*. In fact, I hadn't seen any of the guys since then.

"What's up?" I said.

"On my way home. Just coming from the 8th Street bookstore. Just picked up this copy of *Howl*. Alvin lent my copy to somebody and he can't remember to whom. It was autographed, too."

"You'll run into Allen no doubt and get this one signed, too."

"Yeah, I know. He's around, but he goes out to California a lot, though."

At home I had beer and wine, but I knew Darius preferred to smoke pot. He didn't drink much alcohol, so I said, "Want to come up for a cup of coffee?"

He looked at his watch. "Sure. I promised Josie I'd be back by three, but, hell, it's only ten after one. So, sure, sure."

Upstairs I got busy brewing some fresh coffee in my coffeemaker. Darius sat at the kitchen table looking through the little black book where he jotted down ideas for poems.

He groaned. "Gosh, I wish I had a joint. My contact got busted and I haven't had any weed for over a week."

The coffee was ready, and I placed the pot on a coaster between us with two cups. At the left end of the table, the sugar bowl was beside the salt and pepper shakers.

Darius and I sat across from one another at my kitchen table. He poured coffee in his cup. He didn't reach for the sugar. "James, you got any cream, man?"

"In the fridge. Just milk, no cream."

He groaned and got up, and got the carton of milk, and poured a few drops into his coffee. "You should keep cream, man."

"I should."

"In Morocco, every day, Josie and I got fresh goat milk."

"From a goat?"

"No, from the market, man. When Josie and I were living in Morocco, we got only fresh milk, but we got more first-class weed than we could ever smoke. It was heaven living in the Tensift-El Haouz region of Marrakesh. We were just down the street from where Josephine Baker stayed at the Riad Star during the War."

"Yeah, I read somewhere that she worked as a spy for the French Resistance and when the war was over, France celebrated her with the

Croix de Guerre and the Rosette de la Résistance for her undercover work against the Nazis."

Darius said, "Yeah. You know about the little argan nut?"

"No, what is the argan nut?"

"Well, in Morocco, there are these trees called the argan tree. They farm the trees. Goats climb the trees and eat the nuts, and when they poop out the kernels, farmworkers go behind the goats picking up the kernels."

"Sounds disgusting."

"No, man, it's not disgusting. It's big business."

"You're going to tell me pooping processes the kernels?"

"That's right. That's exactly right! Then the kernels are ground up to make precious oil. You can even buy it here in New York! Women use the stuff."

"What for?"

"They use it on their skin and hair," Darius said. "It's precious and expensive stuff, man."

Someone knocked three times at the door. I wasn't expecting anyone. Several times people had knocked at the door asking for Milo, the guy who used to live in this apartment. I suspected it was yet another person looking for Milo.

I went to the door. "Yes? Who is it?"

"James, it's me, Rachel!"

I opened the door, surprised to see her. She was wearing a pullover and jeans and sandals. She held out my wallet. "You forgot your wallet. It was on the end table."

I was surprised. "Oh, thank you!" I took the wallet and pushed it into my back pocket. "Funny, I didn't miss it. Got to be more careful. Come on in."

She stepped inside. This was her first time at my place.

"Rachel, this is Darius. Darius, Rachel."

She said, "Hi, Darius."

He said, "Hey, how're you doing?"

I'm sure Rachel didn't miss the leer in his voice. I knew Darius was a womanizer. It was something Josephine probably long ago got used to.

Rachel didn't respond to his question, instead, she said, "If you guys are busy, I don't need to stay. James, I just came by to give you your wallet."

"We're not busy. We're just drinking coffee. Want a cup?"

She hesitated. I knew why. She didn't normally drink coffee. Rachel was a tea person.

And maybe Darius's leer offended her. If it hadn't, it should have. She pulled out one of the kitchen chairs, and sat down next to me and across from Darius.

I poured her a cup of coffee.

"So, what do you do, Rachel?" said Darius.

"I'm a receptionist in a doctor's office."

"I mean, beside that, you know, what interests you?"

"I'm interested in music and art and science, actually the whole world, if you want to know. What do you do?"

I thought, aha! She got him there. Darius did nothing but write poems in his little notebook. As far as I knew, he'd never had a job. Josephine worked to support them. She also had family money.

He said, "I'm a poet, I daydream." He was grinning.

"Good for you," she said. She looked slightly annoyed.

I decided to try to change the direction of the conversation. I said, "Darius was telling me about Morocco."

They both looked at me with dismay.

The conversation, after that, got even more awkward, and ten minutes later, Rachel stood up and said, "I've got to go. I've got so much to do. Nice to meet you, Darius."

"Wait," he said. "I'm leaving, too. I'll walk out with you."

She looked annoyed, but waited by the door.

That following Monday, while I was at the typewriter working on a poem, I kept struggling with one line. Should it be:

> My gait faltered, my thoughts fell out of orbit

or

> My stride stumbled; my thoughts dropped out of orbit

After several versions, I gave up and not only junked the line, but the whole draft of the would-be poem. By then, it was close to noon. My phone rang. I was becoming skeptical about answering the phone because lately I'd received so many crank calls.

It was reported in the newspapers and on radio and TV news that crank calls were becoming more and more widespread in the city. The few callers so far caught turned out to be bored teenage boys or girls.

It was now a misdemeanor to make such a call. I picked up the receiver. "Hello?"

"James, it's me, Rachel."

"Rachel. What's up?"

"I'm at work right now. I'd like to stop by after work."

"Sure. Are you okay?"

"I'll tell you when I get there. It'll be around five-thirty."

"Okay, see you then."

Immediately, I worried that she might be coming to say she was pregnant.

I gave up on trying to work on poetry. I went to Cinema Village, down on 12th Street to catch the matinee. A new movie was showing, *Midnight Cowboy*. I enjoyed the quirkiness of it, the humor. It was such a New York movie. The distraction from my own life was a pleasant momentary change.

At a quarter to six, I opened the door for Rachel. She was looking stressed. She was wearing makeup and her office clothes: a proper white blouse with a collar, a pleated blue skirt, stockings, and the block-type black high heels.

"Tell me about your friend, Darius."

"Let's go up to the living room," I said.

I sat down on the couch and invited her to join me. Instead, she sat in the armchair. She dropped her purse on the floor beside the chair and crossed her legs, and as she did so, the friction of her stockings rubbing together made a swish sound.

"What do you want to know about Darius?"

"Does he have a girlfriend?"

"I don't know." I really didn't know.

"Yes, you do. That's all right, don't tell me. He's your friend!"

"What happened?"

"He charmed me into having sex with him. Don't get me wrong, I like him. I just think I may have given in too soon. If I'm going to have a relationship with him, I want to make sure he's serious and that he really likes me. I want to know that he's not just playing me for sex. You know what I mean?"

"I know what you mean, Rachel."

I felt sorry for her. At the same time, I was surprised that she had had sex with Darius, but I shouldn't have been. I said, "When did it happen, when you left here together, Saturday?"

"No, Sunday. He came back over Sunday."

"Oh, Rachel, Rachel. Why?"

"I know, I know! But you and I are not in a committed relationship. We're just keeping each other company and doing so out of loneliness."

She was right about that. I liked her, but I didn't feel strongly attached to her, and I certainly didn't love her other than as a friend. I said, "What happened Saturday, when he left here with you?"

"He walked me home. He's such a smooth talker and I love his eyes. You can tell by his eyes that he's a dreamer. He said all the right things. He was telling me about his idyllic life growing up in Jamaica, that paradise island."

"I guess it is a paradise. I've never been there. I've heard that there is a lot of poverty and crime. A lot of the country is rural, so maybe that's what Darius meant by paradise. He once told me he grew up halfway between Kingston and Ocho Rios, Saint Ann Parish."

"Interesting. When we got to my apartment, he read some of his poems to me. He is quite good, I think."

"Yes, he's a good poet," I said.

"But I suspect he has a girlfriend."

I said nothing, and I felt bad about saying nothing.

She looked crestfallen. "It's just a suspicion I have. There's no way a young man that good-looking and that charming is going to be without a girlfriend. So, tell me the truth: does he have a girlfriend?"

"Rachel, you'll have to ask him. I'm not comfortable talking with you about Darius."

I wanted to save her from Darius. I knew his reputation, but I felt it was not my place to interfere. She'd gotten herself into this thing with Darius, but I was not going to save her from herself, nor was I ready to teach Darius a moral lesson by squealing on him. He was a scoundrel, but I wasn't his reformer.

I wasn't about to tell Rachel that Darius was married and that his wife, Josephine, supported him and herself, and she even paid his child support to Flavia for Darius's daughter, Ermina, five years old. I also was not going to tell her that Josephine had had a nervous breakdown and was institutionalized for six or seven months after she found out about Darius's affair with Flavia.

Yes, Darius was charming, but also perilous, maybe even toxic. Rachel had come to the city for adventure and, in her own words, to not be a good girl for a change. Maybe she would find out the truth soon enough.

One Friday morning, I felt depressed and couldn't work at hammering out lines of poetry. I walked up to the Strand bookstore to browse. For me, browsing was recreational and therapeutic, and the Strand was the perfect place to entertain and treat myself to therapy. I went immediately to the poetry section.

I was checking out titles and familiar names on the spines of the thin volumes. It was both inspiring and overwhelming to see the names: Walt Whitman, Emily Dickinson, Jean Toomer, Gwendolyn Brooks, W.B. Yeats, Langston Hughes, E.E. Cummings, Sylvia Plath, Pablo Neruda, Thomas Hardy, John Keats, Robert Hayden, Ezra Pound, Elizabeth Bishop, Sara Teasdale, William Blake, Edna St. Vincent Millay, T.S. Eliot, Theodore Roethke, and Dylan Thomas.

Then someone tapped me lightly on the back. I turned around. It was David Williams, grinning from ear-to-ear. For years, it was rumored that David Williams was not his real name. Then who was he? What was he hiding? I never found out.

David, for years, was also said to be writing the Great American

Novel, but nobody had seen any of it. Knowing David, and how laid-back he was, I suspected that he had very little, if anything, on paper.

During winter and fall, David taught two days a week at Georgia Douglas Johnson Community College in Harlem. His academic title: the James L. Smith Professor of Literature in English. (The slaveholder, Thomas Langsdon, of Northumberland County, Virginia, legally owned "James L. Smith". Smith published the story of his own life as a slave in 1881.)

David said, "What's up, Mr. National-Book-Award-winner?"

"Being nominated is not winning, David."

"It's close enough. Man, you're famous now. Are reporters following you around these days?" He was still grinning.

"Cut it out, David." I felt insulted by the fun he was having at my expense.

"No, seriously. I've seen dudes get rich and famous and stop speaking to their old friends, but you're not like that, James, and that is to your credit."

"First of all, I'm not famous, and I'm not rich."

"You got a teaching job at a first-rate college. I'm teaching at a third-rate college. The place is run more like high school than college. There are thousands of dudes out here writing poems trying to get where you are. You lucky, man."

"You're lucky, too. You're teaching. Let's go down to the Bowery and get a drink at Bonar's."

He said, "I don't know if I can go in that place again. Herbert and I were in there a month ago and some drunken white dude started calling us names. I slapped him and the bouncer put Herbert and me out, not the white guy."

"Well, you did hit him."

"Yeah, but he had it coming."

"Let's go there," I said. "They probably won't even remember you."

As usual, two or three drifters were hanging around the front of the tavern. They frowned as we walked by them.

Over the door: Established 1856.

We entered Bonar's Old Beer Tavern. Immediately the wet and sour and yeasty smells of beer, with a faint scent of barley, assailed our nostrils.

Inside, it was an old space. There was a high ceiling made of wooden planks. The walls were covered with framed photographs. They were mostly of well known or famous people who'd drunk in Bonar's since the 19th century. There were so many pictures that they were hung side-by-side, up and down and all across all the walls.

There were hundreds of notables: Jack Johnson and other boxers; Mickey Rooney, Rita Hayworth, and other movie stars; radio and TV people; Jackson Pollock, Andy Warhol, and other artists; and Norman Mailer, Truman Capote, and other writers.

The floor was wooden, with sawdust spread across it.

The original lamplights were long ago replaced by electric lights; big bulbs were suspended from the ceiling because it was dark in there, even in the daytime. It was necessary to keep the lights on. An old fan turned slowly in the ceiling.

On a back wall was a big clock with Roman numerals. The bar was the original old oak bar. Even the cash register behind the bar was the original 19th century one they started with back then.

Alongside the cash register was a blackboard on which the bartender wrote the day's specials: fish and chips, burgers, clams, ham and cheese, and the like. Also behind the bar were a thousand and one trinkets, gifts given to the various bartenders over the years.

David and I stood at the bar. Even this early in the day, the place was packed with mostly men, young and old. Most of them were dressed in pullovers or untucked sport shirts and jeans or slacks. Some were obviously students, with backpacks resting on the floor beside their chairs, or young professionals, and others were laborers in dirty jeans and baseball caps.

The bartender, a baldheaded guy, wearing small, round, metal-framed glasses, said, "Yes, gentlemen, what will it be?"

We both ordered the corned beef sandwich. They came with deli-style pickles. I ordered a mug of the house beer. David ordered some type of ale I'd never heard of.

So far, nobody had directed David to leave.

The food and beer were placed before us. I paid for both of us.

David said, "Thanks, man, my treat next time. By the way, James, you will be the first to hear this. I don't want this to get around just yet, but I was browsing yesterday in a little dusty bookshop up in Harlem. You know I go up there to teach. My sister and her family live up on Lenox Avenue and 122nd Street. Speaking of Lenox Avenue, last week I wrote a poem, riffing on Langston's poem 'Juke Box Love Song,' about the IRT Lenox Avenue line. I think mine is better!"

"Is that what you wanted to tell me that's such a big secret?"

"No, man, no. It's something else."

"What?"

"I found a first edition of *Ulysses*. Yes! THE *Ulysses*! It's *Ulysses*, the novel by James Joyce. I mean this is the one, with all the typos, published by Sylvia Beach at her bookshop, Shakespeare & Company in Paris, man. I'm not kidding you. It has a green dust jacket, a little torn on the edges, but it's in pretty good condition. This book is worth thousands, many thousands. I bet it's worth a hundred and fifty thousand dollars. It would take me many years to make that much money teaching."

"David, I don't believe it. You must be mistaken. There are so few of those around, and you found it in Harlem?"

"Yeah, man. It was on a low shelf, way in the back, behind a bunch of other old books. Probably no one had looked back there in sixty or seventy years. I turned to the title page. I couldn't believe my eyes: 1922!"

"Are you sure?"

"Yes! Listen, don't say anything to anybody about this just yet. I want to get it evaluated."

"I've got to see this book."

"I'll show you."

By now, it was noon. We finished our sandwiches and beer, paid the bartender, and headed for David's apartment on First Avenue near St. Mark's Place, not far from my own apartment.

I'd been to David's apartment many times. He unlocked the door. The place was dark and dingy, as usual. You entered into the little living room. The bedroom, I supposed, couldn't have been any bigger than a large closet.

As you entered, the kitchenette was off to the right. It had a small stove and a sink with a tiny counter. David's bookcase stood just inside the entryway. It was filled with dog-eared paperbacks and two or three hardbacks.

David's companion, Camille Armand, was a pleasant young woman with shoulder-length brown hair, and eyes that reflected inner peace. She was at work. Camille worked as a secretary in a law office in midtown. Her hobby was drawing and occasionally doing watercolors.

"Have a seat," said David. "I'll get it."

I sat on the little couch. It was covered with one of Camille's quilts. She'd inherited several quilts from her grandmother. There was a raggedy armchair facing the couch. It was David's chair.

David went to his bedroom and returned with a boot box. He then sat down in his chair and placed the box on the table in front of us. He opened the box and carefully lifted out the book. It was wrapped in tissue paper. With trembling fingers, he unwrapped the book and placed it on the table. "Don't touch it!" he said.

"Okay, but how am I supposed to look at it?"

"Wait," he said, and he got up and went to the kitchenette and returned with two pairs of vinyl gloves. "Camille wears these when she's washing vegetables. Put these on." He handed me a pair and returned to his chair.

I slid the gloves on.

"Now you can pick it up and look at it."

I picked up the book, and carefully lifted the wrapper back to see the soft cover. From having read *Ulysses*, and also from having read a biography of Joyce, I knew enough about the first edition to know what it was supposed to look like. I looked inside. The title page looked right: *Ulysses* by James Joyce, Shakespeare and Company, 12 Rue de l'Odeon, 12, Paris, 1922.

I knew there was no copyright notice. I turned the page and on the back of the title page there was: This edition is limited to 1000 copies: 100 copies (signed) on Dutch handmade paper numbered from 1 to

100; 150 copies on vergé d'Arches numbered from 101 to 250; 750 copies on handmade paper numbered from 251 to 1000.

Below that notice, this: The publisher asks the reader's indulgence for typographical errors unavoidable in the exceptional circumstances.

I had read that the typesetter was French and knew no English.

So far, the book seemed to be the real thing, but was this one of the signed copies? If there were a signature, it was supposed to be on the half-title page.

I turned back to the half-title page and, sure enough, there was a signature: James Joyce. My heart beat faster. "David, you didn't tell me it was signed by the author."

"Is it?"

"Look! Here is Joyce's signature on the half-title page."

"Wow!" he said, holding his face with both hands. "I must have skipped that page going to the title page. I thought it was blank. Wow!" He stood up and placed his hand on his chest. "This is amazing! Do you know what this means? This book might be worth more than a hundred and fifty thousand dollars!"

"If it's the real thing, David, you are now a rich man."

I went home, still doubting that David had found a first edition of *Ulysses*. There were a lot of fakes on the market, but I couldn't stop thinking about the possibility that he had the real thing. What luck for him if it was!

That night I was watching TV. The theater critic, Oscar Cantlay, said, "The comedy *Tools of the Trade* is opening tomorrow night at the Schawartzel Theater on lower Fifth Avenue, in the West Village. The play is already getting a lot of buzz. Yesterday, I went to the preview for the press. The *Village Voice* says, 'Cedric Ainsley Brathwaite is amazing!' Brathwaite is in the lead role as Bobby Walker, the carpenter. Ann Crosby plays the farmer's daughter, Sylvia Greenwood. The veteran actor, Noel Paley, plays the farmer, Joe Greenwood. It's a comedy of manners. Without running the risk of giving away too much of the plot, suffice it to say that race is an issue, and it's about a Black carpenter and a white farmer's daughter. Bobby and the farmer's daughter are in love and want to marry, but her father Joe is against their love and the proposed marriage. Crosby has had several important roles on Broadway. Last year, Brathwaite was in a successful six-week run of *A Raisin in the Sun* at the Wilbur Theater in Boston. I enjoyed *Tools of the Trade*. I predict it's going to be a winner."

The next evening, I was there before the doors opened and had no trouble getting a ticket at the door. It was a small theater with a big reputation. There were about three hundred seats, and by the time the curtain opened, perhaps a hundred people were there. Both Cedric and Ann Cosby were delightful and funny, but the story was a disappointment. Paley, as the father figure, seemed bored with the part he was playing.

When the comedy was over, I waited outside in the lobby hoping to see Cedric, just to say hello and to congratulate him. I only half-expected to see him since actors often leave by the back door, but I waited, sitting on a bench in the lobby. Then I got the brilliant idea of asking one of the ushers to tell Cedric that James Lowell was waiting in the lobby to say hello. She said she would let him know. So I continued to wait.

About an hour later, Cedric came out, smiling and with an extended hand. I stood up and we shook.

"James, my good man," he said, "I'm so happy to see you. How are you?"

"I'm doing well. You seem to be doing well, too. Congratulations on your new role. I enjoyed it. You were great."

He looked down and frowned. "Well, maybe professionally I am doing okay, but my private life has changed since I last saw you."

"Oh?"

"Yes, Regina and I are no longer together." He forced a chuckle. "She left me for someone else." He clicked his tongue against his teeth. "Do you have time to pop across the street to the coffee shop? Perhaps we can get caught up."

"Sure, sure."

We walked out together. At the curb, we crossed Fifth and entered Garland's European Café, which was directly across from the theater. The clock on the wall in the cafe was approaching midnight. There were a few nighthawks hanging out there, drinking designer coffee. Cedric and I ordered espresso.

We were sitting at the counter. I looked at him. "So, what happened?"

"Well, two months ago, shortly after we saw you at the Strand, things started going south. We left the Bronx and moved into an apartment at Broadway and 72nd Street, a five-minute walk from that old subway entrance there at the intersection."

"I know the area."

"Well, Regina got work with the Terpsichore Dance Theater troupe at the Odella Theater in Southampton, you know, out on Long Island. Three nights a week, she didn't finish till late. She started staying there overnight in a hotel. Well, I understood how difficult it was to get back to Manhattan from out there late at night." He paused and looked down into his coffee.

I thought I knew what was coming.

Then Cedric said, "A month ago, she came back one morning and told me she was leaving our marriage, leaving me." Cedric choked on the last word, "me." He looked down at his hands. His fingers were laced together on the tabletop. "I went to England, but I didn't see the Queen."

"What?"

"I went to Rome, but I didn't see the Pope." He was smiling sadly.

"What are you saying?"

"I've flirted with glory, but glory slipped through my fingers. I'm lost without Regina."

"You're not lost, Cedric. You're young, you've got a future."

"That's true, I guess. Actually, I've started sitting in on classes at the Actor's Studio up on 44th Street, trying to improve my skills. It's really been inspiring. It gives me something to do that's constructive during the daytime. In that way I'm not just sitting at home brooding and feeling sorry for myself. For three nights a week I come down here to do the show, and I must say I enjoy doing it."

"See! That's the spirit!" I said.

I waited for him to continue. I wanted to offer him more sympathy in some kind of way, but I didn't know how.

He said, "Almost five years together! I thought we'd be together for-ever, or at least until one of us kicked the bucket."

"Did she give a reason?"

"She said she's in love with Vivian Wayland. Do you know who she is?"

"No, I don't. Who is Vivian Wayland?"

"Vivian Wayland is the founder and director of the Terpsichore Dance Theater, the up-and-coming dance company, based in Harlem, that hired Regina. They've already played the Met. Last spring, they had runs in Paris and Rome."

"And Regina is now living with her, this Vivian Wayland?"

"Yes. Regina was dancing with her company out in Southampton. I guess I didn't make that clear." He stopped and looked directly into my eyes. "It was all so sudden and unexpected."

I said, "Do you know Vivian Wayland?"

"Yes, I know Vivian. I've known her for several years now. Regina and I counted her among our best friends in New York."

"What kind of person is she?"

"Well, not to bad-mouth her, but she's really kind of ruthless."

"Ruthless, or driven to get what she wants?"

"Yes, she has always gone after what she wants. That's why her com-pany is becoming such a big success. She's driven, and I guess she want-ed my Regina."

"Have you seen Regina since she left?"

He laughed. "Yes, I have. She's come back to our apartment to pick up her things. She still has some things there. She keeps coming back to get a little bit at a time and, of course, we, uh, well, you can imagine. So now she's cheating on Vivian with me. Isn't that a fine kettle of fish?"

"Sounds like she's not done with you, Cedric. This thing with Viv-ian might be just a fling, and she may be back home before you know it."

"I don't think so, old sport. She seems pretty taken with Vivian. Re-gina has had a chance to work with many fine dance companies, but this is the one she's chosen. I think she's hitched her career and her private life to Vivian for good."

I sipped my espresso, then looked through the plate-glass window at the other side of the street and the mysterious darkness and the sprinkle of night lights along the row of shops. A few night-strollers were out walking along Fifth Avenue.

Cedric wrote down his telephone number and address on a sheet from his notepad and handed it to me.

Cedric and I talked a bit about our time in Puerto Vallarta. We finished our coffee. I paid for both of us, and we walked out onto the sidewalk, hoping to get a taxi while knowing that two Black men this late at night would have a difficult time getting one to stop.

We waved to seven or eight unoccupied taxis before one stopped. The driver had a Middle Eastern name. He dropped me in front of my place on St. Mark's Place, then drove Cedric uptown.

Time was sailing by. In a short amount of time, I'd have to go back to teaching.

One Saturday at noon, I stopped working on a poem with the working title "Chance," and decided to go see Rachel. I thought of calling first, then quickly decided not to, but what if she had company or was busy otherwise? I decided to take a chance.

I knocked twice.

With a dust broom in her hand, Rachel opened the door and said, "I thought it might be you. I'm glad to see you. We need to talk." She was wearing a kerchief, a white cotton pullover, and cut-off jeans. "I was just cleaning."

I nodded, and walked to the couch and sat down.

Rachel stood the dust broom against the wall by the end table.

She said, "Well, I did some checking around and I found out that Darius is married. People know him. His wife's name is Josephine Cuyp, and apparently he's been married a long time."

"Good, I'm glad you know."

"I understand why you didn't want to be in the middle of it. Tell me about Josephine. What kind of person is she?"

I didn't mind responding to this question. I said, "She's a very smart and decent and kind person. She has integrity."

"Does she love Darius?"

"Completely. She couldn't be more devoted."

"Which makes him not only a cheater, but a slime-ball, too. Sorry to say that about your friend, but that's what he is."

"Does Darius know you know about Josephine?"

"Yes. He stopped by yesterday, expecting to have sex, of course, and I told him to go home and have sex with his wife, Josephine."

"I bet he was shocked. How'd you find out about Josephine?"

"Never mind how I found out. I have my ways."

"You're a good detective, Rachel. Did he leave?"

"Of course, he did. If he hadn't, I would have put him out."

"Bravo!"

"James, do you think you will ever get married and have kids?"

"Absolutely."

"When? When you are forty or fifty?" She laughed.

I wanted to say when I find the right woman, but I couldn't say that to Rachel. She knew why, and she probably felt the same way about me.

She said, "I'm twenty-three years old. Before I know it, I'll be thirty, and then forty, and then fifty. I want to be in a relationship that is going somewhere. I don't want a casual relationship anymore. I've had that experience now. I want to move on. I'm looking for somebody I can fall in love with and marry. I want to have children. I want a family."

As if in deep thought, she fell silent. She looked down at the floor for a long time. Then tears started rolling down her cheeks.

I stood up and put my arm around her shoulders. Then I turned her toward me and hugged her. She sobbed against my chest, and I felt awful, worse than I'd felt in a long time. She was a friend, and she was suffering. The least I could do was try to comfort her.

Between sobs, she said, "From now on, when I meet a guy, I'm waiting a long time before there is any sex involved. I need to get to know the person first."

At this point, I felt that anything I said would be the wrong thing, but I said, "Why are you still obsessing about Darius? Isn't it time to move on?"

Then she said, "Yes, it is, and I have moved on. I've met someone and I'm going to wait at least a month before I have sex with him. I'm going to wait to see if he's the right person."

"Who did you meet?"

"His name is Satoshi, he's Japanese. He's madly in love with me, but…"

I was surprised. I said, "But… what?"

She laughed, and wiped her nose on her sleeve. "If it comes to marriage, my parents would die if I married him, and I'm not sure I want to. I like him a lot, but I don't think I'm in love with him, not yet, but maybe love will come."

"You seem to care for him. So what if your parents would be against it?"

"For a while I thought you and I might get married, and I knew my parents would have disapproved of me marrying you. They want me to marry someone exactly like them. He has to be a lawyer or a doctor or is going to become one of those things. I know what they want. He should not be a poet, and certainly not Black. Oh, you're respectable all right: you're a college-educated person and a university teacher. They would respect both of those things, but they are not enough to overcome everything else."

"Well, maybe they won't object to Satoshi. What does he do?"

"He's a Ph.D. student at NYU. He's a theoretical physicist. He's already doing research. He's so brilliant!"

"That's great, Rachel. Where did you meet?"

"We met at the 8th Street bookstore. I was sitting on the couch upstairs reading the blurbs on the back of a novel when he sat down beside me and spoke. That was two weeks ago."

I thought, okay, so you've been seeing this guy for two weeks. Interesting!

"So, James, I don't think we should have sex again, at least not till I can understand what I need to do. I need to sort out my feelings and see if Satoshi is the right person for me. Having sex with you would just keep me confused, and I won't be able to think straight about anything. What I'm saying is maybe there is a chance with Satoshi. I don't know."

"That's fine, Rachel. We can continue to be friends, though, right?"

"That's just it, James, if I continue seeing you, I'll want to have sex with you. I want you right now, but I have to resist that feeling. I want to be able to think clearly about Satoshi."

"I understand."

"Thank you, James."

Later, after tea together, I stood to leave. At the door, we hugged each other, and I left Rachel standing there trying to smile, but it was a sad smile.

I stopped trying to force the poems to come. Sunday, I went to the Metropolitan Museum of Art. I spent the greater part of the day there, enjoying the ancient Egyptian and the Near East arts. The art works from the Mesopotamia region awed me, and I later ate lunch at the museum restaurant; then, at five o'clock, I took a taxi back downtown to St. Mark's Place. I was feeling empty and sad.

I climbed the steps to my apartment, and there was Sophia knocking on my door. I hadn't seen her since that Saturday morning, last year. Hearing my footsteps, she turned around and smiling, said, "Oh, there you are!"

"Hey, Sophia, how are you?"

With my key in hand, I unlocked the door and invited her in.

We sat down at the kitchen table.

I offered her something to drink–tea, wine, coffee–but she said, "No, thanks."

"How have you been?"

"I just stopped by to tell you that I've been accepted in the anthropology program at the Graduate Center at CUNY."

"That's wonderful, Sophia."

"I'm so excited!"

"I can imagine."

"I didn't get a full scholarship, but I think I'll be able to manage the cost. I'm told I'll be able to get a fellowship later, and they have stipends and grants I can apply for. My dad says he'll help."

"That's great, Sophia. I'm happy for you."

We embraced.

And that was the last time I saw Sophia.

A tiny notice in the *Village Voice* said that my St. Mark's Church-in-the-Bowery reading was scheduled for next Tuesday night at 7:00 p.m.

I knew from street posters along St. Mark's Place that the famous Black Nationalist, Marxist, Muslim poet Malik Dagomba Mbari, privately and legally known as Benedict Jackson, would be reading this coming Friday night at seven. His well-known views were vastly different from mine, but out of curiosity, I decided to go.

His poetry was uneven in quality, even carelessly dumped on the page, and often didactic, but he was worth reading, and therefore worth hearing.

I got to the church at 6:30. The church was set back from the corner with a generous yard around it. People often sat in the yard, on benches under trees, to read newspapers or poetry books or just to relax. The church grounds were paved with cobblestones; so were the sidewalks near the church. Like the Lowery alley, this was an old part of lower Manhattan.

About half the seats in the church were already filled when I sat down. People were coming in at a fast pace. By a quarter to seven, all the seats were occupied. Newcomers began to assemble around the sides and in the back.

Malik was popular among Black poets, the bohemians, and the downtown crowd generally. In fact, he'd for years been one of the Black darlings of the bohemians. Many of them remembered him from the early days when he was a bohemian, living among them down here. In those pre-revolutionary days, he was often seen walking the streets, St. Mark's Place included, wearing a cowboy hat and cowboy boots. Back then, he was pushing a philosophy of integration.

After getting the call to Black cultural revolution and Black consciousness, he'd moved back to Los Angeles where he was born, and where, according to Malik, some of the police were acting like Nazis. According to news reports, they often stopped him and other Black men for questioning. For one reason or another, they were often arrested. If they resisted, they were sometimes beaten or killed.

Now twelve Black men, dressed in black, came from the vestry at the left. They were all wearing dark glasses and their heads were shaved. Six went left and six went right. In a defensive posture, they stood along the walls with their arms crossed.

Two went and stood in front of the door, obviously blocking the exit. Apparently now no one could enter or leave without confronting them. These were obviously Malik's bodyguards and entourage. It was well known that they were always with him.

The audience was largely white, with a few Asians, Afro-Americans, and Puerto Ricans.

In anticipation of Malik's appearance, the church was buzzing with excitement. Then he came from the vestry and stood at the freestanding microphone and faced the gathering.

I'd seen pictures of him in *Jet, Ebony*, the *Village Voice*, and in little literary magazines such as the *Evergreen Review*, but this was the first time I'd seen the real person.

He was a huge man with a bald head and a grizzly black beard. He was reportedly only thirty-three years old, but he looked forty or fifty. He was wearing a red and green dashiki. A heavy gold chain hung around his neck. From where I sat, I could see the medallion pendant, and it looked like a mandala, the Hindu ritual symbol representing the universe.

Back in the late 1950s-early 1960s, when Malik was living downtown, he was married to the celebrated feminist poet, Dora Conrad. She was well published, and she was widely known as an activist in New York literary circles.

Lately, I'd heard that, at the beginning of her readings, she would say, "I want all the men in the room to leave right now. These poems I'm about to read are not for you. They are womanist poems." She would then wait till the men were gone before she would begin her reading.

Malik stood there gaping at us, the audience.

I watched him closely.

"Okay, listen up, all you white folks," said Malik. "Now that I got you all here, you are going to die, die right here in this room." He looked to the left, and shouted to one of his bodyguards, "Turn out the lights!"

Suddenly the room went completely dark. Only the outline of the exit door could be seen. This was because lights were still on in the hallway.

Bam! Bam! Bam! Gunshots? I knew the sounds were coming from cap guns, but they sounded like real bullets. *Bam! Bam! Bam! Bam! Bam! Bam! Bam!*

Immediately people started screaming, and they were running in the dark toward the exit, toward that thin square of light that represented freedom from death. The rapid gunfire continued from both sides of the room. Screaming got louder as people knocked each other over trying to get out of there. Then there was a loud thud.

I sat still, knowing that it was misdirected theater, but a terrible thing to do to people there to hear his poetry. It was on the level of shouting fire in a dark theater full of spectators. The man next to me also remained in his seat.

Five minutes later, we heard Malik's voice again. He said, "Lights! Turn on the lights! Lights!"

The lights flicked back on. I looked around.

People were on the floor by the exit, trying to stand up. Many had already left.

In the next ten minutes, about half the audience was gone. What a foolish, criminal thing to have done to his audience!

We could now see the source of the loud thud. A young woman had run into the wall and knocked herself out cold. She lay on the floor. Several people were bent over her, trying to revive her. Two men picked her up and carried her out.

This was the kind of theater Malik Dagomba Mbari was known to stage at his poetry readings. Most of the audience that Friday night was unaware of his antics. Many of the people here were likely to have known Malik as Jackson from the old days, or known him only on the page. Most probably came expecting a Black bohemian poet, not a Black revolutionary staging a violent theatrical performance.

Now the poetry reading started. Malik was holding a thin volume of poems in his right hand, and shouting and hissing and spitting out the words in a violent and angry rhythmic pattern. He was an engaging reader of his own poetry. Those of us who remained were stunned.

My reading was at the church that following Tuesday. I walked into the same room that Malik had read in, and only seven or eight people were there waiting to hear me. I felt disappointed. I felt it physically, viscerally.

By the time I started reading, there were about thirty people. It was really not surprising: I was not well known. My book was new and well-received, but it was not selling like hotcakes. Yet, for poetry, it was selling better than the average book of poems, probably because of the review in the *New York Times Book Review* and the nomination.

Despite the skimpy audience, I took a positive attitude and read with enthusiasm. The few people there deserved as much, and the small audience responded with enthusiasm. I was grateful.

Wednesday morning, while in the shower, I strained several muscles in my back. I was reaching around to try to wash as much of my back as I could reach when I felt a whole network of muscles back there tighten and lock. After that, I could barely turn or bend without severe pain.

Sitting at the typewriter was painful, walking was painful, and standing was equally painful. Lying down on my back staring at the ceiling was about all I could do. I needed help.

When I first moved to St. Mark's Place, I heard about a masseuse in the neighborhood, around the corner on First Avenue. She was the real thing, not a cover for sexual activity. Her name was listed often in the classified section of the *Village Voice*.

Yet I didn't remember her name, so I went out and bought a copy of the *Village Voice*, and there again was her listing in the classifieds: Ms. Ellen Cromwell, Masseuse, By Appointment Only. Her days were Monday through Friday.

I needed to get to her fast. Bent sideways, I walked to her place, feeling, with each step, that I would not be able to take another step.

I pressed the buzzer alongside Ms. Cromwell's door on the second floor of an old apartment building across the street from the laundromat.

I could see an eye looking through the peephole at me, then a large woman opened the door. Her name was British, but she looked like she was descended mainly from Eastern Europeans. The first things I noticed were her hands, how large they were.

Then I saw her face. She was about forty, and she had a face that was once very beautiful. Now it was interesting, with what seemed a permanent sorrowful look. The corners of her mouth were turned down. Her eyes were those of a sad, sad St. Bernard dog. I started to say she had a self-pitying look, but permanent sorrow is closer to what I saw.

She opened the door and she invited me in.

"Do you have an appointment?" she said.

"No, I'm sorry, I don't, but I'm in a lot of pain."

We were standing in what looked like a living room converted to a waiting room. On a side table were stacks of magazines and newspapers, *Time*, *Newsweek*, *Vogue*, *New York Times*, and the like, and a copy of a novel, *Portnoy's Complaint*, with a bright yellow cover. I'd heard about the new Roth novel. Recently published, it was getting a lot of attention. Interesting that Ellen Cromwell had a copy. Perhaps it said something about the quality of her reading taste.

She said, "You're in luck. I don't have anybody scheduled till this afternoon, so I'll see if I can help you."

"Thank you."

"What happened?"

"I injured my back in the shower."

She smiled. "Happens all the time. The shower seems to be the place. Early in the morning, the muscles are still tight from sleeping in one position too long."

"Yes, ma'am."

"Call me Ellen. Everybody calls me Ellen." She smiled her sad smile. She looked at her watch. "It's 9:15. I can take you now, if you want."

"That would be great."

"Come on in."

From a small table by the door, she picked up her schedule ledger and asked me my name, address, and phone number. I watched as she wrote the information in her book in the 9:15 slot.

Bringing her ledger with her, she said, "Come on back to the massage room."

I followed her into an even darker and smaller room. There was one window with the shade pulled down. The massage table was in the center of the room, and there was a record player on a small table against the back wall. A record was on the turntable. There was a stool at the head of the table.

"I'll leave you to undress down to your underwear," she said, as she turned on the record player and the phonograph record started turning. The music was soft and slow. I guessed Chopin, but I was wrong. It soon became clear that it was Beethoven's Sonata No. 14, "Moonlight," Opus 27, No. 2.

"When you are undressed, just get on the table face down. Put your face here in this opening. Okay?"

"Yes. Thank you, Ellen."

She smiled and left the room.

Getting up on the table nearly killed me, the pain in my back was so intense.

I was on the table waiting for her for about five minutes before she returned. I closed my eyes, waiting for relief from pain.

She came to the head of the table. She spread a small amount of oil on my back and started at my neck and shoulders. She was firm and slow, working deeply into the muscles of my neck and upper back.

Then she moved to the left side and worked at the center of the back on that side.

When she finished with that side, she moved to the other side, where the pain was most intense, and did the same thing. A couple of times I wanted to say "Ouch," but suppressed the urge.

She worked my upper thighs and lower legs in the same methodical way.

I was still facedown. She climbed onto the table and straddled me, sitting squarely on my bottom, and she began, with both of those big hands, to work firmly up and down and into the muscles of my entire back. She dug down deep, but she did it with rhythm and methodical precision.

Then she sat on the stool and worked my feet. I felt the relief swimming all the way up to my head. My whole body began to relax.

Finally, she lifted one leg at a time, then each of my arms, in the same slow manner.

By now, an hour later, I was almost asleep. I felt better, but the pain, more localized and not as distressing, was still there.

She said, "I'll leave the room so you can get dressed."

When she came back, I was fully dressed.

"How do you feel?"

"I feel better, but I can still feel the pain and the tightness."

"You will have to come back. You can't expect the pain to go away in one session. It may take three or more sessions."

"Okay," I said. "So, when can I come back?"

Her ledger was beside the record player. She picked it up and with a pencil poised, she said, "How about the same time tomorrow, 9:15?"

"I can do that."

The next session on the massage table was identical to the first, except Ellen was talking during the whole session. She started by asking me questions about myself. I answered as truthfully as I knew how. I told her I was not married, that I was a teacher, and that I lived around the corner on St. Mark's Place. I said nothing about being a poet.

She then said, "I was once married, but it didn't work out. I got pregnant, but lost the baby. I couldn't carry it full term. Then I discovered that I would never be able to have a child. It just was not in the cards for me. My husband left me. It was a difficult time."

She seemed to be crying. I was facedown so I couldn't see her face, but I heard her sniffling and her voice broke. Yes, she was crying.

"Not having a child is the biggest disappointment in my life. It left me feeling so broken, so unhappy, so empty."

I said, "You never considered marrying again?"

"I considered it, sure, I considered it many times, but each time the man was just not right. They were too old or too young. They were too selfish or too mean. I've had many affairs. I guess that's what you can call them. Affairs! They all ended in disappointment. When I was younger, men were just interested in my body, not interested in me, me as a person. I kept trying to get them to see me as I was. Finally, I just gave up on men. It just wasn't worth it, but when I gave up, I still had sex with them, but I no longer hoped to have anything beyond that. I gave up on love and marriage."

"That sounds pretty sad."

"It is sad, but I keep busy. I took a sculpture class this summer, and I paint. A couple of my paintings are hanging in the living room."

I didn't say anything because I hadn't noticed them.

"Now that I'm in my forties, I'm saving money and I hope to travel to Europe for the first time. I want to go to Yugoslavia. That is the country of my ancestors. My grandmother, Maja was her name, Maja Cackovic, my mother's mother. She was from Yugoslavia. They were Serbian from the area around Belgrade, but not the big city. They were country folk. My grandmother's mother's maiden name was Dizdarevic. My mother Petra kept a pretty good record of her ancestry."

"Good to know the past."

"Yes. There are some Lower East Side families here that knew my folks over there. I met them quite by accident, the Nincics, Bedics, the Majics and Adamovics, good people with a sense of humor. They are regulars at Saint Sava, that Serbian Orthodox church up on West 26th Street. You may have noticed it. It's between Broadway and Avenue of the Americas. I'm not a member, and I'm not all that religious, but I go there on occasion. My mother used to go there."

"I've seen it. It's a beautiful cathedral."

"Yes, it is beautiful, but Cromwell is my father's name. They were from England. I already know about them. It's my mother's side of the family that is the big mystery. I hope to go to Yugoslavia to find out about her family, and her ancestors. It's a country right now that's being held together with glue, and not very good glue. I want to go before the glue dries up, cracks, and the whole thing falls apart. Have you been to Europe?"

"No, but I'd love to go. I will go one of these days."

"A friend of mine says you're not cultured till you go to Europe." She laughed. "I don't know anything about being cultured. All I'm interested in is finding out about my ancestors. That's my reason for going."

On my way out that time, I looked at her paintings. One was a dark, amateurishly painted landscape and the other one was a dark still life with roses and a plate. Just to be kind, I said, "They're nice."

"This is a sculpture I did last week in my sculpture class," she said, lifting a clay female figurine up from an end table. It was about the size of a Coke bottle. She held it up so I could get a closer look.

"I like it," I said, and I was telling the truth. She was a better sculptor than painter.

After three more sessions, my back muscles relaxed, and I was back to normal.

Saturday night, as I sat at the typewriter working on a poem, I heard the typical Saturday night festivities outside on St. Mark's Place. Around ten or ten-thirty, my door buzzer sounded.

I wasn't expecting anybody, but I got up and looked through the peephole. The face was distorted and enlarged, but I saw that it was Ellen Cromwell. I couldn't imagine why she was here. Was there a problem with the checks I had given her? That couldn't be it. I had sufficient money in my checking account.

I opened the door and immediately I saw that she was sloppy drunk. She could barely stand up. Her face was bloated, and her eyes were bloodshot. She was trying to smile, but was grinning drunkenly, and it looked more like a leer than a smile.

She didn't seem to be the same person I'd just seen a few days before. She said, "Hel-lo, I just… I come to see you. May I come in?"

Bewildered, I opened the door wider to let her pass into my apartment. She stepped in and stopped right inside the doorway, and still trying to smile, she gave me what I think she thought was a dreamy look of flirtation.

I said, "Are you okay?"

"Oh, sure, oh, sure. I'm fine. I just thought I would stop by and see you, you know, maybe have a little fun with you." Then she wiggled her shoulders in a suggestive manner.

I was at a loss as to what to say or to do.

Then, suddenly, she looked around. "Nice place, very nice." Staggering as she moved, she walked up toward the living room, and she stopped by the couch for a minute before falling down there. She almost fell on the floor.

I was so stunned, I still didn't know what to say.

"Don't you find me attractive?"

"Yes, you're very attractive, but..."

"But what?"

Again, I was speechless.

"Come and sit beside me. I'm lonesome." She patted the cushion beside the one on which she was sitting.

"I don't want to sit down, Ellen."

"Oh, now, it's Ellen, huh?"

"You said to call you Ellen."

"Yes, and you are James. You are James, aren't you?"

"James is my name, yes."

"I don't know why James doesn't want to play with Ellen. I'm a nice person. What's wrong?"

"Nothing is wrong, Ellen, but don't you think you maybe have had a little too much to drink?"

"Oh, now, you're going to lecture me. That's right, you're a teacher. Lecturing is what you do for a living." She laughed. "I should have known you would lecture me."

"Come on, Ellen, I'll walk you back home. I want to make sure you get there safely. I'm sure you know the streets this time of night around here can be unsafe for anyone who's been drinking."

I reached for her arm to help her up.

She pushed my hand away. "I can stand on my own."

When she tried to stand, she fell off the couch onto the floor.

I bent over to help her up. This time she let me help her.

"You don't like me, do you?"

"Of course, I like you, Ellen. Come on, I'll help you get home safely."

I put my arm around her, and she leaned on me for support.

I helped her down the steps and out into busy, noisy St. Mark's Place.

When we got to her door, she had a hard time finding her key. I waited patiently, keeping my head slightly turned away. Her breath was reeking with the sharp smell of whisky.

Finally, she found her key.

"Will you come in and tuck me in?"

"No, Ellen. You'll be fine. You're home now."

She walked into her apartment, and I reached for the doorknob and closed her inside.

Summer 1969 was winding down.

I kept weighing the words, testing the phrases, and wrestling with the lines of poems in progress, slowly moving toward a second book. It was now August.

But the rest of the world was very eventful: Neil Armstrong landed on the moon, Janis Joplin sang at Woodstock, Sophia started attending classes at CUNY, and I was once again teaching two workshops at Warren Lowery: one graduate and one undergraduate.

On October 13th, I took the train to Stamford, Connecticut, to fulfill my promise to Frank Garrick that I would give a reading at Willem Granville University.

Frank said he would meet me at the station. I spotted him the minute I stepped down out of the train onto the concrete platform. There he was, standing on the platform, smiling broadly. I hadn't seen him since Mexico City, and that seemed like a very long time ago.

"Hey, James, boy, how're you doing? So good to see you, man."

We embraced.

I told him I was fine, and we walked from the platform through the station to his car.

By the time we parked on campus, there was a slight drizzle. Frank and I hurried across the lot and into the Humanities building.

"They're all assembled and waiting for you," he said, as we rushed along a corridor with many different kinds of flyers and posters on mini bulletin boards alongside office and classroom doors.

We entered a medium-sized assembly hall. Frank led me to an empty seat in the front row. I sat down. He walked to the podium and faced the audience. "Well," he said, "we made it. We're not a minute late. Sometimes the trains do run on time."

The audience clapped.

He held up a copy of my book, *Rain*. "This book of poems, *Rain*, is one of the best books I've read in a long time. We're so lucky to have its author with us today. I hardly know where to start. I met James Eric Lowell in Mexico City last summer. He and his friend—can I say girlfriend?"

He looked at me, and I nodded affirmatively.

"James and his girlfriend, Sophia, stopped to visit with my family and me on their way to Puerto Vallarta. It was the first time my kids had ever met an Afro-American."

I closed and opened my eyes. I held and released my breath.

"I'd published James's poems in my quarterly, *Nuevo Mundo*. Many of you are familiar with it under its new title, *New World*. James is such a fine poet. I've admired his work for a long time. I first saw his poems in literary magazines, and I guess he started publishing poems in literary magazines while he was in college back in 1965, four or five years ago. Recently it gave me great pleasure to see the front-page review of his book in the *New York Times Book Review*. James has also been nominated for the National Book Award in poetry. Please join me in giving James Eric Lowell a warm welcome."

Frank started clapping, and the audience joined him.

Carrying a copy of my book, I stood and stepped behind the podium as Frank sat down in the front row.

"Thank you, Frank. I'm delighted to be here, and without wasting any time, let me get right to it. I'm going to read a few of the early poems first, some of them appeared first in Frank's magazine. Then I'll read some of the newer things."

I started, and, at the end, because of the standing ovation I got, I went away feeling that the reading had been a success. I was getting better at public readings.

David Williams called me on the fourth Tuesday of October, and said, "Hey, James, I finally got a letter from that rare book dealer, Hatch

& Goldsmith Rare Books. I took the book to their office in midtown and let them examine it. They said it was real. I had to pay for the appraisal. Part of the deal was they would send me a letter saying it was the real thing. You know they're very respectable and trustworthy."

"Yeah, yeah, what'd the letter say?"

"The letter confirms that my copy of *Ulysses* is an autographed first edition. Do you know what that means, man?"

"That you're going to be so rich nobody can speak to you without an appointment."

He laughed. "They classified its condition as 'very good.' It's not in perfect condition, but it's close to it."

"So, what're you going to do?"

"I'm going to sell it at Sotheby's. I've already talked with the people there. I took the book to their office up on East 72 Street and York Avenue. They were very nice people. I paid a fee to enter it, but, hey, it's worth it. I'm putting a minimum on it."

"How much?"

"A hundred thousand. I'm aiming for a hundred and fifty thousand or more, if I can get it."

"Well, good luck," I said. "Let me know what happens."

Wednesday, three days before the National Book Awards ceremony, I went to Barth & Basil Men's Apparel, a shop on 75th and Lexington Avenue.

"I'd like to rent a tux," I said to the well-dressed elderly gentleman who greeted me.

"I'd be delighted to help you," he said.

"Thanks."

He pulled a tux off the rack. "Let's try this on for size."

He held up a jacket for me to slip my arms into.

I turned my back to him, with my arms back, and he slipped the jacket on.

He then tugged at the shoulders to see if the fit was comfortable. "How does it feel through the shoulders?"

"It feels fine."

"Here are the trousers, and there is the dressing room."

I went into the dressing room, dropped my pants, stepped into the tux trousers, and stood before the dressing room mirror. I was pleased with the image there.

It didn't match my image of myself, but, hey, going to the type of ceremony I was about to go to, this look was necessary. I had no reason to believe that I would need to buy a tux since I didn't think I would be going to this sort of event often.

I came out of the dressing room so the gentleman could check the pants for fit. He felt around the back, he pulled at the front of the pants at the beltline. "I don't think you need any alterations done. How does it feel? Are they tight anywhere?"

"No, the fit is fine."

"Then you're good to go. I'll write you up."

The big day was here. I had a devil of a time getting a taxi to stop for me. I was wearing my trench coat over the tux, and my shoes were classic black, perfect for the ceremonial occasion. I thought I looked respectable enough to get to ride in a New York taxi. I didn't think I looked like somebody out to rob a taxi driver, but you never knew how people saw you.

One driver, again with a Middle Eastern name, finally stopped. I climbed into the back seat, frustrated but grateful.

"The Plaza Hotel, please," I said.

He raised his eyebrows. "How long have you been waiting for a taxi?"

"About an hour."

"I bet if these cabbies knew you wanted to go to the Plaza, they would have been glad to stop."

"I'm not so sure."

He said, "Cabbies don't always think a Black guy is going to rob them. Especially since the riots, often they think any Black person wants to go to Harlem, or to some other Black neighborhood somewhere in one of the boroughs, and they don't want to go to those places for fear of being robbed."

"Thanks for the insight."

"Any time."

The Plaza Hotel was at 768 Fifth Avenue at Central Park South. I saw limousines pulling up and stopping in front. I'd never been inside that five-star luxury hotel. Unlike some who arrived in limousines, I arrived by taxi.

I paid the taxi driver, tipped him well, and entered the grand hotel. I followed the crowd that led me to the Grand Ballroom. A young woman in uniform, working as a greeter at the entrance to the Grand Ballroom, escorted me to my seat.

I'd been assigned a seat at a table with people I didn't know. The card given to me at the door said my seat was at the Williams & Williams publishing company's table. They were one of the three biggest publishers in America.

Normally, one or two, possibly three, people from the publishing company that had published the nominated book came to the award ceremony. No one from Kensington & Livingston University Press would be there.

The National Book Foundation, the National Book Awards' parent body, had assigned me a seat at a table of their choice. Copies of the nominated books, including mine, were standing together, forming a pyramid in the center of the table. No one yet knew who the winners would be. The National Book Awards did it like the Oscars: the winners were announced on the stage at the ceremony.

Unlike the other nominated books, mine lacked a silver round insignia that said *National Book Award Finalist*. I'd called my editor and asked why. He said, "Those logos or emblems or crests, or whatever they call them, cost money!" So, once again, I thought, poetry got the stepchild treatment.

The room was buzzing with bookish chatter.

I greeted the people at my table, editors no doubt, already seated. They were all friendly and gracious in their responses, but they may have wondered why I was seated with them. I certainly did. Williams & Williams rarely published poetry, so poetry was not the reason.

Then the woman sitting next to me at my right said, "Are you one of the authors?"

"I think so."

She laughed. "You think so? You don't know?" She kept laughing. The woman next to her had overhead the exchange, and she, too, started laughing. So did the man on my left.

I hadn't intended to make a joke, but I thought about what I said and realized why it sounded funny to them, but to me it expressed what I was feeling at that moment.

"Which book is yours?" said the man to my left.

"The thin one."

He laughed. "It's pretty thin. It's poetry. Poetry volumes tend to be thin."

"So thin sometimes, it's hard to locate them on a shelf in a bookstore." I wasn't trying to be funny. What I said was true.

He laughed again, and so did other people at the table. Were they laughing at poetry, or at me, or at us both? I thought, no, these are literature people, people deeply interested in books and in reading.

The woman on my right pulled my thin volume from the pyramid, and miraculously the pyramid did not collapse. She opened the book, and started reading the first poem. When she finished, she said, "I like what I've read so far."

"Thank you," I said.

"Do you write fiction, too?"

"No. So far, no."

"Well, if you ever do decide to write a novel, send it to me. I'd like to see it. Here is my card."

I took her card and looked at it. Her name was Marie McCreary. "Thanks. Maybe I will write a novel someday."

"A lot of poets write novels," she said. "D.H. Lawrence, James Joyce, Thomas Hardy. Gosh, so many!"

The man on my left said, "Langston Hughes, too."

Marie McCreary said, "Yes! Write a novel about a poet!"

The chatter in the room was intensifying.

Then I noticed a tall man with silvery grey hair was now on the stage, checking the microphone.

He spoke, "Greetings! Welcome to the 1969 National Book Awards ceremony. I'm Maximilian Neville. I'm going to be your master of ceremonies for this evening, and we have an exciting lineup of books and authors to celebrate!"

Everybody clapped.

Neville was one of the best-known book editors in New York. He was also something of a celebrity because he appeared often on radio and TV. People wanted his opinion on many topics.

Servers were placing food and drinks on the table before each of us. I hardly noticed. I glanced down at my plate with its steak, peas, and small potatoes. I was hungry, but in no mood to eat.

The chatter became a whisper as the people focused on what the MC was saying. "I'm going to read the names of the fiction nominees first, then the nonfiction, then poetry, and finally the writers in the young people's category. When you hear your name, please stand and let us congratulate you."

He slowly read the names of the four fiction nominees, and they each stood as they heard their names, and the same for nonfiction.

I stood when I heard my name, and so did the other three poetry nominees. I knew their poetry: Clara Fleming, Martin Neal, and Joe Radford. Blowups of our faces were lined along the far wall.

As I stood there, I remembered the name of last year's winner, Robert Bly, and I thought, don't get your hopes up. This is likely to be a total toss-up, but I'd written an acceptance speech just in case. Yet I thought it highly unlikely that a first book of poems would win. Fleming had three books, Neal, six, and Radford, sixteen.

Neville read off the fiction names again. He opened an envelope and read the name of the winner, John Lee Goff. There was wild applause. His novel's subject: two rural men spending a great deal of time together. They were in the high-country sheepherding; it dealt with the conflict and friendship between the two. It also dealt with humanity's interaction and conflict with nature.

More celebratory clapping when the winner of the nonfiction award was read: Susan Nestor. Her book questioned the existence of God, and explored all deity theories in relation to the Christian god.

When the MC got to the poetry finalists, I held my breath. My hands were sweating. Then Neville said, "And the winner is..."

"Success is just as difficult as failure."

—James Baldwin, in conversation

⳾⳾⳾⳾

The author wishes to thank my editor, Jennifer Joseph, for her sensitive and thoughtful readings of this novel. I also thank her for her professional and expert advice, and for seeing the book with sensitivity through all of its necessary editorial stages. Thanks, as always, to my wife, Pamela Major, for her skillful and careful readings of the manuscript through all the stages of its evolution over a period of a year and a half. I also thank her for her empathetic help with the editing process.